MOTTAK

*An African Tale
Of Immigration and Asylum*

MOTTAK

*An African Tale
Of Immigration and Asylum*

NATHAN HADDISH MOGOS

Diasporic Africa Press
New York

This book is a publication of
Diasporic Africa Press
New York | www.dafricapress.com

Copyright © Diasporic Africa Press 2015

Library of Congress Control Number: 2015936442
ISBN-13: 978-1-937306-35-9 (pbk.: alk paper)

Special discounts are available for bulk purchases of this book. For more information, please contact us at sales@dafricapress.com.

Diasporic Africa Press uses environmentally friendly book materials, including recycled text paper that is composed of at least 30 percent post-consumer waste, whenever possible.

Printed in the United States of America on acid-free paper.

Contents

Intro

Coming from a continent where the coldest temperature would be ten degrees, give or take, living under constant subzero was a nightmare. Besides, the snow-covered landscape looked so much more glamorous in the movies, like a white carpet treatment from nature. The distant mountain range encircling the northern arctic town resembled giant bowls of professionally scooped ice cream, served on a massive blue platter. The flavor switched to suit the season. On those cold winter nights following a heavy downfall of snow, if one spared a second to glance upwards on a moonlit night, there stood massive chunks of vanilla cream whipped onto the cone, frozen and chiseled to perfection by a flawless gelato king in the patient hand of nature, served on the dark blue, steel tray of the still Northern Sea. As mouthwatering a prospect it was from an artistic point of view, the moment often escaped the overwhelmed and preoccupied tropical minds thrashing their way past the massive piles of caked ice. Ice cream was just the last thing they could imagine.

"Man, I don't think we are still on Earth!" snapped the heavily breathing Cliff. "Na wa! Last I rememba, we took off from Oslo, we flew up and up, but I de fear we no come down. Ah ah! I tell you dis must be anoda planet dey kept it hidden from us, mtsee!" he added in his typical Nigerian pidgin English. He was still shuddering and shaking from the biting cold Monday of the odd, mid-December arctic winter. Even though the trip to the nearest convenience store, REMA 1000, was a ten-minute affair, we had been dreading it all day, hoping for some magic microwave to heat the place up for just half an hour.

It was the three of us, walking as cautiously as we could over the glazed, narrow footpath to buy the groceries we needed so much. It was our second arctic winter experience, yet we still had to come to terms with it. Baked by the sun for far too long, my body was still in shock, trying to adjust to the new environment. Though we came from different backgrounds—Eritrean, Nigerian, and Congolese—African-ness brought us together. We faced too many of the same stereotypes and prejudices to be overly proud of our tribes, anyway. Though this attitude was not shared generally, as some tension still existed between people from warring nations and tribes, one had two choices: to stay in the close comfort zone of one's tribe or ethnicity, or enjoy the salad-bowl diversity that the Mottak delivered. Besides, as one Nigerian friend sarcastically put it, "For dem, we look alike, anyway."

After quite a few minutes of slow-motion plowing over the wet pile of snow, Cliff, who was leading, slipped and fell flat on his back. As it is almost a shared custom in Africa, all three of us burst into loud laughter. They say when you fall and everybody around laughs at your bad luck, you will forget about the pain and pick yourself up to join the excitement.

"Eeee dey, my back it painin' me," Cliff whined playfully, while we kept laughing at him.

Jean Thomas, who we just called Congo, had the weirdest snickering laughter I had ever heard. He would get overexcited literally about anything, and a smile never left his face. "You killing me, mon!" To me, he added, "I like the way dis guy falls. Flat on his ass all de time." He laughed loudly. "Good thing you wid big ass, my friend."

Finding another topic to joke about, we slowly wound our way to REMA, forgetting for a couple of minutes the unforgiving, treacherous wet snow and cold breath from the ocean.

Congo was a laughing machine. He would laugh if he saw a stranger laughing from a distance. The funny part was, it was never a fake laugh. It was a genuine one; a very contagious one. He could never finish a story. If it was funny, he would just start a sentence, "You know what happened... kiikiiiii... De man... kikikikii... He... kikiki..." and would go on for some time, dancing and stomping his feet as if having an epileptic seizure, while you waited for him to finish the story. Even if the story was not that funny in the end, you would end up laughing at how worked up he got over it.

The scary part of walking on such cold December days, which were dark round the clock, was that you might not find a single soul along your path. At times, it was so hauntingly still that it reminded one of a scene from a horror movie, just before the monster appears from nowhere to unleash its fury. Once in a while, though, a car would pass by to remind you there were people still living in the town. The houses looked empty, the trees dead, the sea quiet, and the faces long and reserved. Talk about culture shock; we were freezing and shocked at the same time. It was not a nice feeling to relive!

Inside REMA, we caught our breath, and at last, relieved we were inside and warm, with people around, Congo snickered once again, remarking, "Mama Africa, forgive me!"

We laughed in agreement, reminiscing on the things we once took for granted; all the times we looked for shade to escape the scorching furnace up in the sky!

Searching for the cheapest products on display, since our budget was limited and our needs too many to fill, we separately gathered our basics and headed to the cashiers. Keeping the weather in mind, primarily lightweight goods were preferred. Luxuries were ignored and discount foodstuffs piled up. With all three of us smoking cigarettes and occasionally drinking some beers, the 1,550 kroner allotted for asylum seekers was barely enough. We were struggling really hard. The money might be of real value if you had it exchanged somewhere in Africa, but now we lived in one of the most expensive countries in the whole world. It was annoying when people repeated the cliché, "That is a lot of money back in Africa," whenever one of us complained about the lack of it. It was just never enough anyway, anywhere!

Cliff had gone on a spending spree when he had first arrived. He selected expensive beers, foreign cigarettes, quality foodstuffs, and branded soft drinks. He thought maybe he would be left with at least half of his two-week pay. He was astounded to find out that he was actually short by 400 kroner. Infuriated, he just bought the beer and the cigarettes and a few frozen foods, and returned the rest. As soon as he came back from the store, still astonished by the price, he announced to everyone watching TV in the reception, "Attention, broddas! I have exhausted my money wid drinks and cigarettes. I bought sleeping pills; I be sleeping for the next two weeks." Having grabbed the attention of everyone, he added emphatically, "So I beg you neva wake me, unless for emergency. Undastand?" And he hurried down the stairs to his room.

Walking the way back with some extra weight was the worst part of the trip, though: The cheap Chinese-made gloves barely contained the cold; our fingers were near frostbitten. The plastic bags carrying the goods got heavier and heavier, and the safer road was a steep hill that made everything worse. But we always laughed our way back!

❧

As there is time for grief and sorrow, there shall be and must be time, no matter how short, to rejoice and praise the life one is blessed to live. We are not numbers, nor decorations to linger as a burden on Mother Earth's back, until the day she shall claim us again. We are here for a reason. Every man has a destiny. Every man was born with willpower. Every man is tested, though the tasks might be tough for some of us. And, of course, every man is entitled to happiness and peace of mind; no man can deny this. Every man finds and seeks happiness in his own way, as pleasure is an individual quest, not a social solution. It seems like there are not enough happy, peaceful plates handed out to us in the queue of fate. You just can't make everybody happy!

Being city boys and used to the African hassle, we were almost inseparable. Each of us had our own mother tongue, so we used English as a common language. Besides the obvious reasons of tribal, religious, or regional choices of affiliation in the Mottak, some of us had been drawn to one another because a positive, laid-back attitude resonated across city boys in Africa.

In a continent where most governments have long neglected the voices and needs of the very people who most probably helped it overthrow its predecessor, as they are busy usurping wealth and piling on debts for the next in line, one faces a challenge when he or she lives in an African city. If one is lucky to have rich parents—regardless of how the money was earned, as there is a wide, blurry line between legitimate and illegitimate— all doors are open; unless disaster strikes, in which case shit can happen anytime. For the gifted, regardless of their upbringing, they can make a decent living, if they can bear to look the other way in response to all the injustice, corruption, and abuses of power at every level.

Then, there are those who give us all headaches with their self-proclaimed call for patriotism. They promise change for the people and take up arms, heading to the bushes or deserts or wherever they strive to catch headlines. Yet, faced with the paltry prospects offered by government funds or public schools, most disadvantaged and dissatisfied inner city youth turn to the streets for wisdom and fend for themselves. Even for those with a college degree, one's ethics, morals, and years of intellectual molding fail to deliver a decent meal to the table. With times testing even the resolve of the most decent, law-abiding citizen, people tend to bend the rules in desperation; none has faith in the system. Everybody is playing for keeps.

For the majority, who either lack the brains or the opportunity to pursue higher learning and lifelong skills, they depend on the streets. They find lots of shortcuts and loopholes to use and abuse! The middlemen of middlemen for the simplest of tasks feed many bellies. Bureaucracy is the largest employer, with the widest network base in the whole of Africa. The chain of command travels most often across tribal lines, where riches go from a gushing flood to a mere drop. Siphoned all the way along the pipeline of the economy, the majority only hears the gurgle as the riches rush past, heading to the taps of a selected few. "It's not what you know but who you know," people say. Some call it business, some call it hustle, some others call it petty crime, but it is a success to be envied if one makes it in the end.

With few ever utilizing that wisdom to create a lucky break, some dream of going overseas to test their fate. Most go on a short-term mission; few ever go for good. Even though few ever do so, the high expectation back home is that you eventually return with something. Whoever succeeds abroad, only good news makes it back to the hungry ears of brothers and sisters desperate to hear about the happy fortunes of their loved ones. Besides, unless on uncontrolled tantrum, no one would dare call or write back home of their failures and hopelessness.

Stuck in a big city, once a city boy, always a city boy! Full of broken dreams and limited opportunities, one found oneself surrounded, yet the prospect of heading home empty-handed was a suicide that few would attempt. If one gives up or is forced to go back, the humiliation, shame, and disappointment would torment one forever. Thus, with the hostile Babylon and tough competition for every second and dime available, one had to remain focused to play along in the plot, as if you knew your role.

The spacious building that housed around sixty asylums is perched on a hill at the intersection Asbjørns Selsbanes Gate, which meanders left and right through the narrow sloping landscape and merges to the main street, Storgata, and the Divisjons Gate that eventually winds its way up to the biggest hospital of Harstad, farther uphill. The brick-walled, two-story structure ironically stands in front of a Coast Guard Defense building. I guess you never know what to expect from us. As one friend from Mali joked, "Broddas, don't think you are free! We are in the middle of the town, but surrounded by the military!"

The front entrance facing the Defense office led straight to the multipurpose reception room. With a big, flat-screen TV entertaining the busy sofas that encircle it, the far end was the reception stand with a whiteboard hanging on the wall. Mail notifications were marked with initials for the recipients to collect from volunteer receptionists.

A narrow corridor led to the first kitchen, a spacious corridor with three ovens, and all the utilities required for cooking and baking. At the other end of the kitchen was a door to the office. The office accommodated six staff members who ran the place, and had two adjacent rooms and a basement store. The second room, separated by partitions and occupied by department managers, had an inside door that led to a wide meeting room with huge windows overlooking the town center and the distant Northern Sea. The exit door of the meeting room led to a tight corridor, with a closet room serving as the secondhand clothing store in a corner before returning to the reception.

The most popular hangouts were the reception or TV rooms and the Internet room, a tiny space at the far right end of the reception corridor that wound up and down the dormitories.

The residents were assigned space by the Mottak management, upon arrival, in the twelve rooms evenly distributed in the basement, ground, and first floors. Each room, with the exception of two small ones, housed four residents in the double-decker beds that were identical in all rooms. The cream, dull-colored walls were lit by fluorescent lights hanging from a high ceiling. With an air conditioner in the winter and ventilator in the summer, the rooms were modern and livable. The two bathrooms accessible to the residents were crammed in between rooms on the ground and basement floors, and the one toilet near the main entrance of the reception was designated for staff.

The Mottak had three exits: besides the entrance, there was one from the ground floor that led to the narrow Divisjons Gate and another through the gym in the basement. The rooms had simple, shared amenities: the fridge, a square table with two chairs, two sinks, and adjoining, separate closets with drawers. The roommates awaited their fates to be decided by the authorities, like thousands of others.

Enough about the place: Setting was nothing but a distraction, anyway. It was just a space. It never really justified nor defined an entity, if one had the right state of mind. As soon as someone realized you live in the Mottak, his or her whole perception of you changed dramatically, no matter how well the person might have known you. That was how it was; you were where you live. I might sound ungrateful, but don't get me wrong here. I have been through worse. This would be heaven compared to what I had been living before, in terms of material efficiency. Still, it was not the space; it was the state of mind that mattered in the end.

Many of us came from disaster zones, places without reliable electricity, water, and other utilities that the ordinary Western would think of as essential. The very thought of living without it would drive some insane, let alone if they had to live through it for a day or two. Well, in those "unforgiving circumstances," as some would say, was where some of us learned to adapt, rise up, and keep going. Some among us made it through horrible incidents where life was valued too cheaply; and wound up numb and unsurprised at the sight of another person gasping for the last breath on Earth. Life went on; some passed away, and some passed on.

"Pass on to where?" was the million-dollar question. Was it a stage, a level one got elevated to as soon as one overcame one obstacle along the way?

In any case, throughout the journey, some of us sought one thing genuinely: peace of mind. We just wanted to be free from the mental shackles that had starved us of our rightful destiny. So, the space in which we found ourselves confined, no matter how comfortable it might be, was a prison, no matter how artistically the encircling walls have been built. Yet the worst prison was the body itself. There were just too many battles on different fronts that some of us had to face. Feeling like a blind man doing a life sentence, as one friend had put it, "It is no easy in Babylon."

❦

Speaking of camps, I had been to some camps back on my continent. They are ugly. Some had been misplaced; others had been displaced. Run by NGOs or the UNHCR, the services are appalling. The best they can do is to keep you alive. Thatched roofs and ragged tents pass for shelter. With resources limited and residences often overwhelming the supplies, water and basics were a luxury.

The funny part is that a shanty town will often sprout alongside the camps to provide all sorts of services for the privileged. If a man has the money, he can get everything he wants; a decent meal and wash it down with a couple of beers, foreign brand cigarettes, a rented bed for a couple of nights until his documents are all sorted out, and all while the condemned languish inside the camps.

But then, many flee their homeland due to the millions of reasons you may or may not witness on your TV: the never-ending civil wars, tribal feuds, famine, extreme poverty, military conscription, political instability, and a whole lot of disabilities. However, not all refugees share the same ambitions. Some bide their time with patience in the camps until the situation stabilizes, so they can go back to wherever they came from. These groups rarely complain, regardless of how they are being treated by their hosts. It might take years or decades, but they make up their minds, "There is no place like home!"

Then there are those who look beyond, to the greener grasses. With their minds set upon the good and comfortable life awaiting them, they are never satisfied with the so-called safety the camps provide. Survival is not the quest, but the glamorous life they have been dreaming of their entire life. Some go to extraordinary levels to reach their destiny. But one thing is sure; there is always another way. The doors are always open for you, if you wish to fend for yourself.

That dream is what had brought most of us to Europe and beyond.

Many are sacrificed along the way. The journey is never easy. Some routes have deserts to cross, seas to navigate, armed guards, twisted bandits, and prisons you have to evade to get to where we were. It had been a long journey for us; only the lucky and the well-backed made it out the easy way.

So, now that we were here, we were just hoping for our misery to stop. Maybe it would be time for some reward that justified our suffering. But then, it never stopped!

The lack of opportunities were frustrating for us. We just needed a break to prove something. Not that we need to prove our worth to anyone; we were survivors, we could make it anyhow. We just needed to prove our worth to ourselves. We understood that we were intruding, yet we had legally and willingly surrendered ourselves to the authorities, hoping they would understand our burning desire for a fresh start. Nothing more! We were just humble Africans. We would be a colorful addition to any culture; not a threat.

Well, I speak for myself.

❆

Another year was coming to a freezing conclusion in the desolation camp. We had spent the whole of the first December, a Monday night, glued to the TV watching one horror movie after the other. Occasionally, Cliff would jump from his seat and growl, "What is de problem wid you people? Change it, na ah ahah!" He would grunt in disapproval like many West Africans, and would look around at the startled faces produced by his sudden outburst and say, "I tell you, dis vex me. Mtsee white people killing each other on de film at night, black people killing each other in de day on de news!" He would shake his head while still watching the gross Hollywood production, which failed to evoke the faintest of emotions. The least he felt was irritated while the rest of us had stayed until five, shuddering and wincing at our own will.

The Drama Inside: The Mondays

The next day was always the worst. Gloomy Monday; recycled every day of the week. It always felt like the first Monday of school. The same cycle of thoughts rushed all about you. Just another day! You woke up for nothing. Most of us slept away the day and half of the night.

I reached out and moved the thick dark window curtain, and lazily glanced through the thick basement window. The pile of snow was ever-present in the darkness outside. I wished I could remain in bed snoring in a deep sleep, but I had a sleeping disorder that prevented me from sleeping long hours. I envied those people who could just doze off at any given time of the day. Besides, my conscience never rested, reminding me of every misstep in my life.

The routine of the residents in the Mottak was so boringly redundant that it made me want to kill myself every time I thought about it. On those cold winter days, I and many others usually woke up, sometime around 1 in the afternoon, unless I had some chores or the language class to attend. Failure to do so would result in fines of 100 kroner for every absentee, roughly a day's pay of the 3,000 Kr allowance per asylum seeker. Fidgeting, tossing, thinking, and turning for as long as I could, with an occasional glance at the clock, I would force myself slowly to one of the two bathrooms shared by dozens. If lucky, I might find one of the booths free. Otherwise, it was a wait in a queue of two or three, fighting the smell of fresh shit from the toilets next to the shower booths. December was the toughest, though, with the arctic winter completely sucking the light and energy out of the skies and our bodies.

Usually, after a shower, I headed to one of the two kitchens to cook the day's meal. Some, frustrated by the occupied stoves, made stew in large pots that would last for days. After that, I only had a few options: head to the TV room to watch movies and sports nonstop to wear myself out and sleep, or spice it up with some Internet time for 5 kroner per hour, take long walks (only in the summer), work out in the crammed and crowded makeshift gym in the basement, chit-chat with my fellow asylums, or read books from the library.

While taking my shower in the basement bathroom, listening to some Persian, high-pitched song played by a couple of newcomers barbering each other over the sink, I was praying that I would run into Congo. The guy was my belly god; he had always been there when I was starving.

❁

Congo was stationed at the first room to the immediate right of the basement toilet—the dungeon, according to most of us. He had been living with a couple of French West Africans upon his arrival. Speaking French very well and being the friendliest person, he was a dream to have as a roommate. He often woke up early in the morning, for no apparent reason, though the old habit began to fade away the longer he stayed in the Mottak. Congo could be heard shuffling around the Mottak's marble tiles with his distinct humming and whistling of some catchy Congolese tune, often interrupted by a loud snicker. He would stop by every friend's room to see if they had woken up; and though he was sure we were dead asleep, he checked every morning.

Giving up, he would head down to the Mottak office and chat with the ladies at work. Leaning over the high wooden desk at the entrance that serves as a buffer reception to the boss's inner office, he would charm the workers as they slid and shifted files in and out of the crammed silver file cabinets. They were quite fond of his presence. A smile was written all over his dimpled, round face, regardless of his temperament. His innocent questions about why Norwegians often did things in a different ways, followed by his uncontrollable contagious laughter, was probably a welcome way to start a day before they began to encounter the grim and raging faces of the rest of us. Having passed some time charming the ladies, he would head back to the TV room. Splaying across one of the dull, cream, leather sofas, he would watch attentively all the news stations, so he could update the late risers when they woke. Glancing occasionally through the French window overlooking the parking area shared by the Coast Guard and the Mottak, seeking any insider gossip, Congo followed Al Jazeera, the BBC, and CNN to collect full coverage of whatever went on around the world from different angles, often exclaiming on his own, "Ayee, aye, whad is happening in dis world, mtsee...? Whyyyy small small boys and mothers dying every day? Eeyyyy!"

Fed up with catastrophe and chaos all over the world, but stocked with enough headlines to spark a conversation during awkward moments, he would return to his room to prepare a meal. He was very elaborate when it came to preparing meals. His roommates still in dream number infinity, Congo would cautiously withdraw a polythene bag and fill it up from the closet and the fridge with whatever he planned to cook for brunch, and then tiptoe his way out.

There was no such thing as quick breakfast or a snack for lunch; he took his meals very seriously. He would begin making a light breakfast while slicing and dicing onions and vegetables for lunch; all along, listening through earphones to some Congolese music and moving to the rhythm and talking to whoever was listening about some good times in Africa. He was a good and creative cook, being open to cuisines from all over. Whenever he ran into somebody cooking something peculiar, he would pay attention to the recipe and the process, and make the dish the very next day.

Having made his lunch, he would check once again whether any of his friends had awoken. He hated eating alone. If none had awoken, he would forcefully nudge any one of us. "Ehehe, I don't know whad your problem is, sleeping like cats all day. Wake up naw! I made nice lunch, come eat!" Knowing his cooking talents, few turned down the proposition. Most jumped up at once to wash their faces at the sink and dig in.

With the growl of my empty belly growing wilder by the second, I knocked at the door, hoping and praying he was inside.

"Come in, it is open naw," came a muffled shout from inside.

Voila, my prayers were answered as the two Frenchies—as we called them, for they only *parlent français*—and Congo were just finishing up lunch. Having needed no invitation, I headed straight to the middle cupboard where they kept the common plastic plates and spoons.

"You eat," said Congo. "Der is plenty. I made a nice fish sauce wid rice," he added, pointing towards the two pots on the table. "If you want to eat boiled potatoes, too, you have in de fridge."

I joined them at the table, with a mountain of rice dripping with spicy hot fish sauce.

He was a very good cook. Surprisingly, though, he spent very little on food, considering the quality of his diet. He was a bargain shopper, often leafing through the daily newspapers in search of ingredients on sale. He would announce, "My broddas, goat meat and chicken is on big sale," to which Cliff would chide, "I don't know who is paying you to advertise dis or dat on sale. Are dey giving you for free, coming here every day telling people buy buy buy? Why, my brodda!"

He always found something to keep himself busy, to the annoyance of some. A room in which three other men slept, ate, and hung out most of the day is expected to be a little messy; but not Congo's room. He scrubbed every smudge, washed thoroughly every unwashed dish and placed it in the closet neatly, swept the floor, and mopped it afterwards. These were routines he gladly and joyfully fulfilled. To top it off, he rarely complained. When people left a mess, he just gave them a disapproving look and his signature snicker, followed by, "Ayy, African men, we always messy. Expecting our women to clean up afta' us. Ayyye, mtsee!" he would mutter in that peculiar utterance most Africans share, and then pick up a rag to wipe off the mess.

Finishing off my day's meal, I sighed with relief. The three of them shared a good laugh after an exchange in French, probably at my expense, as I had heard even my mother complain that I ate like a drought-starved kid saved from the brink.

While I was washing the dish at the sink, Congo asked me, "You seen Cliff today?"

"No, man! I just woke up, you know!"

"Aaay, I don't understand you, man. You missed some drama in de morning!"

"What drama?" I was geared up to catch up on the action I missed, knowing anything that involved Cliff definitely had some hilarious story behind it.

"You know dat little boy, de Kurd? Aaaay, he almost turned de Mottak into Baghdad today." He broke out with a signature snicker and went on to narrate another Cliff mishap.

Cliff, who hated watching the news, had run into him and others watching the news on Al Jazeera of some suicide bombers who had blown up a Kurdish town market, killing dozens, including women and children. Restless with the news coverage that had taken too long, he had joked, "Mon, change de channel to music; dis no news. Dis people blow each oder up every day. Dey wake up to bomb blasts, not alarms!" With many laughing, it had encouraged him to go on. "Dey go, like, 'Ahmed, we meet tomorrow afta de second blast...'"

At that, most of the growing crowd burst into a loud laughter. For those familiar with his constant banter, none took him literally; he joked about everything. But there was a Kurdish teenager who, unnoticed by the others, was witnessing the scene in his hometown with horror. He could not control his anger at being made fun of. He jumped on Cliff with both hands, giving a raging, agonized growl, which took them all by surprise.

"It took five of us to subdue de man!" Congo said, raising his stretched palms, showing all five fingers for further effect.

Though feeling a bit guilty at his insensitivity, the irritated Cliff, after the surprise lunge, threw another punch line. "Hey, search dis man! Ah ha! Maybe he has some bomb in de belt, ready to blow," and he left the reception room before things got out of hand.

"Dey will kill him one day, I tell you," said Congo. "Dat man knows how he dies, I tell you." With a look of genuine worry, he got to his feet, gesturing me towards the door. "Let's go see him in his room na."

I was already smiling, imagining his animated version of events—it was always he who was the victim—as we headed to the farthest room in the basement.

⌘

Cliff's room was a ghetto. He shared it with two of his countrymen. All three of them were distinctly huge in physique, loud and expressive by nature. Though intimidating, at times purposefully, Cliff was the nicest of the three. His crescent-shaped, wide-open lips revealed perfect white teeth and canceled out the intimidating effect of his bushy eyebrows, restless big eyes, and dark, egg-shaped face.

Cliff was a messier and more passionate version of Congo. Clothing of all sorts was strewn across the room and the table cluttered with unwashed dishes of all sorts. At times everything the occupants owned would pile up like an abstract Lego creature an artist spent hours perfecting. Once in a while, though, he would be in the mood to clean the place inside out, spotless. Yet with dozens of visitors a day, it would take just hours to resume its ordinary, messy appearance.

He was the most irregularly regular person I had ever met. He had a unique rhythm that he stubbornly clung to, yet it worked out perfectly for him. The way he dressed, the diet he consumed, the cigarette brand he smoked, and the jokes he shared all mirrored his ever-changing moods.

These moods revolved around money. When he was loaded, he became the happiest man who ever lived; dressed up in his best and wore a smile from ear to ear for everyone to see. He would cook his famed spiced chicken sauce with smoked fish and rice and invite us all to join in a celebration of life. "In life, you have to enjoy, me broddas." Drinks were bought, music played at full blast, and the mood inside the Mottak was transformed. He made sure he lived for the moment, with full commitment. Whenever he was in the mood, the whole Mottak was alight, as he went from door to door, joking and kidding with whomever he ran into, even the officers with whom he often argued. When he was happy, the entire camp was brighter. He had this magnificent effect on people. Backed by the ever-snickering Congo, they were the most sought-after company, especially on those cold, boring nights.

Cliff was reclined in his favorite chair that he had dragged all the way from the disposable furniture plot. "Eeeey, me broddas," he said. "Was thinking of coming to see you people, you know." He threw both arms in the air in his welcoming way. "You have cigarette wid you?" he asked, looking towards me. Since Congo spent more on groceries and being a so-and-so smoker, we never pressured him to buy his own pack.

"No man," I replied. "I smoked ze last one in bed, man. Will buy from ze merchant later, man." I had a distinct Habesh accent, noted for its lack of the "th" sound. "Now, tell me what happened wiz you today in ze reception," I added, to his disappointment.

"You have money wid you?" he asked. "I finished completely aaaay. De merchant won't borrow me naw. You buy for me, I complete you after tomorrow." He decided this without even waiting for a response. Watching me still standing, he snapped, "Go on, naw! I tell you about it later. I tell you one thing, mon, I understand naw why dis Kurdish people have no country..." He trailed off as he rushed us out of his dorm.

My wet towel still hanging over my shoulder, we headed to the next dorm where I resided so I could change and scrape up what was left of my allowance.

In the first of the two rooms on the ground floor, Cliff knocked firmly and stepped aside, while narrating his version of the morning melee. "I swear to God, de boy was possessed. He jumped at me like he seen de devil. De boy gone kolo." Laughing uncontrollably, he stamped his feet before he went on. "I tell you, it is juju. Neva have I seen a person scream like dat. De boy needs Jesus, I tell you!"

While we were laughing along, an ever-agitated man cracked the door open with caution. "What you want, *kompis*?" he snapped. "I tell you *welahi*, no borrow. You buy or *muaselama*," he threatened, with his usual strategy of trying to put off a potential loan-seeker in a mix of Arabic, Norwegian, and English. Noting the indifference in the trio standing in front of him, he changed his tone and demanded, "What can I help you?"

"Look at dis man," Cliff exclaimed. "Why you always nervous? Maybe we come here to greet you, huh? Mtsee, you hopeless. We broddas. Why you do us dis way? We don't understand," he said, taking offense and hoping to rouse conscience of the man we called the Merchant.

"*Welahi*, I did not know," he answered. "Bror *beklager* now." Pity was not in his character, and he wiped the smile to inquire firmly, "What? What you want? I know you, Cliff. Why not you pay me money back?"

Giving up with the cajoling, Cliff snatched the fifty-kroner note from my hand and handed it to the Merchant with a plea. "You know I will go crazy if I don't get my cigarette, now give us two and I pay next tomorrow!"

His bartering over every issue was what made us call him the Merchant in the first place. "Why not you two smoke one pack? *Vet du* you share? Africans love sharing."

After a tiresome argument, he finally gave in and handed us a pack each. "I write it. You, Cliff, have now six pack. *Welahi*, I wait by door when you get money." The over-emotional Merchant noted the debt with a blunt pencil in the accounting notebook he carried in his back pocket.

We made our way upstairs towards the TV room, which was already packed with residents. Merchant followed us upstairs, jiggling his key chains and flip-flopping to holler at some poor soul who had been avoiding him for days. With the sight of the Merchant in the TV room, many faces squirmed, reminded that half of their allowances would be handed over to him. Otherwise the badgering never stopped. His presence would double when payday was near. He was not a guy to run or hide from.

The Merchant surely was the best businessman without an office in the Northern Hemisphere. He was a yes man. Whatever you needed, whoever you sought after, whatever time and cost, he was the man to see. He was renowned for the auction he held every Sunday. He lived on the first floor of the Mottak with a reticent Arab who barely uttered a word.

Every day, he would get up early at around six and get on with his daily patrol. He would begin with the Elkjøp electronics disposal ground. There, the Merchant would rummage through the pile of electronics the good citizens of Norway had deemed surplus. He would scan for portable electronics of all sorts and haul any he found back to the Mottak on his bike or on his back. Seeing what he found, one came to understand why Norway is consistently at the peak of the Human Development Index, with commercialism at its best in the never-ending race to keep up with the latest version. Given that the items discarded in an inviting open space, respectable yet less advantaged people often dug through the pile before the elements could ruin its contents.

Most items were in good condition, just outdated—like a couple of years off. Where I come from, few people ever get to change their TV sets let alone cars in a lifetime. You use them until they break down irreparably. Here, laptops, DVDs players, plasma TVs, mobile phones, refrigerators, washing machines in a relatively good working condition are left to rot. That's where the Merchant came into the picture, an environmentally productive yet undocumented member of society.

He would pick up every salvageable good, every day before the others had a chance. He would pile up his finds in his shared room, stocked for assessment. A gifted diplomat by nature and amazingly fluent in his three languages, he had been able to earn quite a reputation among the asylum seekers and foreigners living in that small northern town. Born in Ethiopia, but raised in Yemen, Saudi Arabia, Iraq, and a couple of stints in Southern Europe, he was a good middleman. With a short, skinny figure of light brown complexion, kinky brownish hair, sharp pointed nose, buried yet commanding eyes, and parted large lips that rarely came together, he had a familiar appearance that most cultures around the Red Sea area show, and he used this malleable look to his convenience.

Apart from salvage, he would buy anything else that caught his eye for next to nothing and bide his time to make a profit. The Merchant would scour many stores in town, flea markets, elderly homes, and ordinary neighborhoods to collect anything worth selling. Then, every Sunday at around noon, making sure all the staff members were gone from the Mottak, he would hold a massive auction.

It felt like African open market, with the street vendors displaying everything from cloth, to ornaments, to electronics, all colorfully crowding the pavement. Sprawled across the reception desk, potential buyers would hover in search of valuables and essentials at a reasonable price. Everyone always found something interesting they had been looking for some time, and then the bargaining began.

"How much for this jacket?"

"My friend, look at it! It's very good condition! *Jedid, welahi.* For you, because you are my friend, I give you for 200 kroner."

"Hey man, this is old. Give me for 50!" a disgruntled asylum would reply.

"Fifty? No, *kompis.* Try it on. *Jeg viser deg,*" and he would force the buyer to put on the jacket, hurrying him from behind and exclaiming for everyone to hear, "*Habibi,* you go out tonight to disco like zis, all women want you! Zis is classic, my friend." He would caress the jacket and try to comfort one. "No zis one no get old, my friend. You give to your lil' brazer one day."

With most owing money, they dared not differ.

"Yeah, you look good," another would add nonchalantly.

"Two hundred is fair, man," said one more, waiting impatiently.

"My friend, why don't you buy? Every time you complain. Dis man stingy ahh ahh!" He would finally convince the buyer to dish out the 200 kroner for a jacket the Merchant had gotten for free from an elderly person's house.

As convincing as he was, the Merchant was relentless, with his fidgeting hands often touching you gently on the shoulders and the jaw to show his compassionate side. He often sold out and quietly headed to his room to count his profits. He never divulged how much he was making, often complaining, "*Habibi*, I make no money. I give you for *gratis*, my friend."

On weekdays, he would sell cigarettes—LM, the cheap expired soggy Russian cigarettes that smog the Mottak constantly. Thanks to frustration and boredom, LM was the sixth finger of the asylum boys. Buying them from an undisclosed Russian source at the lowest of prices, he sold them at half the price of the cheapest cigarette sold in stores. The expiry date never bothered anyone; we were living on expired dreams, so the numbers were just like a decoration. In fact, half the money from the two weeks' allowances went to his pockets, thanks to his credit system, which he strictly enforced.

He would show up twice every second week until you gave in to his demands. There was this one time I had been unable to pay my debt on time, and man, was he nagging me every chance he had. He would show up first thing in the morning, wake me up from my restless sleep, saying, "My friend, why you not give me? I know you good man. Why I give you cigarette anytime, *welahi*? Pay me now! I want to send money to family."

I convinced him that I would borrow from friends and pay him later that day. The Merchant went out and closed the door, shaking his head in disappointment.

While I was still in the bunk, tossing and turning, he came back again, now able to speak some Amharic: "*Ante lij* money *stegn*. I saw your friend Cliff today, he has big money. *Tebeder tolobel, habibi.*"

I told him I would.

But he would not leave the room, and continued harassing me, on and on, switching from one language to another every other second. "*Kompis jeg er blakk.* Me poor, my friend, family need money. I am sick hospital, *mehed albegn, ikke bra habibi.* You have *kjæreste* ask money. And why you sleep all day? Cliff *er ute inehid...*"

I finally gave in and got out bed. "*Shower ladregna genzebhen estehalew.* I will borrow and give you your money, okay, my friend?"

He went on and on, narrating about who owed him money and how nobody ever paid him back and how badly he needed the money now. Oh man, he followed me to the toilet, reminding me that he would come see me later. "I know you. You are good man. You not like others," he said, appealing to my humanity. "I know you! *Welahi*, I know you give me money. *Bhwala metalew.*" And then he marched right back to badger somebody else. The funny thing was, he played the same trusting, nagging, and friendly trick on everyone, knowing they eventually gave in.

He also sold prepaid mobile phone minute cards for all the telecoms the residents used, spices not ordinarily sold in stores, bus and plane tickets that were booked by mysterious fellows on the cheap, and alcoholic drinks just after the curfew hours of 8 in the evening. He could help anyone that needed anything fixed, from watches to laptops, for a fair charge. The Merchant was by far the most sought-after fellow in the whole building. He was valuable in the Mottak, so few people crossed him. You could end up needing something badly on any given day. Life would have been a whole lot more inconvenient had he not been around. There were some who bought everything they ever needed from him and never left the Mottak.

It was common, the sight of him swinging his round head, like a lollipop, shuffling his big flip-flopped feet, size 46 for a guy 1.6 meters tall, screaming at the top of his lungs in that high-pitched screech, "My friend," "*Kompis,*" "*Ere jeles,*" "*Habibi,*" or "*Amico.*" I never heard him address anyone by name; that was how we understood that he just meant business.

❧❧

That particular Tuesday night in the TV room, the usual suspects had already assumed their positions. A heated argument ensued, provoked by the strong spicy aroma that circulated in the air from the kitchen by a group of Eritrean and Ethiopian residents cooking the infamous *dorowet*.

One West African exclaimed out loud in disgust, "What dis people eat? Disgust me!"

Another one added, "I don't know what they eat, taking days to prepare. Is it bomb or what?"

Once the ranting in dismay began, it was contagious.

"Dey fill it wid spice! Dis people are crazy! Never seen no one eat like dis people!"

The already bored-to-death Cliff finally found a subject to drag on and mull over. He spit out, "Dey leave the kitchen too dirty. No bother to clean. Den dat modafoker wake us up from sweet sleep for us to clean der shit. Mtsee!"

"Hey, like you don't leave mess. Come on, it's not zat bad," I interjected, hoping to diffuse the tension and to kind of defend my culture.

But my attempt drew the ire of mostly West Africans, led by the lively Cliff. "Ayyy, I don't know why you put so much spice in your food." Staring at me, with his inquisitive bulging eyes, he went on. "I like your food. But it takes four hours to prepare and dat what you call injera takes a week and after you eat it, my friends," he looked around to make sure everyone had his attention, "it is torture to the mouth, the eyes. Burning, my God." He looked up into the sky and sarcastically added, "I thought you people spilled de spices accidentally."

The West African side of the reception burst into loud laughter, satisfied that Cliff had delivered a fair verdict.

"And when it comes out, me brodda! I thought somebody was lighting my ass on fire. Burning hell! Oh God!" He broke into another round of animated laughter.

The Habeshs, Eritreans, and Ethiopians, outnumbered in the reception room, fidgeted in our seats, having been made fun of for our traditions, but we knew better than to do anything but let it slide. Engaging in a discussion with Cliff was a lost cause; he was relentless. Eventually, the laughter ceased and most eyes returned to the TV where a tennis tournament was being played live. In those times, we watched anything athletic—except golf and cricket, that is.

❦

However, the two kitchens were a battleground. The upper kitchen, used mostly by people residing on the top floors, is bigger and more accommodating. It has spotless, creamy brown tiles maintained constantly due to its proximity to the office, and is often a busy area. The spacious, farmhouse, stainless steel sink has wide-enough double bowls and adjoins double-decker bakery ovens and stainless steel kitchen cabinets full of utensils. The bakery ovens are seldom used apart from public holidays that involve mass cooking. On the other end are four, separate, modern electric stoves with their complete sets and appliances to cater to the appetites in the building.

Given all this space, it was funny how little things led to bitter fights. As we all came from different cultures, we all had our unique dishes we prepared for some home-away-from-home comfort. Yet the flavors and odors of a special dish were often repulsive to others.

If an Eritrean or Ethiopian happened to cook the spicy roasted beef or chicken sauce or bake injera—the staple thin sheath of highly yeasted and fermented bread—the odor would reek throughout the entire kitchen and make its way to the reception area. Those not familiar with the odor, while sitting probably brooding over their delayed reply from the authorities, might be incensed by it; and there went another exchange of words and hateful looks.

The same went for everyone, such as when the Arabs and their Middle Eastern friends got their turn to cook. Some of them were experienced chefs who at times worked in some Norwegian or Italian restaurants. They cooked their favorite dish, fish, for which they constantly headed out to sea by themselves in the summer. In the kitchen, some of these cooks would take all the space for hours, baking their homemade breads, their sauces, or their unpopular fish stew in the oven. As they, at times, cooked at odd hours, the entire Mottak might be offended by the smell of fish; and there went another drama...

"I don't understand why zis people have to make fish like zat!"

Another would add, "I don't know what dey do with de fish. It smell so rotten!"

Some others might be infuriated by their full occupation of the space for too long. "Are you cooking for the whole village? What is dis! De rest of us are suffering!"

But the same went for every culture: What is not yours looks and smells weird, but it is only strange to a stranger.

However, the longer we lived together and befriended one another, some of us dared to try out others' food. Still, stereotypes were difficult to wash from one's perception; be it a Nigerian fufu with some stocked fish-spiced sauce, which actually tastes exquisite, or the Habesh injera and wet, or the East African cassava, mattokke, or Arab couscous with fish, or Somali spaghetti with unique meat sauce or whatever Western food one desired, every culture had some new spice or sauce that it prided above the rest. Thus, most of us stuck to our familiar customs or the common dishes that didn't have "weird" ingredients. But the fact remained, few of us cleaned up after use, to the disgust of whoever cleaned up the next day. The funny part is, everybody blamed everybody else for the mess. The East Africans blamed the West Africans, the Muslims blamed the Christians, the Africans blamed the Arabs, the Arabs blamed the Kurds, and vice versa.

The same went for the other kitchen, with bitter fights over who had claimed a shelf of the oven first. At times, someone would come out enraged from somewhere else, crying, "Who switched off my pot?" to unconcerned, indifferent looks from the others in the kitchen. It was funny to watch at times—unless you were involved, that is. Since everyone was living on the edge, a simple exchange of words could escalate to any level.

At around nine, tired of a rerun of football games and redundant action movies, the three of us decided to head out to town on our evening routine of patrol. Though it was a weekday, the nightlife was as good as any city's under curfew; you just never knew who you might run into. With a charismatic duo by my side, some local folks were often curious enough to have a conversation or two, followed by a round of beers.

After a quick dinner at Cliff's, we headed down the main gate. A breathtaking cold gust of ocean wind welcomed us outside. We trudged down the slope of Asbjørnselbans Gate without a word. Stabbed viciously by sharp air knives, even the motor-mouth Cliff was tongue-tied.

It was biting cold; still, we managed to stretch and slide out of control, just for the hell of it. We had not been out for a couple of days and things were too boring around the Mottak for us. The jokes were getting stale, groceries running out, and cigarette vendor getting sore, and the tension was escalating in the TV room. Besides, you never knew what a cold, blacktop, white-down night had to offer. So we had overdressed for a stroll.

There was a dreaded spot a hundred meters down from the camp where you would definitely slip; you just didn't know when exactly. You just hoped you fell down in style. A frozen pothole of water was covered by a thin layer of snow, totally undetectable at night. At times, it made us wonder if it was a malicious prank by some bored pensioner, who was probably cracking his ass up in his living room watching us on a hidden camera. Though we had been advised to wear ice studs over our shoes, we were skeptical, as usual. Every time anyone wearing a pair of those walks behind you, it makes you jump because they sound like police horse hooves clicking and clanking every time they come in contact with the hard ice.

The night lamps illuminated the white path ahead. We took a right turn down Sigurds Gate, rather slipping and sliding along the sporadically salted narrow street.

Cliff found his tongue. "I don't know why dey don't salt dis way to de Mottak. Mtsee, dey probably laugh through de window every time dey see us fall. Some entertainment. I tell you dis is a conspiracy!"

Congo slipped and rolled on the wet snow, unable to control his snickering. "I know, man," and he broke out once again with a muffled laugh. "Am picturing it. Like Channel 3. De open de window and de three of us de black musketeers..." He trailed off on his own. Laughing and pointing at one another with the dire excitement of our imagination, our feet finally hit the warm cable pavement of Hans Edegate Street.

The stone buildings that line the street and eventually merge towards the sentrum, the town center, were dangerously quiet. With most buildings being offices and business centers that rarely came to life even in the dark daytime, it was at times unnerving to walk alone. The skeletal trees across the street from the Bingo Building in the park were decorated with Christmas lights, flickering a gloomy combination of colors, yet it was the cold breath swooshing past the heavily cottoned trees that grabbed our attention.

Crossing the intersection that led to towards the sentrum came the lonely figure of a black man. He walked cautiously towards us. He had the entire flashing outfit we had been advised to wear at night. He had a white ski mask, the yellowish vest, a flashing key chain dangling from his waist, a flashing armband, and one tied to his left ankle.

It was Congo who broke out with his snicker. "Look at dis man looking like de first black man to walk on ice."

"My friend, it's not bad enough it's cold," replied the man. He was a new resident from Guinea, and defensive. "I am slipping every other meter and I have to look to de side to see cars too. Dat is too much work for a walking man." He shook his head in dismay, a bit ashamed that he kind of looked ridiculous.

"E, dey paying you for the advertisement, my friend?" Cliff questioned. "Or you doing this one for free too?" he added, giving him a thorough look.

"Ah ah, protection, my friend."

"My friend, all the flashing is for white people, not for us. Trust me," snapped Cliff, irritated.

"Mtsee, trust you. Do you know how many are killed by cars who can't see dem in dark?"

"My friend, you are de blackest man I know, walking on white sheet of earth." Cliff bent over to let out suppressed laughter, and went on, "What more of a mark dey need?" Looking towards us with a smile, Cliff added, "Maybe even betta, you look like a moving tree from a distant. And you telling me they still don't see you..." He pointed at the shining logo. "Ah ah, what is with de company logo on it, huh? Is it advertisement?"

"No man, it is the name of company giving it for free," replied the agitated boy, trying his best to end the conversation as soon as possible.

But Cliff was just getting started and we were thoroughly enjoying the encounter. "Company giving it for free! Look at look at dis fool!" He looked back at us with a gleam in his eyes and a poking finger at the new boy, who was so embarrassed that he could barely face us. "Nothing is for free in Babylon, my friend." Mockingly, he laughed and added, "I tell you, my friend, you are advertising der company for free. And dis man still thinks dey is doing him a favor. Wake up, my friend..."

We all laughed in amazement at his interesting thread of a theory. He always had a different way of looking at things.

But the boy did not give up yet. "Oooh, I know you! You always try to criticize everything I do. Everything I do is wrong, according to you, Mr. Professor," he snapped in an irritated tone.

"Professor! Ah ah, I school you anytime, my friend," Cliff said, "but I understan' why dey, dis company, chose you particularly." He pointed at the logo of some insurance company glistening in the dark. "Dey might have watched you walk up and down, up and down, for no reason all day, my friend... Walkin' around like legedisbenz in Africa, ah ah!"

Even the boy was grinning at that comment, while we were nearly in tears, laughing our asses off in that cold night.

But Cliff heated up whenever people were laughing at his jokes. "I tell you, my broddas, de saw opportunity. 'Hey, why not use dis man to advertise our products for free? He covers more area dan de mail man.'" And he trailed off, cracking up and stomping his feet uncontrollably.

"You are crazy. I don't know why am freezing here, listening to your bullshit," the boy said, and he was off, leaving us still grinning from Cliff's quick punch lines.

❧

Though we had thought of taking a longer tour around the town, the wet breath was whistling on our faces, barely hindered by the rows of wooden houses that stood between us and the raging North Sea. First stop was Nordlys, the spacious pub with a huge garden perched on Havne Gate, opposite the Harstad University College, overlooking the North Sea. It was a famous hangout for the more financially stable, single, horny women. The place had the charm of a country pub, the kind one always sees in melancholy, Midwestern American movies: wooden everything in a dimly lit cabin full of bench seats strewn around hard timber tables in every corner. Yet the place had a homey atmosphere. It was a karaoke night, with only a few regulars relaxed in the spacious, classic bar. The spot was still not used to having the likes of us walking in, as we often drew glances that seemed to ask, "What the fuck are they doing here?" But we had thicker and darker skins, and strolled in without a bother.

An old man was attempting to sing country music in a sleepy stupor. None seemed to care, except what I assumed to be his drinking buddy, who was applauding the off-key number, bobbing his head from side to side with his eyes closed—nostalgia. Given our unspoken rule of never buying a drink outside the Mottak on a weekday, we avoided the condescending look of the bartender and sat around a booth at the farthest corner. We had never heard of the song, but the screeching voice pouring out of the old man's throat, abused by its decades of tobacco and alcohol, strangely resonated with the night's weather; a graveyard symphony.

"Ayy dis is a blasphemy," snapped the irritated Cliff and gestured us towards the exit. "I tell you, if dis happened in Nigeria, you would be stoned to death."

We followed Cliff out onto the smoking couch, outside under a heated awning. We lit our LM's and were somehow drawn towards the distant, dark, raging ocean to our left. With the old man's number playing in the background, the ocean had turned on the show, blowing steam in natural frustration. Some phenomenon must have provoked it, stirring its vastness from a nap. It was frightening; for some reason, out of the dark blues, everything about the night reminded me of death.

Dragging a lungful of the soggy LM, my thoughts were suddenly consumed by the uncomfortable thought, animated in the form of the vast sea. They say death looms from afar, like the clouds when you are young, then descends to a visible fog; a stench reeking closer in your mid-thirties, then lurking behind you like a shadow in your forties, if you make it that far, and then you begin to feel its every move, like an echo inside you, like the lub and dub of the heart, teasing and cajoling, left and right, before sweeping you off your feet in the end. It was the only constant rule of nature; the rest was subject to change. And the immortal ocean felt like it was mocking my temporary existence, reminding me of my passage. "Even the mountains crumble down in a fraction of a second, only I remain," it bellowed. Standing from a safe distance along the coast, one can see its charm as it laps at the beach, like a baby on all fours so adorable, fooling you for a second before it grows deep, way too deep and fast, epitomizing a young man's life. You only head deeper, lost and out of touch, stranded in the middle between the beginning and the end, navigating the undiscovered depths, swimming in exhaustion. It waits and waits and snatches you down into the thick, impenetrable darkness when you least expect it. "You are just another insignificant drop in the ocean, nothing more!"

I quickly shook off the thought that had become more frequent of late; my demons had crept up on me.

It was a flat night as we headed back, with a last lap around the sentrum before we cut back and headed up to the camp. On our way there, retracing our route, we ran into the lone figure of Knut, or Chucky as Cliff had dubbed him, sipping his pils, lost in himself as usual, probably contemplating death. It was probably in the air that night, I figured. He looked withdrawn; maybe he had some mushrooms and believed he was imagining us. He barely looked up from the freezing doorstep of the town mall. The cold was too much to bear as we waved from afar and headed back straight to the Mottak.

That night, lying in my bunk, the demons inside me ran amok. Whether self-inflicted or in complicated circumstances, it was one of those days when something powerful just sucks your energy from the marrow. The mini-depression moved in like an unfriendly roommate in the tiny rom; I wished to ignore it, but it was always there, doing something annoying. With all the uncertainties in life—my case was taking too long to be decided by the authorities—it reverberated in my thoughts during those sleepless nights, making me wish to wake up dead at times. All the dark thoughts beat me down hard. I mean real hard, man!

It was one of those days, which often lurk in like the dark arctic winter, when I felt like mourning for my own death. How fucked up this must sound, but it was like waking up to dress up all in black, to head to one's own funeral every fucking day! The coffin open and welcoming! The world was hostile as quicksand in a desert storm. As sick as it sounds, I felt there was nothing to wake up to, just loitering around. Numb and stiff as a mummy. Betrayed by time and circumstances, no space to either park or spark. Just wasting oxygen for nothing. No prospect to serve, I floated along, still looking for my spot. "I sure must have a destiny and a purpose to breathe," I questioned myself over and over again. Yet, I felt like I was walking around for no reason at all.

Lying back, staring at the dark ceiling, I didn't know where or with what to start, as my grievances in this wretched path they call life never seemed to cease until the day I would capsize. I tossed and turned in my bunk. I was tired of drifting aimlessly. Sick and tired of getting sidetracked and just pretending as if everything was all right. I wished to stay focused but visions got hazy and clouded; I was so confused that I kept seeing mirages at times, even lost in the jet-black darkness where no light was in sight, in any direction. Was it fear of the unknown or was death so close by? I had no clue! There was nothing worse than the feeling of losing yourself inside yourself. Feeling so empty, I wanted to scream out loud; maybe it would help. But then, I could not risk being labeled. It was no fun being a little "kuku" around Africans. You just had to hold it together, to yourself, and wake up with that empty smile the next day. Hoping to wake up, I forced myself to begin a happy thought that would end up in a happy dream.

I waited and weighed, but my conscience had a tight grip on my conscious. With no idea where to begin or where to turn, it was like the winding cord of fate had entangled and strangled my mind so tight that I could not breathe. It never finished me off, though, just left me by a thread with a faint pulse. I felt like ceasing to exist, yet kept breathing. The night was so agonizingly long, but that too would pass and I would finally drift away.

Chucky was in fact our first white friend in town. Some people thought he was probably a Russian or some Eastern European refugee whenever they saw him loitering in the camp. At times, he would crash on the reception sofa and snore wildly as if he were on his king-size bed. He would wake up and stretch his hands, yawning and lazily gazing at the black and brown faces glaring at him. He was a drug addict—with a good heart, though. He was the first and the only native Norwegian who had really felt and understood what it was like to live inside the reception center. The depressing feeling of being invisible in a high-rolling society, the freedom and the recklessness of living a hopeless, strive-for-the-day attitude, was something one could not understand until fate forced you to see.

He was disowned by his family and the generous welfare state for abusing drugs, thus becoming a nuisance to the community. The offer of psychological assistance—if he committed himself to a psychiatrist yard, which would have enabled him to rehabilitate himself and his image and slowly work his way back into the safe and comfortable hands of his people—had never appealed to him. He was just a small-time, harmless rebel and loving every second of it.

Being scorned by his countrymen inspired him to rebel even more in every way, and against what the system stood for. He was infamous; people recognized him and he did whatever was possible to infuriate them. We knew quite well it was not through pity or compassion that he was spending time with us in the camp; it was rather the common feeling of rejection by the system that bonded us.

When he was high with whatever he was injecting himself with—crack or crystal—his demons took over. His shoulder-length, unkempt, blond hair would shadow half of his bushy, heavily bearded, pink face. The raging, bloodshot, bulging eyes restlessly scanned the surrounding to lash out; the gritting teeth; fists clenched tight, ready to throw a punch; striding with purpose with his beat-up army boots stomping the ground—these would scare the daylights out of a stranger. Yet the worst he would do was kick an empty trash bin. He wished he were violent, though. Ranting on and on how he would make the system pay. "They will pay, I tell you. I will never sell my soul. I will die a free man!"

For some unknown reason, he despised ordinary Norwegians, openly criticizing and making fun of them. Though we understood little of what he would say to them, their sudden change in demeanor and at times near-confrontational incidents told the stories. But you felt their discomfort in his presence; at times, they would try vainly to appease his demands, just to get away from him in peace.

Wednesday, another Monday takes over where it left off. I had those days where I woke up stiff and longing for the need to penetrate. My ever-flexible soul mate, the woman of my dreams, meticulously crafted by my fantasy, would pop up at intervals during the self-deprecating and soul-immolating sessions like an advertisement break during the night, and take over the show for the day. The cravings for the need to penetrate would become overwhelming. The intermittent scenes in my head, switching from my stagnated fate to daylight erotic fantasy, would swing my petulant mood to the other extreme, and demand an outlet. Every unforgettable, haunting quality of the women in my life would be juxtaposed to make a montage of the woman of my dreams, whom I would penetrate on and on unnaturally while I toss, wince, and turn in my bunk, eyes glued to the milky ceiling.

I had missed many language classes in the past few weeks, already incurring a fourth of my two weeks' allowances. The gravity on my bed was like quicksand, pulling me back deeper into a fuzzy slumber. In those odd, dark, arctic morning hours, to add to my dilapidated state of mind, my speech department was on strike. Words even in my mother tongue came out laboriously. I needed the money, but I was rock hard under the bed sheets.

The frustrated and more stagnated I got in life, the more I longed for release. The scenes got more perverted. On those days, with every woman who got away, every woman who had rejected me, and every woman I had been unable to make an advance on, as well as the woman I despised and wished to humiliate, my mind would recreate the scenes where I made amends. It had been weeks since my last encounter with my sugar mommy. After agonizing moments of cajoling my penis to sleep, I forced myself up while telling myself that I definitely needed to make up with her and blow off some steam.

Out of habit, I drew the curtains open. In the total darkness a distant street lamp illuminated the narrow street. Mumbling my displeasure in my mother tongue, I limply shuffled towards the sink and washed my face. The water was electrifyingly cold, sending tremors up and down my nerves. The image staring back at me had lost a couple of kilos and aged a lot since the last time I paid attention to it. My hair had made a dramatic retreat in matter of months, yet being unkempt, had shabbily dreadlocked itself. My big, bloodshot eyes were even intimidating to myself. I had not shaved in a while; with my beard hanging down, even the Somalis had been greeting me with a smile, *"Aselam alikum,"* thinking I was one of theirs. We looked so much alike, anyway, from having been part of the great Aksumite Empire in the glory days.

I looked around at the other bunks. The occupants had already left. They were both annoyingly early risers, specially the Korean guy; I had no idea what he did afterwards. I checked the time and it was already 8. The classes began at 8:15. The Voksenopplæreingen, the language school for adults, was located some 500 meters down the street.

❦

Even though the Mottak was a temporary residence for asylum seekers, some had made it their home. According to the Norwegian Directorate of Refugees, the procedure to decide upon the asylum case of an individual takes from three months up to a year. Within that period, those who fit the criteria of the directorate as legitimate cases requiring protection are granted their residence and work permit. Priority is given to those who come from a crisis region, where their lives are under threat due to political or civil unrest; those ones came and went in a couple of months. They were the forgettable faces that soon were replaced by others. For the rest whose cases were under investigation, the longer you waited, the greater your chances of getting rejected. It was a common belief that once you passed the six-month mark without a reply, you should start contemplating a plan B. Likewise, the rejection letters poured down on the residents more frequently. The bad news was often relayed by the residence officers or a letter from the Immigration Police.

For the more or less forgotten and rejected ones, the resident paper issue was a forbidden subject. You had the sleepless long nights to mull over it. When you woke up, you scurried around nonchalantly in the Mottak. The future had hit a dead end for the rejected. Unable to get a job without a permit and having already surrendered fingerprints to the authorities, you'd be restricted from trying your luck somewhere in Europe.

With the stress inside and the mistrust from outside, roommates shifted like sand dunes in the desert. Naturally, people from the same country were assigned to the same living quarters, yet that did not ensure they get along. To coexist peacefully inside close compartments, it was best to live with someone totally different from you. It kind of balanced out; though you began at odds, ridiculing each other's eccentricities, you eventually grew accustomed to each other's ways and finally learned to compromise. Think-alike friends often started off great but most times ended bitterly, as they began to find and magnify the differences that had been camouflaged and tolerated before. Two short-fuse roommates would end up with shorter fuses after getting into each other faces over irrelevant issues. It would be ideal if one held the brake of reason while the other stepped on the gas for some entertainment.

I had assumed I made great company until I went through multiple roommates in a couple of years. Being an extrovert and moody at times, I must have driven them crazy, waking up every day with a different demon steering my mood. But some of the guys were really weird, and I had trouble holding back remarks. There was this one who was a professional martial artist who freaked me out with his blank stare. I would wake up in the middle of the night to his bald head and beady eyes fixated on the wall behind me, or at me directly; I couldn't tell. With the stress and at times paranoia that came with the place, I had no idea what went through his mind. It was him, and an old guy, and I who had been assigned to a basement room when we arrived. They were from Ethiopia, the country where I was born. Having lived more than half my life in Addis Ababa, I related more to the light, humorous attitude of the Ethiopians than to the courteous yet suspicious demeanor of my fellow countrymen.

As it was in the beginning, we got along pretty well. We joked freely to stem some of the stress of arctic cultural shock. But then the drama started ...

"Ante yeselam new mindin new inde bich belilitu ymtafetebgn?" (What the hell are you staring at me for in the middle of the night?)

The guy would just blink and glare blankly at me. I would cuss in my mother tongue in a whisper, because provoking a martial artist in the middle of the night was not a sensible thing to do. It would take me a while to go to sleep, though. I would wake up every time I heard the slightest of sounds inside the room. The guy was ridiculously and unnervingly quiet.

The old guy was mesmerized by "Korea," as we dubbed the martial artist. At times, he would practice his abchaki, yubchabi, kumsa one, and kumsa two, brandishing two knives and tearing up the air at a blazing pace while we watched without making a sound.

After rumors trickled into the Mottak that two former residents had already been transferred to a psychiatric ward following threats to the rest of the residents, every little sign of weirdness was deemed a possible case of insanity. After one resident had been reported carrying around a knife to protect himself from the devils trying to steal his soul, these were alarming. Though Korea was as calm as they came, we were not really comfortable with the knife show. The older roommate of mine used to tease Korea in his absence by saying maybe he should use his extraordinary knife skills in slicing and dicing the onions and vegetables we struggled with in the kitchen, instead of torturing the air.

Even some of our friends were a bit alarmed when they opened the door and stood face to face with a short guy jumping and kicking in midair with two kitchen knives in hand. After stumbling into Korea during his daily practice and receiving a steely glare and an angry huff of air, Cliff had replied with a slam of the door and hurried past the corridor, "Eey eey, dis Blacki Chan in your room, whad is he planning to do? I don't know and don't like it. I don't like it!" Smiling and shaking his head in a mocking concern, he said, "My friend, you live in Chinatown, bedder watch dat man. Me don't stay in dat room, neva. Huyyya wid a knife if he gets angry. Not very good, my friend. You have to once again seek asylum inside anoda asylum center, my friend."

In the class of a dozen, the language teacher gave me a scalding, disappointed glance before I took my seat at the back, by a window on the third floor building. It had been weeks since I last attended the obligatory, twice-a-week classes. I had not done the assignment nor read the textbook, so the old woman kept muttering in frustration about the lack of interest. Even though I had been attending the course erratically for over half a year, I still had only an elementary knowledge of the language. It was just not sinking in.

Out of the dozen, only two were enthusiastic participants, and unsurprisingly, both had been granted residence and work permits. The rest, either pending or rejected, were just there for the attendance, including me, constantly checking the time, occasionally flipping through the illustrated pages, and seldom shaking or nodding our heads in reply. I wandered in fantasy. My dream girl came to mind and I drifted away, while the teacher had the ones sitting in the front read a passage. "Det er et rødt hus..." Sometime in the day, I reminded myself that I would have to call my sugar mommy and make up. She was pretty sore after my last outburst at one of her parties.

The arrangement I had with my sugar mommy was manageable. She was in her early forties, married and divorced a couple of times, and had no desire to ever get married again. She was very skeptical of men; not surprising in a country where more than half of the married end up divorced. Having set her career goals long ago, she had firmly stuck to her principles not to ever compromise for a man. Men, in her words, were "weaklings that never stop sucking up the titties of body and mind until you dry up. Then, when you do dry up, they walk away in search of another victim." She had her tubes tied long ago, in her twenties; a grave decision for such a young woman, yet never did I sense any regret from her. For her, kids were just noisy, demanding distractions that enslaved women. Her life was her career and her three cats; she had no room for any one but occasional drop-bys. Had it not been for her sexual appetite, she would have done without men for the rest of her life.

She had no affiliation with any religion, yet had in-depth knowledge of faith institutions, which she kept to herself. Deep-rooted, proud nationalist that she was, she rigorously followed current affairs. Yet, instead of stating her opinions in the open, she left anonymous critical comments on Internet news article that incensed her, a practice in which she buried herself for hours.

Her plump, opaque face rarely betrayed her emotions. It masked her emotions and opinions, making her often hard to read. Blinking blankly, she would let even the most offensive expressions roll by. She often played with her long, curly, blond hair with her fingers when pondering a thought; this somehow made up for her rigid expression. At first glance, her thin lips gave you the impression that they had never cracked a smile in her entire existence, with a twitching pale nose not helping with that impression, either. Full figured and remarkably agile that she was, she was very aware of her bulging waistline, for which she adjusted her clothing style. As dully organized and cautious as she was, though, this camouflaged a rebellious streak that came to life during intoxication. After a couple of glasses of wine, the opinioned self would come alive. Animated and unreserved, she would engage in long conversations with any stranger who had the ears for it. Yet, she was very tolerant and had a better understanding of other cultures than many I encountered in Europe.

I never caught her eye on the occasions I frequented the local jazz club, Nordlys, where we fished for sugar mommies in our weekly night patrols from bar to bar, looking for some action. It was the liveliest of the handful of other pubs and clubs in that small northern town. Congo had been the boldest, initiating a conversation in French with the three ladies that were sitting at the adjacent table that rainy autumn night. The place was packed with out-of-towners who had come for some event we were not quite aware of. Yet they were buzzing and quite generous; we barely paid for a drink, yet the beers kept coming the entire night.

We paved the way toward comforting the ladies with our presence, through the charm of Congo and his fluent French, and through Cliff and his quips. The ladies invited us to an after-party. We gracefully accepted the offer and took a taxi to what was soon to become my every-other-day house, a stone's throw away from our beloved camp, near the hospital. Inside the first taxi, I sat next to a younger but shy girl who happened to be the niece of my sugar mommy's colleague.

Her two white fat cats and a tiny black cat sprawled on her sofa, welcoming us. Cliff was never comfortable in the apartment and dubbed her Thatcher, for her Iron Lady–like composure. He despised cats of all sorts, especially black ones, which were considered a curse in his culture. I never trusted them, and Congo was not really that comfortable around them, either. After having the cats locked out on the balcony at Cliff's insistence, the party ensued—beginning with the ladies joking at our superstitiousness.

"I don't understand why you people keep cats in your home," Cliff said, looking concerned, while lighting a cigarette from the candle fire. He continued, "Dey are de devil; you see dogs in de eye, you see loyalty. But de cats, eeeey, you see evil, ah ah." The three woman were giggling over our reaction.

"Cats are clean. You just have to love them the right way," replied Thacher, "and you don't need to train them like dogs or men. They do it themselves." The three of them went on exchanging funny comments in their language that further animated them.

I went on to relate a theory that a cat would eat you alive if it were locked up to starve for weeks, while a dog would never leave your side, even after your death. It must have something to do with women and their intuition that escaped men, this natural attachment of cats to women, as they dismissed the theory without a second thought. But we saw cats differently, the veiled rage, caged within the tiny body that never fooled us.

The cats were the talk and joke of the night until Congo put the issue to bed with his cynical remark. "I have one question. Why de two white cats are fat and de black very thin? Don't you feed dem equally?" He broke into a snicker and said, "Dat is cat racism, my friends."

"No, it's de two white cats discriminating him," said Thatcher, giggling. She quickly added, "I am kidding. It's a year younger than the other two." She looked at us one by one and finally said calmly, "He is my favorite cat, as a matter of fact. I like anything black." And the rest was history.

❀

Having not had a good night sleep, I was barely awake, to the annoyance of the lady whose look had changed from concern to contempt by the end of the lesson. Hoping my roommates would still be asleep, I just wanted to get back to the warmth of my bunk.

Without even stopping to greet any of the so-called camp friends, I quickened my steps up 10 Normanns Street, leaving behind the courthouse where the Voksenopplæringen was ironically situated. I felt like being prosecuted over charges I was not quite sure of every time I climbed the courthouse stairs. Coincidentally, the police station overlooked the courthouse. I hurried past and headed straight towards the hospital, bypassing the Mottak and the Coast Guard base.

Making my way down the narrow path, I slipped and tumbled twice to rise up cussing in my mother tongue right in front of a fenced, old, gaping dungeon. I held on to a dismantled fence that bordered the path that led towards the base entrance. The dungeon brought back memories of my soldier days as I thrashed my way down the hill. It seemed everywhere I went, the Earth carried the scars of the past battles won and lost by people long gone. All around, the hills still retain the bunkers and dugouts that jutted over strategic points that were used during the Second World War against the Nazis.

I finally made it to the flatter, yet still slippery parking lot of the defense employer's right across from my dungeon. It was like a battle, getting around the town as a pedestrian at that time of the year. Infantry always paid the price in any battle, regardless; I nodded in agreement with myself. I had to get back to have a little nap and make that call. I decided this when I entered the camp and reached the warm, cabled front steps of the Mottak.

Inside the Mottak, the usual suspects were loitering around the reception. With a quick glance at the whiteboard and its list of names, I saw that my name was once again missing. Even if it appeared, it would be a post from either the office informing me of a fine over some stupid violation or the Immigration Police issuing me a renewal of the temporary refugee ID card. The redemption letter was elusive! I looked into the TV room and found Cliff and Congo sitting in the corner listening to some Angolan newcomer who had become an instant hit among many residents for his funny outbursts.

"Man, this modefoka disturb me in de morning," blasted out the infuriated Angolan. Since he had a long name, we just called him Angola. After some Portuguese tantrums and murmurs, he continued, "...was dreaming sweet dream. Me back home in Luanda, with me baby walkin' by the beach—" already some of us had begun to giggle in anticipation of where he was going, and at the animated way he told the story—"...and dis fokin' Arab wake me up, tellin me cleaning! I say what! Where am I?" A huge round of laughter followed as he went on, relating how the cleaning attendant kept spying on him like a cartoon character, to make sure he had fulfilled his chores. "He come from one corner and ran hurugugug past me. I look around; he is on de oder side, looking at me. I am thinking, should I clean him up too with dis mop? I tell you, dat man is making me *grande problema,"* Angola muttered in irritation.

⽤

The cleaning chores were such a pain for those of us who went to sleep late at night. The cleaning attendant, an Arab Norwegian, reminded the room on duty to clean the common areas, as scheduled by the office. He was not a popular fellow among many of us who had our sleep interrupted. Especially in the cold dark winter times, most of us sleep through most of the day, and any interruption was considered an offense.

Though it was for our own good, keeping the Mottak clean, it was a common source of disagreement. With the duties only being on weekdays, whoever had to clean the toilet or kitchen on Mondays did not have a pleasant task to start their week. Yet we had lived in less hygienic conditions in the past; still, I found it amusing at times why we found it insulting to clean up other people's messes.

To tell the truth, though, some were way messier than others. Some failed to flush, and the shit formed a nasty crust that needed to be scrubbed hard. For unexplainable reasons, some others defecated while crouching on their feet, leaving dirty footprints all over the seat. Cliff, disgusted by his find, said, "Mon, I just lost de appetite to crap. Der was big feet mark on the toilet seat. I don't understand what kind of style it is, mtsee." It was irritating. While cleaning it, you'd curse and lay blame on the group of people you suspected of having done it. Some even had the nerve to walk in to one of the booths which you just had cleaned, and you'd hear the defecating melody begin while you were scrubbing the next booth.

One time a guy was cleaning and one of the residents walked in on him. The resident was suffering from nasty diarrhea. Hearing and smelling all the commotion in the other booth, the cleaner lost his temper. They exchanged few words and the next thing we knew, a fight had erupted. After others had interfered, those of us who had heard the commotion headed down to the toilet to find the unlucky guy lying flat on his belly, with his pants still down, while the rest were struggling to restrain the other one. Knocked down but not out, the resident said, "My friend, you clean after me finish." Then looking at the rest of us,

he added, "Zis man crazy. He broke door, pull me out by force..."
followed by Arabic explanation to his peers.

Someone siding with the one on duty hurled insults at the
other. "You shut up! What man would use toilet while oders
clean?"

Another added, "You make him clean up his own mess, eff it
stinking the whole place!"

The angry man finally calmed down, and ushered everyone
to the door so he could get on with his duty, but dropped a final
insult. "It is the food dis people eat, shitting five times a day
that the rest have to clean." He got another knock for unfinished
business.

❀

Later that day, after a much needed nap, I joined my two friends
in the TV room. Cliff was in a serious conversation with the
Merchant and a mystic man we called the Nomad, while Congo,
two Somalis, and one Eritrean fellow were arguing over the
premier league football. I slid unnoticed to a space next to the
Nomad, who was engrossed in whatever the Merchant was
saying in a mix of Arabic and English. I casually looked back
at the Nomad, who had his back to me. He was dressed in an
expensive looking coat over a white shirt and black tight fitting
jeans with matching, shining, flat, black shoes, a type you rarely
see around the Mottak. The guy even wore cologne when he
went for the shared toilet from his ground-floor room. Dressed
immaculately, he was a rare sight at the Mottak but a delight to
watch. The way he held himself made many look up to him.

"Hey, I no no see you today. Where you be all day?" inquired
Cliff, when he realized I had slipped in without greeting him.

"Man was at school in ze morning and went to sleep when I
returned." I faked a yawn.

"Ayyy, you missed de drama here today." Cliff repositioned
himself on the sofa to get on the story telling mode. "Today, a
lot of letters came, my friend! It was bonanza!" He chuckled
sarcastically. He produced a folded letter from his back pocket
and raised it up in the air, for all to see. "You see here, some of
us get letters for hospital appointments to run blood test on us.
While some oders get positive letters accepted by de government
for work permit!"

Some grinned at the irony and soon a gloomy silence followed. It was not enough that we had to worry about one positive reply from Immigration regarding our asylum cases every day, but there were also letters along the way announcing mandatory blood testing to find out our health status. Mostly all of us were hoping to avoid being HIV positive. It was just too much shit to worry about. Life stuck in the extremes of two positives! But I was glad to hear some of the residents had received positive replies from the authorities—well, with a pinch of a salt, that is!

❦

The ultimate source of ecstasy in the Mottak was getting the acceptance letter from the UDI, regarding one's asylum—the very reason we had set foot on Norwegian soil! As it often happens, it is one of the three office women who breaks the good news. Other times, the news arrives in an official UDI letter.

I never forgot those tense moments when one of the ladies strolled around the Mottak with a folded yellow paper in hand. That yellow never looked so magical; yellow was for freedom. Everybody would wish she was heading towards him with that news each had been waiting for. The Oscar moment! Then she passes with a nod, or worse, greeted you with a smile. And all in that fraction of second you would be thinking, *This is it, the wait is over, it is my day today,* and she would ask, "Have you seen so and so...?" Then all the hopeful dreams and near-ecstatic feelings would deflate. The pensive looks of defeat, in those fractions of a second, were the worst to experience collectively. As much as I hated to admit my envy in those moments, I was also happy and relieved to watch a load lifted off the faces of the chosen ones, in seconds. It somehow compensates for the agony of waiting, that some change is at least happening around you, if not directly to you; and especially when it happened for those who had been through hell all their lives, the ones who deserved a second go at this poker game they call life.

Some would break down in tears over the prospect of being given a decent, second chance in life, a clean break, the privilege of joining the community with the highest standard of living on earth. Others would just stare in disbelief and wait for a second or two for the news to register, or would check if the woman was joking, and then either scream out in delight or give a surprise embrace to the bearer of the good news. The locals were not that excitable; rarely did one witness any sudden explosions of affection!

I have seen so many reactions in my time in the Mottak. It was especially exhilarating to watch those who had received their blessings earlier than they had expected. They would scream out in delight, throw whatever they were carrying, break down into tears... Those who had come from a recognizable, manmade disaster zone with a legitimate claim for asylum, according to the UDI, would often show a momentary relief.

As for those who had waited two years or so, watching and waiting as the others were accepted and rejected, week in and week out, theirs would be more of a reincarnation. Two years with no reply, not knowing when or how long it would take for the decision to be made, was the worst state to be in; only those who were in that position knew how it felt. As one victim explained, "It is worse than being in prison, my friends. At least in prison you know how long you will be serving."

But there, myself included, one saw people come and go; sometimes one even felt like one was working in the Mottak for free. Have no work permit, you could not go to any other country with your fingerprints already in the database. Couldn't go back to one's country. It was a dead end in both directions. But the worst part was waking up every morning, wishing and praying it would be the day; the salvation day. Sometimes I felt even a rejection would bring me some closure to my agony. But then, sometimes I believe good things come to those who wait. And wait I did.

Well, those witnessing another's fate change for the better, after a moment or so of disappointment over one's own fate, would rise up to congratulate the relieved, whether one liked it or not. Sure, some would feel gutted to see a person they disliked or a person who had only been around for few months get the nod while others kept waiting. As we all tend to see our own suffering more than others', some of us felt we had been treated unfairly by the authorities. Not all UDI decisions would be appreciated by the majority. There would always be a rumor circulating to discredit one's reputation out of envy or pure hatred.

But Cliff once again was the first to give a rapturous, genuine, congratulatory hug. His disgruntled demeanor vanished at a snap of a finger as he sprang off the sofa with full enthusiasm to greet two Somalis who had just been granted their papers, one after the other. "My brodda. You deserve it," he said. "Finally de day has come. You feel big stone lifted off your chest, I know, my brodda! Look at you, man. I never seen dis man dis happy!" This was followed by a warm embrace and soon all of us took the cue to do likewise.

Some never tried to show their contempt for the disparity of fate. The Nomad, who had never been fazed by the residence papers, rose up and hastily shook the two Somalis' hands in a congratulating manner and stated towards the rest of us, "Fuck their paper, man! I came here to get some green paper, not some passport. I don't need a fucking paper to move!" And he stormed out of the Mottak, perhaps for a couple of nights, to his mysterious hideouts he rarely spoke of. In reality paper was no proof of existence, yet you had to have it to convince others!

On the ground floor, the residents were constantly changing. Still, there were familiar faces that graced the Mottak with their colorful addition. The Nomad was a North African, and might look like an Arab from afar, but he was a real sub-Saharan. He was a modern-day nomad. He was in his mid-twenties when we first met him, yet spoke six languages competently. He had the sharpest brain, which he used to his own good, remarkably. He was always solo, trusted none. He strived so much to be independent and never got emotionally involved, as he knew deep inside that he would have to move once again. He had a handsome, innocent face which he manipulated to his great benefit. He could pass as an Italian when he was dressed in his suits and spoke and acted like an Italian from the movies. When he was under an Italian alias, his expressions would mimic Italian, greeting us, "*Come stai, mia amico?*" At times, he would be straight from Andalucía, with a fluent Spanish that one would believe without a doubt, and mingle with a couple of Latino immigrants who had lived longer in the town, for greater effect. And, of course, he could be a devoted Muslim Arab, with all the traditional attire and beads you would normally see and assume came straight from the mosque. As a natural Arab, he would be conversing passionately with his Arabic-speaking brothers, as passionate as they come, often exclaiming, *Welahi lazim!* He was another real survivor.

He said he was not cut out for the Mottak. He abandoned the system from time to time, yet never left for good. He considered the Mottak an oasis he visited when the water dried somewhere else, but never his permanent residence. Noting his peculiarity, he often switched rooms during his short stays in the camp. He worked and traveled wherever he sniffed an opportunity to earn a krone. The man knew no fear and every interaction was business, never personal. We met on the road and had been around to know him enough before he once again set off on his endless journey. The Nomad was a strange fellow. Besides the many things he could do, he was a professional pickpocket.

The Nomad had the quickest hands I had ever seen in my entire life. He would strike like lightning at a moment he felt a potential victim had let his guard down. His boyish groomed looks never raised any suspicion as he strolled by, doing his business selectively. Had it not been for one good friend of mine who told me about him, I would have never suspected this gentle man could be that cunning. My friend, who spoke of him with mixture of admiration and mistrust at the same time, had seen him in action so many times yet had never seen the Nomad ever lose his composure. "My friend, dat man is like a cobra," he had said. "You have to see it in replay or you won't trust your eyes de first time you see him in action," he said, shaking his head in astonishment. Even when the Nomad was caught in the act, he often took offense and distracted attention from the issue abruptly.

There was this one time when he was caught red-handed by a man he had mistaken for a drunk. The older looking man was actually limping naturally; the Nomad mistook it for drunkenness. He got close to the man and watched him closely for a while: the usual drill of where the target put his wallet after paying for drinks. I had heard the Nomad jokingly say, "Zis people don't like to carry zat much cash. Make it too hard for me to spot zose who carry cash." Later on, when the man headed to the men's room, the Nomad saw his chance and bumped into him, knocking the man off balance, giving him the fraction of seconds to fumble into the man's jacket for the wallet. But the man was fully aware. He grabbed the Nomad's hands before he could snatch the target. Somehow sure of the other man's intention, the old man staggered to his feet. Incensed by the attempt, the old man began hurling all sorts of curses and accusations in Norwegian at the top of his lungs. "*Jævla tyv. Satan du prøv å stjele lommeboke min!*" That caught everyone's attention.

Normally, a person in his position would lose his cool and try to walk away or run if he could, before the authorities were summoned. But the Nomad had other ideas; he went on the offense. He shoved the man and went on a rave in French. When people converged around them to calm the situation, he had already turned the tables. He demanded that the police come quickly because he had been wrongfully accused of stealing, just for helping an old drunk fool up from the ground. It was a racially motivated, deliberate attempt to humiliate him in public. And people were swayed in his defense, apologizing on the old man's behalf. By then, the old man began to doubt if he had maybe imagined the attempted theft. The older man ended up buying him a drink to reconcile. He did not get paid that night, but at least got a free drink out of it.

But what I admired about the Nomad were his principles. He never targeted the poor. Though he kept himself distant from others, on the occasions when he socialized, he was a warmhearted man with a great sense of humor. He would be an ideal friend, if not a business partner.

Like the Nomad, there was another intriguing fellow who had once shared a room with the Nomad. As usual, Cliff had baptized him Hilton, as the guy resided everywhere as if it were home. No one was sure where he was originally from, nor in which camp he stayed. I can't blame him, though, as name, age and nationality were negotiable when you were subjected to constant migration, like the seasonal birds. We met him through a Nigerian friend, who had introduced him as coming from Northern Nigeria. He had been staying occasionally on the ground floor with Dudu and another West African. When pressed for his hometown and certain aspects of culture and identity that all Nigerians should definitely know, he would back off and narrate another shady story. But he knew some Nigerian cities and Igbo language to back up his claim. Soon, he switched allegiance to Niger, claiming he was originally from Niger but grew up in Nigeria. Since there were no asylum seekers from Niger, there was no one to confront nor confirm his stories. Later on, our friend from Niger got tired of the jokes about West Africans and decided to befriend Sudanese guys and moved in with the Nomad. That guy was flexible. He somehow convinced them that he was from Chad, but had been living in the Darfur area of Sudan for some time. The guy spoke some Arabic and had an unquestionable stare and confidence. The guy was having fun; or he meant no harm, anyway.

However, the lies often caught up with him and he disappeared for some time. Since many asylum seekers from small towns are welcome to stay with us during their weekend visits, you often see many new faces that vanish just as fast. So his disappearance was no cause for worry.

Then came a friend of ours from another camp for a weekend, with a spicy story about our Continental friend. He had shown up one day out the blue and been a constant presence. Posing as a Zambian preacher, he had been spreading the good deeds of the Lord at the top of his lungs to all the desperate souls packed helplessly in the small town, Mottak. "Repent! Repent!" he had cried out. "The deliverance of the righteous from the evil grips of sinners in the Mottak is near. Babylon shall fall! Only those who cleanse their soul and give their heart fully to God will be spared. Evil thoughts and money-chasing dreams are the highway to hell. Thou shall not put a price on the infinite love our Lord the Savior had blessed us with! Refrain from all the temptations of what Babylon has in store." He had been able to restrain most of the women from spending money, and collected it for himself in the name of Christ.

Of course, they found out he was just a fraud and got him into trouble. Then, after a couple of months, I ran into him in another Mottak. This time, though, I was taken aback by the audacity of this brother. He sure was the Continental transformer.

Cliff and I were paying a visit to some friend who had a residence permit, and who was celebrating his birthday in a nearby small town. Before we headed straight to our friend's place, we decided to visit some of our distant friends in the Mottak. We asked for some directions and got to the Mottak, and guess who was on the front step to welcome us? The transformer himself! We just could not wait to hear his latest alias, but we played it cool. He greeted us without a slight hint of nervousness.

We went inside and found our friends, who were watching a movie in the reception area. Gripped by the movie and hospitality of our hosts, we had forgotten about Hilton. It was the Ramadan fasting period and some of our Muslim hosts were preparing to pray before they broke the fast. For some strange reason the transformer shuffled calmly towards the prayer room. Cliff and I exchanged a look, waiting anxiously if this boy was going to do what we really thought he would do at that moment. He did not disappoint us, either, as he slid naturally to the prayer room and slipped off his shoes. His hands, feet, and face were still wet from the ritual water the Muslims splash before every prayer. He blended in amazingly well; no one gave him a second look. Since others were still rushing in for their prayer, the door was ajar for us to witness that character prostrating calmly until the session began. Just before they closed the door, he caught my wide-eyed stare and gave me quick wink.

⯲

When my mood finally settled, and my animal urges were still unmet, I decided to make the dreaded call to my sugar mommy and make up. Besides, I had to get away from the camp. I just felt so suffocated. I was terrible at apologies. After stuttering my way through the apology, to which there was merely a derisive sigh every now and then, she finally gave in and told me to come by on Friday, since she had an old friend staying over for the week. Deflated, I withdrew myself to my bunk and sulked, contemplating nothing but sex.

Vehemently obsessing about sex during the waking hours, my every thought revolved to arouse the deep, suppressed animal inside, conjuring scenes of inhuman copulation in my already-occupied mind. Every probe would play back, on and on. My nostrils would pick up the scent of female perfume or their body odor from afar, like a canine, from the deepest recesses of my memory. My eyes would instantly dart to any revealed female flesh, no matter her age or race, as women passed by my basement window, which in turn would instigate thoroughly erotic flashbacks from the past. Imagination would run wild, temperature rise, muscles twitch, flesh expand. The cravings for the need to penetrate would become overwhelming. In my mind, I would rip off the clothes and romp in the open. The scenes got more perverted on those frustrating days. With the intermittent scenes in my head switching from my stagnated fate to daylight erotic fantasy, my mood swung to the extremes.

Then the cravings picked up at night, during the self-deprecating, soul-immolating time pre- and post-sleep. The haunting images that had been busy like the camera of a birdwatcher were replayed with extra-special effects, like extraterrestrial nude powers. It was some sort of therapy; for those intense moments, the mind shifted to another dimension where no thoughts race to jam the traffic. Nothing beats the calm therapeutic effect of a heavy romp. The cravings receded but never were extinguished, yet the energy seemed to uplift the spirit for a day or two. But I had to wait for a couple of nights to get my natural release, by the look of things.

Cursing my own fate, I shuffled back up to the vortex, the TV room, where the mood had finally lit up. A Nigerian friend of Cliff's was telling the full reception crowd about hometown adventures. Once again, it was Cliff who dubbed him Tallest for his towering, well-built figure.

"My broddas," Tallest said, "we used to eat a lot of money, ayyy!" He held the back of his head to elaborate his point and looked around to face Cliff. "Cliffo, no business here. You knew what dey used to call me in Lagos."

"Ah ah," exclaimed Cliff. "Man, every time dis man come around me, I feel like I am sitting at de petrol station!" Cliff jibed, backing his friend's story, which was often met with skeptical reception.

"Ee, Cliffo, you are funny man!" the Nigerian said, trying to brush off the joke, knowing where he was going with that remark.

"Dis man been siphoning oil from pipes for years. Dey used to call him Total, my friends," he said, referring to the French owned Petrol Station.

"Good times, my man. We used to make lot of money, my friend; it is no joke, I tell you." In a hopeless attempt to steer the story back to him, Tallest continued, "It's no easy as well, ah ah. You had to have a gang dat tamed de police and security. Den you have to tap de pipe and guard your spot every day, my friend." Emphatically, he went on with his story. "Once it was done, de oil flows to own tank and to de greedy government tanker."

"You mean, you used to steal oil from the government all the time?" asked the often fascinated Knut, who was squirming and twitching in a corner.

"Steal? What you talking about?" snapped the Nigerian. "We in Nigeria have oil, but de government export it all to you people and again buy our own oil back and sell it to us." In irritation at having been questioned by a white man, he added, "Ah ah, dat is not de way it works, me brodda. Tell dis boy!" He took a support-seeking look at us, hoping we would clarify the point, but sensing he was the only expert in the field, he proudly proceeded with the narration. "You see, my brodda, most of de region de oil come from, de people still poor. Dirt poor. Even fuel is very expensive. Imagine de oil is coming from under their land, yet dey pay more for fuel. Why? So we take de oil and sell it for cheap back to de people." Having achieved his original goal of captivating everyone's attention, he got up, staggering, straightening his giant figure, which was clad in a clinging dark brown t-shirt, and went on with the story. "It is community service, not theft! You understand, we make some money out of it, too. De police know, de government know. But when dey decide to catch you, my friend, it is shoot on sight. No mercy! So you must have connections and a gang!"

"Eiie, Mr. Mobil. Are you distributing oil to de people? Ayy, mtsee, dis man comes to Europe and now saying he did it for de people. I know, you huh, you greedy; you neva think about people!" chided Cliff trying to distract from the subject. He was often bored in a subject he could not direct, or with any political talk that dragged on for too long.

"Cliff, why you always have to joke abut dis thing? It was you who brought de subject. Ah ah, dis Igbo people have problems, I tell you," he declared, disappointed at having his limelight taken away.

"If you care about people, why you not you give me back de money I owe you so I could buy drinks for dis people? Eeiii, look at his face changing already... People's man! Mtsee." Cliff was satisfied he had shut down the Tallest show.

Tired of the movie, the three of us headed down to the gym and let off some steam. In those grueling winter nights, we needed to move the muscles. With the gym at the end of the dungeon, one found three treadmills, two bicycles, a bench with all the weights, and a set of dumbbells lined up in a tight corner of the supposed basement/utility room. With the mobile heater being stolen a couple of weeks back, one had to carry one's own heater from the room whenever you wished to work out.

That night, we had a special visitor, Sleepy. He shuffled his way into the tight closet gym with intent. None of us had ever associated him with athletics or any sort of movement in that regard. Sleepy was made for bed. Even most of his conversations began, "I was on my way to bed..." or, "I got a call that woke me from my sleep..." or, "I will take a lil nap..." or something similar. Besides, whenever we crossed paths, he always had on his signature light blue, sweat suit pajamas, regardless of the weather or time of day. But they had said to never underestimate a sleeping giant. Who knew? He might have been a heavyweight lifter back in the good old days. That particular Wednesday, he had on black shorts with a matching grey t-shirt and black sneakers, with a white towel resting on his shoulders. All three treadmills were occupied—one by an Iranian veteran, one by Cliff, and the third by a Somali fellow. Congo and I were benching in turns.

Cliff, taken aback by the new arrival, welcomed him sarcastically. "Are you looking for the toilet, mtsee? Dis guy probably sleepwalking."

Sleepy laughed at the remark and announced, "From now on, I no longer be known as Sleepy!" He carefully folded the towel and placed it on top of the fuse boxes that dwarfed the far corner of the camp gym. He cracked his knuckles and twisted his neck about while maintaining a firm eye contact with Cliff. We assumed this guy probably used to work out big time; maybe Babylon put him to sleep. He went on to stretch his legs, leaned on the wall to his right, and stretched his arms. He sprang up and down for a minute or two, as the rest of us quietly followed what he was doing. He was already sweating profusely, as he stood with his hands on his hips like a landlady I once knew back in my hometown, just before she raised hell in the compound. He breathed heavily and walked back towards the fuse box to pick up the towel and dried his face and neck, as if he had been working out for hours. He strode around the bicycles and the treadmill, looking up and down the sweating figures, and cracked a smile.

"Ayy, Sleepy, what now? Are you benching or biking first?" asked Congo invitingly.

"My friends, Rome was not built overnight," Sleepy stated, before he hastily left the gym. That was the shortest stint in the gym by anyone.

❧

Sleepy, Fili, was an intriguing fellow. He had been one of the longest-serving residents of the Mottak. He was on his third year when I arrived, though he slept through most of it. He had come from Ethiopia, though his parents had Eritrean heritage. His wish for a share of the northern riches had met the northern slumber. He would literally sleep for more than sixteen hours at a time. He would reappear at some odd hour in his famed light blue pajamas, shuffling his way towards the TV room. He was always in the reclining position on the sofa, ready to slide down easy when the inevitable sleep took him. As Cliff teased him, "Look at dis guy! Do you have a sleeping sickness? Dat tse tse fly bite you? Why you always ready to sleep?"

Fili was quite a funny guy when he was awake, though, often teasing and joking hilariously before he dozed off on the sofa. He had lost his ambition long ago—one could read it from his eyes. The sleep was his way of hiding from reality.

The few hours he was awake were spent conversing animatedly with his girlfriend of a couple years. His light at the end of the tunnel sustained his dimming desire to live. He would be on the phone for hours, smooth-talking until he paid her his conjugal visit. At every chance of a break, he would fly down to a town in the south and reimburse his diminishing spirit. Having no other task he performed freely, he had been exempted from the obligatory language course, citing health issues, and woke up early whenever he had cleaning duties. Otherwise, he was tossing and turning in his bed, regardless of the day. Yawning at all times, even after his fifteen-hour nap, he waited for his girlfriend to come back from work for his therapy.

His round, chubby appearance gave him a contented look, yet his half-smiles told the story. The funny thing was, no one had heard him complain about his state of affairs; having being rejected for asylum once by the authorities, he awaited a second rejection even though he had appealed. Being a close friend, Cliff often pressured him to get off his bed and join us on our endless adventures, to which Sleepy would reply, "I am really tired. I have to rest a little."

"Rest a little," Cliff would say mockingly. "Ah ah, I don't know what your girlfriend say when you tell you will rest a little every time she want to do some jigi jigi."

"My friend, everything done in bed, I am a master. I turn like Korea in bed, my friend. You know, I am maintaining condition!"

"Condition. What condition you talking about? You sleep more, your dick will fall asleep on you, my friend. You have to do some training on others before you go to your woman."

To which he would yawn and stretch his arms in defeat and roll back to his hibernation. Some run; others sleep away their troubles!

❦

Ever since sleep had finally crept its way into the TV room sofa at around 4 in the morning, I was dreading the early tap-tap of the cleaning chore on Thursday. Exactly at 8, the infamous Arab would knock at the door and jiggle the knob, or worse, open the door with his master key to remind us of our cleaning duties. As was often the case, I struggled to drift away, knowing I would be rudely interrupted. My demons never took a break. The saying *life is a bitch* kept ringing in my head. Destiny was just one unreliable whore sometimes, more like the prostitute for whom you had unfortunately fallen head over heels. She was always out there, spreading herself for the rest of the world, while you constipate and masturbate, wishing she were there when you needed her most. We are all prostitutes, anyway! Everybody out there looking for something in return, so I figured, why wait to have my destiny delivered into my hands when I could scrap on my own? It was all a game, anyway. Agitated and exhausted, I was tired of it all. I just wanted an ending.

The devils had wreaked havoc inside my head. It had been nearly a year since I had begun waiting for a verdict. Though I was a young, intelligent, and healthy individual, I felt like a leper in a colony. Cordoned off in the camps, I was in a losing battle, suffering from the endless barrage of thoughts that bombarded me from all corners of my head. For a long time, I remained optimistic that some good would come my way, some day in the fork of life.

All the friends I had made while I was in the Mottak had all moved on, at either the behest of the state or on private business. I seemed to be the only one stuck in the middle, waiting for lightning to strike me. Cliff had once joked that lightning even strikes a moving shiny object, so a static dull figure like me had no chance. A lot had happened. Our comfort zone had been diminished. Times were hard. New faces poured in and old faces were disappearing by the day. A good friend of ours from Burundi had been deported. "I am done with Babylon. I find me some nice girl and live me far from de city, my broddas," he had said at his farewell party, which had felt more like a funeral.

Usually, people from my country were granted asylum within a couple of months, but my case had mysteriously taken longer. Maybe that was a sign! In my stay, I had been presented with plenty of opportunities that I had been unable to take—maybe that had cost me my way forward. The more I thought of it, the more I would begin to be disappointed by my own weak conviction. After surviving what I had been through in life and what I was still going through, I had almost reached a point where I had no wish to go to heaven. So what was stopping me from getting what I wanted? Maybe I was a coward. Had I had balls, I would have long ago abandoned the Mottak and been out trying my luck somewhere else. Sketching schemes and plans, executing them at ease in my dreams, I finally drifted away!

The knock was often a timid, yet firm, tap with the back of the key chain. "Cleaning, my friend," he would squeak, and hasten off. He was well aware of the hatred the residents had for him. Though his profession made him a hated figure, the guy was not a bad person; the fact that he kept a close watch of his task was what irked us.

I replied on the second tap, when Korea whispered my name, in a sort of a plea to get me going. Cussing had long become my morning ritual. I shuffled in baggy cotton shorts and an oversized sweatshirt up the stairs to collect the mop and bucket. The basement toilet was my morning chore. The devils ran amok. A slideshow of my struggle, the dark side, replayed in my head. The voices inside my head were pushing me.

Man you have been through shit in life. You have been labeled. You have been scorned on sight. You have been discriminated and cast aside, even by your own kind, so why should you expect any favors from those who had been innately sworn to look down on you? In life, you have learned one thing: you live it by yourself; you die it on your own. The bunching and the munching were just for the cowards who can't find their feet to stand on their own. You ran away from your country, tired of the empty promises and the constant herding from morning to dawn! Once one finds his full individual self, there is no need to confirm to any group or to prove his worth to others. Can you stand on your own or will you still be bitching about it?

I had no answers as the cleaning master mixed several detergents from the tiny closet into the half-filled water bucket.

Cliff, who was an early riser, had already awakened to take a morning shower. He was taunting the preacher, a devout Christian new arrival, when I walked in. The bathroom door burst open and the stumbling Cliff walked in. Preacher was startled by the huge, half-naked figure suddenly emerging from behind and laughing out loud with an index finger pointed towards him.

"Ay man, what de hell is dat thing?" Cliff said. "You are not an African, my friend."

"What? Close ze door don't disturb me, *Yhe ebed*," pleaded the tiny naked figure of Preacher, feeling uncomfortable around the giant West African.

"Oooy, my brodda. Come see dis man dick." He ushered me for a closer look of the infuriated, squirming Preacher.

I joined in the fun. "Look, look, am sorry for you my friend."

"What are you talking about? Am taking cold shower, it gets smaller, you know..."

"No, I don't know. It looks like three testicles, my friend. Where is your dick?"

"Cliff, am not playing! Close ze door!" he cussed under his breath in Amharic, while covering his privates with one hand.

"I tell you, I no longer consider as an African. Maybe Indian or something, man."

"Fuck you, man. I saw yours, man. Zat is a leg, not a dick. You made it yourself, huh? Please close it, man."

"Attention, everyone. Our friend here has been deleted from de African race immediately. From now on he be considered..." Cliff trailed off, lost for a nationality to label his victim. "I think you look like more Tamil Tiger or Papau New Guinea, until further notice."

"Just close it, Cliff. I get sick from ze draft, please!"

With Cliff around, the gloom was lifted off of me. I cleaned the sink and the toilet seats, listening to their animated exchange. It sure was a blessing to have him as company. He once told me that people meet for a reason and that there is no such thing as a coincidence. "Dey just meet for a reason, for both good or bad reasons. Der is no such thing as accident. Don't take any chance meeting lightly, my friend. Especially when your spirits tell you something," he had said, tapping his heart all along. Our meeting on top of the world was sure a confluence like the river Nile at Omdurman, where the White Nile meets the Blue Nile to form a formidable force and flow upstream, constantly braving the desert for millennia. But I was not sure if I had the same prominent effect on him. He had no idea what his presence meant to the Mottak residents. He was the subliminal comical vortex to the chronically depressed souls in the camp.

The two were often in a war of words, literally on everything, as they entertained the rest of the Mottak with their relentless banter. Preacher was a new addition to the Mottak, but he was quickly taken under our wings for his energetic and informative personality. He was a staunch pan-Africanist, yet slightly biased and too proud of his Ethiopian heritage, which he made the base of every argument he never backed away from.

According to his claims, he was born into a proud Amhara family with a lineage traceable to the late emperor. Though he was an academic lecturer in a Dire Dawa university in Economics, his reasoning and logic spiraled strongly from his strict Orthodox Church upbringing. A quote by a philosopher was often followed by a verse from the bible, which he often leafed through at testing times. He often organized little get-togethers to celebrate and cheer the residents, even though his son-of-the-emperor, intellectual attitude had alienated him in the beginning. He soon toned down his airs and blended well.

The Mottak warmed to him after an unforgettable episode that stunned everyone. A week after his arrival, he was already asking too many questions of the officials, who were feeling nervous around him. Then, one day, two Norwegians came to visit their compatriot who worked in the office; Preacher overhead them utter the word *neger* in the middle of their hushed conversation. His perky restless figure, leaning over the reception desk to demand an explanation, finally found a subject with which to make his mark in the Mottak.

"Excuse me, did you use ze word *nigger* while you were talking about us?"

The two Norwegians looked at the tiny African with his beady eyes and pointed nose. After a short pause, one of the Norwegians replied, "You might have misunderstood. We were not talking about you or your people!"

The other one quickly, perhaps too quickly, added, "In Norwegian, the word *neger* is not an offensive term like in the US. It was just taken from the Spanish term *negro* for the color black. So relax, my friend."

Having cornered them on the spot he wanted, Preacher licked his lips in delight and stood up to give a speech none of us would ever forget.

"You know I am not a nigger. And don't tell me it is just a word with no meaning to you. More zan a century ago, when you people were still freezing without ze technology in ze winter, my great grandfather, along wiz hundreds of thousands, demolished a strong army of Italian invaders—17,000 were killed in one battle. My grandfather still keeps ze skull of one of his victims on top of his bedroom shelf." The entire Mottak fell silent all of a sudden, with the two visitors stunned, looking at each other over the development of events. The Preacher was in full command as he paced around the reception with an inflated chest. Noting he had gripped the attention of the residents, he proceeded, louder. "After, ze advances continued by your other neighbors, who came by with zer bible. Zey came with zer Bibles only to find out ze Bible was written in our own unique language, and accepted Christianity way before you people even knew about it. But ze missionaries never stopped coming. You know what we called you white people in those days, Ali? It iz a derogatory term spat in contempt just like you people use ze word *nigger*. It waz only King Menelik ze Second who stepped in and made it a punishable offense zat ze people became less hostile to foreigners like you. So now, my Ali friend, now zat I came to your country, you think you have every right to call me a *nigger*?"

The dumbfounded Norwegians were left pale-faced as the glaring, questioning eyes, buried deep in the sockets of the Preacher, awaited a response.

Satisfied, he threw his hands in the air and walked away towards the gate, with a glowing smile plastered on his bony brown face. He became an instant hit with the residents, and the officials were wary of his presence after that.

His endless personal war of words with Cliff had begun after just two weeks in the Mottak. He had convinced the camp officials into arranging an Ethiopian New Year's party on September 11. We all sat facing the TV once again, watching some Nigerian movie Cliff had borrowed from an old friend. As usual, with many African movies, witchcraft was intertwined with the plot. Myths and folklore are still revered and respected. And above all, one should be watchful of the evil eye. It might appear in a different name, juju, zahir, budda, or more, yet we all had it entrenched deeply in our traditions. Even the highly educated were wary of it, regardless of how dismissive of the subject.

In the movie, a woman is bewitched by her envious neighbors and becomes the laughing stock of the town. Cliff, though, was highly animated during the funny scenes, often uttering, "Mtsee, you think id is a joke. In Nigeria, der er powerful people with evil powers, my friend." He went on narrating a story where a good friend of his had been bewitched by a former lover for his money. The friend had been fed a juju by a well-known sorcerer so that he lost everything he had in a short period. The friend finally died of madness. Hearing that story, one by one we began to relate a story about others we knew. You can't risk telling an evil eye story as a personal experience. As the strict Ethiopian Orthodox he was, Preacher blurted out during the conversation, "It is because people have a weak faith in God, zat evil can get to zem. Wiz God on your side, if you believe 100 percent, no evil can come near you. If you are afraid, ehh, I tell you... You are giving an invitation to evil and its followers." He gathered his breath and went on, "All of you should be ashamed of talking as if you are glorifying ze devil and open ze door of your heart to God!"

Stunned by the rebuff, Cliff gave him one cynical look and exclaimed, "Look at Preacher. After watching de movie, scared as a rat, you start talking about God or evil. Go pray to Bomboclad, and tell him to give you your residence paper."

"Eeey, Cliff, very wrong," replied the Preacher. "God is not responsible about residence paper. Maybe he is punishing me through ze law for my sins of ze past."

"Oh, you give me headache. All I know is, I do good, then good things happen to me. I do bad, you understand me, evil eye or God will punish me. Not de law."

The healthy debate went on for a little while. Cliff never backed away from an argument he firmly believed in, not until the other gave in. Preacher tried to change the subject and said calmly, "Yo, Cliff, tomorrow is ze New Year, Ethiopian New Year. We would like to invite you for a lunch program we prepare here tomorrow."

"What! You people crazy. It is September, you know!"

"No, Cliff, we follow different calendar. It will be 2003 tomorrow." Preacher was trying not to drag out the conversation.

"Today is 2002? Ah ah, dis people. Look at look at dem!" he said, looking towards his Nigerian and other West African friends, who were equally perplexed by this new find. "So you say you follow different calendar. De whole world is 2009 and you people 2002. If white people hear dis, dey will laugh at you face. Please don't embarrass us!"

"Uufa, Cliff, don't be difficult! It has been like zat forever." The tired Ethiopian looked around for some of the younger ones to explain how it really works.

One of them took the cue and began explaining. "You see, we follow Julius calendar while European calendar follows Gregorian calendar."

"So we Nigerians follow what? Chinese calendar?" interjected an impatient Nigerian friend of Cliff's.

"No, no, my friend. Listen to me first! Catholics follow Gregorian, and Orthodox Christians follow calendar like ours..."

Cliff was agitated. "Dis man make no sense. Yo don kolo! So, if I am a Muslim, who do I follow?"

"Uufa, I meant how it began. Every religion began counting the days from ze birth of their messiah, my friend. Ze Chinese have their own, ze Muslims have their own, we have our own. I am not sure about ze Indians. But due to ze European influence, most of the world follows the Gregorian calendar."

"Is it de same. Like seven days, fifty-two weeks?"

"Of course. Only zat we have thirteen months instead of twelve. Every month has thirty days with the exception of ze thirteenth Pagume, which has six or seven days! Not exactly Julian calendar but based on ze gospel of Enoch and book of Kufale."

"Bagume! I like dat one, very short, my friend!" A snicker followed from the indifferent Congo.

"So you celebrate Christmas de same day or what?" the curious Nigerian asked.

"Two weeks later. Ze same with Easter," narrated Preacher to a growing audience.

"Two weeks off, huh? So you people must have been real slow," interjected Congo sarcastically, to the annoyance of the Ethiopians and Eritreans, faithful Orthodox Christians. "De news trickled about de birth of Jesus after two weeks."

"You are hopeless," Preacher fired back. "Do you know we accepted Christianity way before Europeans did, let alone Africans?" He was getting infuriated.

"Okay, okay, Mr. Google. Thank you for de piece of history," Cliff said. "So what are you preparing besides food? Do you have beer?" He'd already lost his interest in the calendar, which put the heated conversation to rest.

"Two each for every guest. You are all welcome!"

"Dat is nice. You people don kolo, very crazy, you count backwards, but not my problem. I will come, my friend." But once Cliff found someone with a strange thing to offer to his taste, he never let up; he would always try make fun of it every time he ran into you.

The next day, a lavishly prepared lunch was underway in the meeting hall. During public holidays of certain cultures, the Mottak sponsored a get-together. It was a noble thought where some get a chance to celebrate and bring an almost homelike feeling to the Mottak. Likewise, it gave others the chance to get a taste of another's culture; traditional attire, music, and of course the food and ceremony.

Cliff, after having tasted every spicy and weird-looking sauce and bread of the Ethiopian culture, danced off rhythm to the Habesh music, while the rest of us from that part of the world joyously shuffled our feet and shook our shoulders to the beat.

Laughing uncontrollably, while still trying to dance along, Cliff joked, "Look at you people, are you dancing? Eey, or are you, are you sick? Shaking like dat, like you got electric shock!" he said, pointing to Preacher. "Eey, specially dis man, he dancing like he was in some juju, I tell you! I thought you were giving God 100 percent of your time?"

Sensing another hysterical exchange, we slowed our dancing and faced Preacher.

Preacher, a little embarrassed, said, "Cliff, zis is a holy day for all of us. We are celebrating ze beginning of our Lord's new year. I am not drunk and ze musik was only rejoicing ze name of ze Lord." Agitated, he added, "Why you always have to challenge me?" and headed to a group who were eating from a traditional tray. As it was a tradition to feed a maximum group of eight from one big tray in many African countries, Cliff, sensing defeat, approached with a smirk on his round face.

"My friend," said Cliff, "dis Europe. Why you people still eat on one plate for four of you, huh?" He added, "What you think? You go on a drought next season?" The whole room burst into a deafening laughter.

"Hey, hey, zis is our culture, okay," blurted an irritated Habesh.

"*Yhe dmo ymeche new bakachu,*" added another in Amharic.

"In our country, we like eating together, my friend," added another.

Preacher, though, kept quiet, though his irritation was obvious on his face.

"Sharing is happiness, my friend," added an Eritrean who was taking a mouthful of the spicy dorowet.

"Why? Plates are expensive der?" quipped Cliff.

"You people don't share like us because you are greedy. We like sharing like zis, man," Preacher finally answered.

"No, no, my friend. Now why I understand why you people are all skinny. Rather be greedy, my friend. Der is plenty of food in Norway."

"Leave us alone, man," said an annoyed pair, standing and ready to strike if the verbal assaults persisted.

The satisfied Cliff walked away, as the rest of us tried to calm Preacher and his friend. He had won the argument! There was also this other side of Cliff, where he would often ridicule another's culture in a harmless way: After the laughter had long passed, though, it would make one look at the subject from a different perspective. His wandering thoughts always looked at things with humor and suspicion, yet they never stopped him from fearlessly venturing into the unknown.

The unique Habesh dish and the ceremony behind it were apt to draw comment from Norwegians, though. Often, it was the curious Knut who was watching from afar, failing to hide his growing revulsion at the dexterous Habesh fingers peeling off the thin pieces of white flat bread, injera, from a large shared tray. They rolled it around the steaming hot sauce, wot, and then would delicately place it into their mouths. He asked, "Why do you people eat with your hands? I mean, would it not be easier to use the fork and knife?"

Preacher almost choked in hastily swallowing the scalding injera and wot. "You know, you people have no passion for your food," he fired back with a defiant tone. "For us, we want to feel what we eat with all ze five senses before we put it in our mouth. You just don't buy injera from ze store. It's homemade, wiz passion. Zere is like many steps ze woman specially, carefully follow. Have to buy ze right flour. Combine ze perfect mix of ground teff, sorghum, and baking powder. It takes more zan two days to prepare ze best injera. It has to ferment in a yeast mixture sealed in a container, constantly stirred by hand to make it a lump free thin paste ready for ze oven; we call it *mitad*. So, my friend, our women spend a lot of time on it before it's served. We want to appreciate before we chew it down. Ze soft texture of a fresh baked injera, ze thinner and more flexible ze better, as you feel it embracing ze sauce, absorbing ze fat and the grease in ze process. Ze eyes of injera have to be tiny and not overlapping, with no lumps. It iz art, my friend. An irreplaceable, unique, and exotic form of art served on the plate every time that no civilization can replace. So, better appreciate before you start shoving your prejudice down our throats!"

Knut and his friend shrank in their seats. Preacher, having delivered a justified explanation to which all the Habesh people felt really proud of, placed large chunks of tightly rolled meat stew into the mouth of the guy sitting next to him.

The act of *goresha* incensed other cultures, having a finger-wrapped roll of injera and wot stuffed in to your mouth by someone else; it would be an offense to decline it, as it was a highly regarded, affectionate gesture among Habesh. For us, it was a gesture of respect and act of endearment towards close ones. The larger the roll, the more warmth and affection behind the *goresha*. Having to share symbolizes the togetherness, which might be somehow perceived as stinginess by other cultures. But then, things are only strange for a stranger. Thousands of years of tradition kept families united during meals around a plate into which, time after time, multiple food-greased hands dipped until it was empty. The meal was a ceremonious part of the culture, with more emphasis and norm applied during holidays or among guests. Though fading gradually, it was still a custom to wait in one's seat while others finished up; following an after-meal grace to the Almighty, one would get up to wash the hands. Even though some of us were cosmopolitan Africans, massively influenced by Western culture and more pronouncedly by the African American culture, some customs and habits were deeply embedded in our identity.

The City-Boy Weekend

It was Friday, my favorite day of the week. Back at home, when Friday came around, you did what you had to do to get enough money to last you for the night. That is what a real city boy does. It usually got crazy, whether you had been working or bumming on the weekdays, even though no one minds having some fun at any time and any day of the week. Same shit, different place; no matter the circumstances, I didn't see the reason why I couldn't have fun. And thank God I was not alone. I had come across cultures that even celebrate death, the graceful departure of their beloved ones, as if it were a wedding day! So, no trouble is big enough to stand in the way of celebrating life!

Thinking and worrying never solved all problems. The nights were to be celebrated, regardless of what might have happened during the day. In my travels across different cities in Africa, I had noticed one uniform mood in the city that never made it to the BBC: No matter what was going on in the country, be it a riot, civil war, raid, protest, or a blackout, the bars and kiosks were always open for business. Thus, there was a great need to let loose whenever you had the chance, under any circumstance. Problems were a constant partner, like a nagging wife, and were always waiting for you when you went home.

On Fridays, the city asylum boys were in a better mood. No matter what kind of fucked-up week you had, you could make up for it on the weekends. Some of us might have not even left the Mottak the entire week, but on the weekends, we might end up being seen in every open door in town. Some other city boys from nearby, smaller towns would join us for the weekend to spice things even better. They all came from different countries: Congo, Angola, Rwanda, Kenya, the Sudan, Eritrea, Ethiopia, Nigeria, Mali, Morocco, Senegal, and some others I may have forgotten; still, the same city vibe got us together. It would be all jokes and fun. English being the medium of communication, one heard all types of accents and pidgins, even new grammatical rules and new expressions. No stress, so long as we understood each other; language is nothing but a tool of communication, anyway. We never ran out of subjects to joke or even bicker about.

The party would take place in Cliff's room, or any room where we were welcome. Some just did not like to see us have fun, but when they saw us together, they knew better than to stay away.

The drinks would be bought early, with stacks of the cheapest beer, Gran's Bare Øl, packed in the fridge and under the bunks, with a bottle or two of the strong local homemade vodka; we were often loaded for a busy night. Whoever wished to be a part of the group was expected to bring at least a six pack or more, or else you would have a long night taking all the punch lines thrown at you. We did not care for scavengers when we were barely scraping for the crusts ourselves. Taking advantage of what little we had was a mark of one's character, and we usually let it be known.

Congo played the music. He had thousands of songs downloaded on his laptop and blasted it through two speakers, which we'd found discarded outside a convenience store. The guy knew how to manipulate our moods and read our tastes as he switched from reggae to ragga, oldies to hardcore hip-hop, classic to modern African. Few of us ever complained. Congo barely said a word while attending to our musical requests and demands, apart from his occasional snicker. At times, he made us forget where we were, even what situation we had gotten ourselves into. He would just guzzle his beer and bob his head to the beat as the rest of us got crazy. The dim fluorescent lights were wrapped up in purple and black polythene shopping bags to give the place a pub feel. Improvisation is the best skill most city boys in Africa acquire in life, to make up for what's missing.

At the beginning of the party, after an exchange of pleasantries, we talked about the status of our cases. It all got serious and everyone paid attention.

"Did you hear about dis guy, dey gave him negative. Now he is very sad and depressed."

Then some would analyze the situation. "Yeah, very sad. I hear dat man has five children back in his country."

"Zat man deserves asylum. He tell me his life. He was living in hell all his life. If he go back zey kill him."

"Maybe the case he presented was not good enough."

A couple of us would defend him. "What are you saying? Dis people don't care about individual case. Dey only care if your country is at war and the media shows it."

"You see what zey give you," an angry one added.

"Are you mad? You don't know dat man. Look at dis man judging others!"

Trying to calm the others, the friend would say, "I am just saying some people fuck up their own cases when they panic during the interview. We don't know what he said."

It was always a touchy subject; we all had our different opinions when it came to the UDI and its decision-making body. Thus, as it often happened, it used to be the Burundi guy, the oldest in the group, that pacified arguments. "Broddas, broddas! Let us not forget that it is out of our hands! Whatever they decide will not prove our existence. It is just paper; life goes on, no matter what the decision might be. Let us not get carried away. The best we can do is stick together and help out one another." His words often stung and gave you something to think about. He was often right; he had been in Europe for a decade and knew his way around. He was wise and calm. He had been expecting imminent deportation to his motherland after his asylum was rejected twice. Still, having being used to the "refugee business," as he often called it, he was unfazed by his situation. Though we often teased him, we gave him a lot of respect. With that and the drinks working their magic, it would soon be a joyous party again.

The party would drag on until we ran out of drinks, with some party crashers adding color to the already colorful congregation. The mood generator, Cliff, was always full of energy, trying to keep everyone engaged. He would jump from chair to chair; chatting with one brother after another about whatever the other was interested in talking about. Cliff was cool with everyone; he would laugh at a dry joke as if it were the best in the house. He would listen attentively to a sad story from a drunk as if it were the will of his rich grandfather being read. He sympathized with everyone's sadnesses and joys. Even when he teased, no one was offended for long. The big smile over his round chocolate face was a total contrast to his intimidating, well-built, tall figure. With Congo tagging along, he would snicker over a joke he had not even heard. With the two giggling and snickering, one after the other, they would transform the asylum brothers' gloomy moods over protracted or forgotten cases into reasons to laugh.

The topics were, at times, informative. As we barely knew one another, everyone was obliged to introduce and at times defend his beautiful culture to others. Though there was some ego and hyperbole in the narration, especially if it was about the cities and the women, it gave us some facts and ideas about the other, regardless of whether one believed the other's story.

Nigerians led by Cliff would praise Lagos as if it were constructed by the hand of God himself. "In Naija," as they called it in the pidgin English, one would start, if he sensed he should let others know his background, "na wa! De city is more beautiful dan London, mon. De clubs are so nice. De restaurants very cheap, de cars we drive you cannot find in the rest of Africa at all. And everyone knows we have de most beautiful women in de world." Encouraged by his countryman, Tallest would add, "Naija has money; it is only de government that is eating it, mtsee." No one ever conceded; we all had something we loved of our cities that we found to be priceless and unique.

Nostalgia often brought back the good flashbacks. Despite the obvious heavy military presence in my hometown, Asmara, the inflation, and the aggressiveness and violence of drunken locals, its nightlife was what kept us sane. No matter what kind of mood you had been in that day, once you hit the bars, your mood lifted. Even on an empty pocket, you could go to your favorite bar with your head held high, saying, "Some days you have, some days you don't!" When you were loaded, you couldn't wait to meet with friends. You'd start making calls early to your core group to let everyone know the night was on you. And once you were assembled, you'd rain beers on the table until the night gave in. The next night would be somebody else's turn. There were even times where you would walk penniless into the bars where you were a regular, and people just bought you drinks the whole night.

Man, I had me some good times in the city center of Asmara.

Begin with root beer in Bar Zili and warm up with jokes. You down a couple of the root beers and wait until the friends fill up the table. It's a laid-back, guys' hangout with a clear view of the pedestrians heading to and from the city center. Situated under one of the most symbolic architectural imprints of the Italian colonial era, it was strategically set adjacent to the Shidda roundabout that spreads to the four corners of the town. From the main thoroughfare to the busy streets lined by bars and businesses, from Red Sea Secondary School to Sunshine Hotel, you could see the movement of the entire town while sipping the soothing meloti root beer. The homely wooden tables were filled with people of all ages. The city, regardless of the so-called security police that crouched at every corner, went about its business in that relaxed, "am taking my time" attitude.

Depending on finances and the mood we were in, we would head towards Bar Peacock or the surrounding bars in Gejeret for some upbeat trendy music and fine women. Joke and chat for hours until midnight, then it was a debate: head to Hollywood Pub for the hottest women and music, Bar Diana for familiar faces and classic oldies music, the cozy Rim Pub for the reggae and the atmosphere, and a lot more. When the bars closed around 2, if you still could afford to not call it a night, you head to the open clubs—Mokambo or Warsai—any day of the week and get wasted until the sun came up.

Most of us had vague images of other African cities, mostly bad, imprinted by the few occasions those cities got media coverage. Still, to hear the same biased story of one's beloved town from another African could be infuriating. Knowing that, the Burundi, Big Brodda as we called him, would come in once again to moderate the mood, saying, "My broddas, I have been to many African cities, believe me. I been to all corners. Been to the South Africa, Kenya, Nigeria, Libya, you name it. I lived, struggled, and had fun everywhere I went. Life is so different from what we see on TV. Every city got nice modern part with comfort and standards of a Western town." Looking around at the brown faces, he went on. "But we have to admit, most people live in de ghetto and struggling. But den when you go to de ghetto, you find people who have nothing, with dim future, no prospects. But der is lots of love; love no money can buy. All dey need is respect. All cities have dem in Africa. So stop dis stupid bickering over whose city is de best. We all left de cities we love for different reasons."

He would glance around with those big eyes of his to see if his message was getting through, and continue, "Until we get back, we have to make de best out of de places we travel. We would not have left if we had been all rich and powerful der. We come here because we had been deprived one way or de other. Believe me, me broddas, if you are homesick, you will neva feel at home anywhere, no matter how well you do. Babylon is tough; we have to be tougher and rougher to make de best of it." He emphatically hammered the words to a quiet but attentive audience, hitting the nerves right.

We would feel guilty and stupid, and would let the subject drop and proceed with what we did well: have fun regardless of the situation on the ground.

❁

That December Friday, though, the party had begun way before we had anticipated. I was awakened by loud Nigerian bass thumping from Cliff's room. I ignored the noise, along with the rest of the circus music that went about the Mottak, and wallowed in my fantasy. A Nokia ringtone then forced me out of my trance. I tried to ignore it twice, but it was persistent. I figured it could even be the office to congratulate me on the acceptance of my asylum. I hastened in a hurry and picked the phone out from the clothes near my bed. Sadly, it was just Cliff, who invited me over to his place for an early celebration.

He had said, "Come na quick, quick. We shakin' and shakin' beer here." I figured I had to buy some groceries, and forced myself up.

Not bothering to ask the occasion, I barged into Cliff's place with my shorts and towel, straight back from the shower. Congo, Tallest, Preacher, Angola, and a couple of new faces had already assumed their positions. P-Square brothers screamed to the Afro tune "Ee No Easy to Make Money, My Brodda," but unlike the other times, the table was full of all sorts of drinks already. The room was as messy as ever. The floor had turned from cream to dark brown, with hundreds of footmarks from spilled beverages. Clearly, the party had been begun early in the morning.

Something was clearly off. Cliff was stumbling around in his attempt to open drinks for his guests. His bloodshot eyes struggled to open a bottle with the spoon he often used. Baffled, Congo rose from his chair to snatch the beer away from Cliff's hand and pop the cork open with his teeth. Handing the beer towards Angola, to pass it on to me, he questioned with brotherly, warm concern in his voice, "Eh eh, Cliff, my brodda, we did not know we were here for de after-party. You not tell us why you hosting de party?"

Stomping his feet with an uncontrollable laughter, Cliff rushed to hug Congo and pulled him back to his chair. "You ask too many questions, my friend. Just drink." Looking at the rest of us, he said, "Everybody please sit down and drink." We left it at that and got on with the business.

After like a couple of drinks, Cliff got up and announced with his hoarse voice, "Everybody, dis kind people had told me today dat dey rejected my asylum for de second time." With a muffled drunk smirk, he sat down back into his chair with a thud to blank faces staring at him. It meant deportation was imminent. We knew right then it would be awkward to talk about it. We all vented our disappointments in our own way, but it registered instantly in everyone else's mind that we could be next. But we were city boys from Africa, and knew that you win some and lose some, but got to move on. Move on we did. Going in turns, we stacked up the fridge with the ammo for the day.

At around six, Knut came by with two heavily bearded Norwegian friends. The newcomers were reserved upon arrival. Cliff had become the magnet to all the lost souls in that small northern Norwegian town, especially on those dark, winter days. Thanks to him, the atmosphere was so relaxing that you wished never to leave. After scanning the brown faces of all sizes, the loud Afro beat music, and the smoke haze, the guests soon relaxed and enjoyed the festivities. Everyone was at ease and engaged in lively conversations, eating, drinking, and smoking whatever was available.

"Oh, my broddas, welcome to Kalakuta Republic!" Having noticed the way they were scanning the room, Cliff stated this proudly, looking at the guests with a beaming smile.

The two new white faces exchanged a puzzled glance. One of them could not help hesitantly correcting Cliff. "Did you mean Calcutta?" he asked, followed by the signature Norwegian standard smile.

"No, mon, I mean Kalakuta." Cliff stood firm.

The young man was around twenty, and relentless. "I think it is Calcutta, the ghetto in India. You know, the Mother Theresa thing!" he said, looking around the rest of indifferent faces for approval.

"Ee dey, look at dis man. I tell you, it is Kalakuta in Nigeria, not the one in India!" Cliff's attitude had already begun to give way to a mild irritation.

"Oh, I thought wrong, man!" said the still-unconvinced white boy, smiling.

Cliff, sensing his dissatisfaction, got up from his bed and slid past the crammed encampment towards the window, where his iPod was attached to the giant speakers. He had recently borrowed it from a Nigerian friend who had lived in Norway for two decades. It had around eight thousand songs in dozens of genres. He sifted through the playlist and finally played Fela Kuti's song, "Teacher Don't Teach Me Any Nonsense." The mesmerizing, soft, catchy Afro beat reverberated in our ears, while Fela delivered poetic emotional verses with a message.

Cliff waited a couple of minutes, before narrating the significance of the singer and its relevance to the topic. "You see, my brodda Fela is de Nigerian version of Bob Marley," he stated. "He died recently. Dey killed in him in frustration, like dey killed all our prophets, you understand me!"

The white boy looked at his friend with a hint of discomfort.

Cliff proceeded with the tale. "He always sing about de poor people and criticized de government about corruption. Dey imprisoned him plenty times, my friends. He once locked up in a bad prison cell dey call Calcutta. After coming off prison many times and going around de world, he went back to Lagos and declared his big compound de Kalakuta Republic. Wid its own flag, independent of Nigeria. De compound had everything inside. Free clinic. Free library. His band playing live music all de time for de people in de ghetto. My friends, once you go in, you never come out of de republic!"

I had heard a little about Fela, but never had I known he meant that much to ordinary Nigerians. The rest were geared up to hear more of the legend, especially the two white boys.

"Yo, man, that is cool. Robin Hood, like hero of the ghetto, huh?" the Norwegian said.

"Robin Hood, you say, mon? Dat man loved his people so much. Think about it, my friends. Republic inside a republic. De media went crazy about it. But for dose who knew him and loved him, he was our president, not Obasanjo," said Cliff, checking the audience to see if the subject had gripped their attention. "De government sent de military to bulldoze de republic down. Dat man was everything, man. He married twenty-seven wives on de same day. Imagine, my friends, most were his singers and some working inside de republic. After de government demolished da place, da women had no job. Dat is why he married dem all! He wanted to take care of dem all! Dat man is a legend!"

The overawed audience listened to Cliff's telling of the legend while the unusually long Afro-beat songs, at times running for a half an hour, played in the background.

⚅

The party wound up at midnight. With the drinks exhausted and the gang feeling tipsy, we made our way to the town. Unlike most cities we were used to, Harstad was a quiet town even on weekends. Then, the town came to life. All the hidden and hibernating souls came out, most intoxicated for a night out. With the few bars and clubs all packed within the narrow city center, which you could cover in three minutes on foot, you were likely to meet anyone who was out that night.

From the brothers in our party, though, only a quarter would dare to go out in the weekends. There were tons of reasons that stopped them: some held back due to financial constraints, but most others due to inferiority complexes that arose from fears of racial abuse by drunk locals, self-consciousness about being surrounded by white faces, the language barrier, and any other issue that the Mottak's walls seem comfortable.

The rest of the city boys from Africa had been through too much hardship to care about what others had to say. We tried to look our best, mingle with the crowd, and have fun. There were some clubs that didn't allow us to go in, due to the lack of an official Norwegian ID, which were not issued to asylum seekers. Despite being regarded as loud parasites crowding the spot, wherever we went, we tried to dance our asses off to whatever music was being played. Though not huge fans of oldies music, we twisted on the floor, headed to the next pub or club for pop or techno or break or hip-hop... Whatever it took for a city boy with rhythm to release the stress and feel the music. In clubs, we saw people nodding along to the songs they know, others who loved the music and danced to it, but a man with "riddim" becomes the music. And the music set us free.

❀

The night shift crew, along with the three Norwegian friends, braced ourselves for the cold as we cautiously slid our way down the slippery Asbjørnselbans Street.

Knut, having noticed Cliff addressing every one of us with nicknames, asked, "Yo, Cliff, why you always give everybody another name?"

Cliff, still nursing the wound of having been rejected by one club, lashed out. "Mtsee, look at dis white boy asking me why I rename. You people came to Africa and renamed everything and everyone; why?" Every one of us was already cracking into a loud laughter. "You people do mogo mogo, you think it was because de rivers and de villages did not have names! No, you wanted to name it so you can remember Chucky, my friend!" Bursting into a grin, Cliff joked, "I dey laugh, oh boy. Besides, my mind is jammed; I don't have time to remember strange names!"

Whenever the talkative Knut had a story to tell, he narrated the same ones he'd told his Norwegian friends. Failing to achieve the same reaction, he would try to explain the story once again, irritating the already hysterical Cliff.

We passed the intersection between Rikardkaarbøs Gate and Hvedelings Gate, still laughing at Cliff ridiculing Chucky, and Knut relentlessly trying to reason in return. We walked down the Rikardkaarbøs and made a left at the Ming Restaurant, leaving the town mall to our backs.

"I don't understand you people, man," Cliff remarked. "We and you guys are always different, man."

"No, come on," protested Knut, "stop exaggerating! Why you always do that, to make fun of the white guy or what?"

"No, man. I tell you, it is de truth. Look, hear what dis man tell me de oder day I call him." Cliff looked around the flock, who was following their exchange closely. "He say he going for a Frisbee with his friends. And ask me if I want to come. I say what? What de hell is Frisbee? He say, you know, we throw stick for de dog to fetch it. And when he fetch it, dey throw it once again. I am angry, am wasting my credit talking about dog and stick together, so I say no and goodbye." After an animated, foot-stamping good laugh, he looked up and down the skinny figure of Knut in a sort of appraisal. "My friends, what kind of man throws a stick to a dog and call it sport? And worse, I have to bring my friends to watch him do it."

"Come on, man," Knut pleaded, "don't you have a dog back at home?"

"We have dogs, my friend."

"Okay, what were their names?"

"What name are you talking about? Dey all look alike; just call them Bobby or something." He looked towards us, hoping we'd back him up. We were enjoying the exchange, so no one interrupted.

"Didn't you have, like, your own dog you used to, you know, be around the whole time?"

"No, my friend, we had dogs. When you come into our compound, dey bark. You scratch deir noses a little bit once in a while and walk inside. And de dog stays outside."

"Why? I mean, why can't it come in inside?"

"Look, it is how it is. Dey stay out and play and wander wherever dey want. Dat is why dey call dem dogs, my friend."

"Okay, I guess you never play with them like we do, huh! You are funny, man, but seriously, it is cool to play along with the dogs. It just shows that we care for their being. They are not just animals for us."

"Wid a stick, huh," Cliff mockingly replied. "Look, where I came from, we call it chasing afta the neighbor's dog. And it is no laughing matter, my friend, no Frisbee. De dog probably snuck in and ate your lunch while you left your room to borrow some salt from de neighbor." After laugh, he added, "You know, back at home, we borrow everything to one another, man. So, my friend, you will not chase de dog with a smile but angry to bit de shit out of it, my man. And all de nabos would be cheering behind you. And you said dat you care dey are not animals, huh? Tying and pulling dem around is caring? No, my brodda, you people just like to change and control nature. We just let de dogs be dogs, you understand me?"

"You are funny, man..." And he left it trailing, but I knew he was dying to say something more.

We kept walking down past the open parking lot to our right, the giant, stone, low-rise cinema and the gallery to our left. We jaywalked towards 4 Håkons Street, made it down the street that bisected the Grand Hotels and the two bars underneath it, turned left, and finally reached the heart of town in Strandegata. The cobblestone street had a cosmopolitan feel to it; the nexus of our night life.

Standing on the polished marble beneath the Grand Hotel balcony, you could monitor the rhythm of the night. Just across the street, to our far right, across the tiniest of roundabouts, stood Metzo, a trendy club with high-tempo music and a cool crowd. A hundred yards away, a wooden one-story building housed an exotic cafe and a couple of restaurants that were irrelevant and almost nonexistent in our CBPS (City Boy Positioning System) before reaching an area of great interest to us, The Black Sheep. It was a beat-up pub with pool table and a diverse audience, albeit the worst taste in music.

On the edge of a downslope intersection, towards the university college, was our favorite spot, Nordlys. The soft rock music and the laughter of the regulars spread out in its open, lively garden.

With most of the hotels and cafes around the town being out of our price range, few of us barely knew their names. Apart from the boutiques inside the mall and the two nightclubs and one bar, the rest were irrelevant. Not one asylum boy I knew had been spotted in one of the indoor cafés drinking a latte. You need coffee, you just rush your ass to the Mottak and make one in the kitchen; that was the deal.

It was funny, though; we assumed café coffee was a luxury, but we would go on a spree in the hotels and clubs, drinking shots or buying rounds and rounds of beer. It was expensive, and would also come with severe consequences on the following morning!

❀

Haunted by the alarmingly still cold Friday night, Cliff blurted, "Where I come from, no way you find anywhere dis quiet. Especially in de city! It is full of noise all de time, full crowd."

Even the white friends agreed—probably this was the thing that bothered them most about living in the small northern town.

It was an experience we had yet to come to grips with. As in many cities, especially in Africa, if you were taking a stroll, be it at night or in daylight, turning a corner into a quiet street set off alarm bells. The prudent thing to do was to walk back the way you came and take another route. It was an instinct thing: Silence meant trouble, as if evil were lurking. Here, we came across many alarmingly quiet streets at an alarming frequency, as it was the order of the day in this part of the world. Still, you couldn't shake off your instincts—you kept looking over your shoulder to make sure you were safe, especially when one was on his own.

Norway was one of the safest places in the world. Crime was as distant as a hot sunny day. I kind of missed all the drama I was used to, in a crazy way: the police chasing culprits, the muggers and prostitutes lurking and patrolling the corners, drunks and vendors crowding the narrow footpaths, minibuses honking and hooting, beggars and bums sitting idlly in the middle of the street, the bars and clubs blasting music to the fullest. Now, it was a different story. The pace of life was slow and methodical for us.

Noticing all this wasn't the same as being ungrateful, as what some would think. We nodded to the guards and glided past the gates of Metzo. The place was packed and the hip-hop music made us feel at home already.

With loud music playing, a drink in one's hand, and beautiful women to dart the eyes at, a brother soon forgot the world and its endless troubles. We Africans followed the drum. The drum is the heartbeat of Africa, the lub and dub set the mood of the people and the times. The body moved according to the beat, following the tempo; you let yourself be finally transported into a trance. The mind could be at rest, surrendering to the heart. The music was in full control of the body, like a beating heart.

Most dance moves were meant to depict the movement of animals; hence, they were natural animal expressions of affection and sorrow, just as the ancestors used to do. Though the times had changed, the essence remained. The world was turning into a small yet divided village; rhythm had become more uniform and more contagious than ever, at times spreading faster than a virus and more extensively than religion.

With very few black faces around in the town, we were not that difficult to pick out in a crowd. In fact, we knew every black face that frequented the town center. The locals knew three kinds of black people living in their town: the first were the citizens who had migrated long ago and assimilated. Then came the American basketball players playing for the local team, who often hung out with the locals. Finally were the asylum seekers, who were treated like untouchables.

However, the asylum city boys wanted to be perceived differently from the rest of the asylums. We were more social and more independent. Our appearance was somehow trendy, managing to stay stylish with what little resources we had available. Even though the locals could tell us apart because we did not speak the language, we did not feel like strangers. We did not expect—even detested—sympathy. All we needed was a break. Due to the locals' perception of the asylums as awkward and uncivilized, we strove hard and at time distanced ourselves from those stereotypes. Thus, we unintentionally created some sort of deviation and self-denial of ourselves from the rest of the asylum seekers. We had nothing against them; we just wanted to be free from all constraints, while they wished to refrain from all sorts of temptations that happened to bring us joy. As Cliff would state, "Am no refugee, am a tourist just passing through."

Thus, with a confidence and swagger, we got by well. We were entering the clubs without raising the guards' suspicion. We were able to make friends from all over. Some of us assumed different nationalities so we could gain certain benefits. Congo would, at times, pose as a French journalist who was on a business trip in town, with his excellent French convincing the locals. I, at times, get by as a Jamaican who was around for a concert or visiting a friend. "Yes mon, I and I mean nothing but love!" Tallest would change professions and nationalities every week to suit his audience, given his excellent knowledge of many languages and cities. Most of it was done to pass as ordinary fellows out to have fun, especially if we met a Norwegian woman in one of the clubs. Admitting your asylum status would usually leave you sitting alone at the bar, unless the woman was really interested in you. There was some sort of mistrust or pity—we didn't really know—but I suspected it was due to our lack of jobs and residence permits. Some were just outright racists.

In a way, though, our night outs were a cry for recognition. To remind people that we were still out there. As dormant and inactive as we were during the so-called productive weekdays, we made sure we made our presence felt on the weekends. In a funny way, it was the only time when we could mingle freely and feel equal, listening to the same music, drinking, and dancing on the same dance floor. It was therapeutic. If I missed out on a pair of weekends, I would feel the difference; but a good weekend would at least dampen some of the frustration from boiling up until Tuesday, at least. Moreover, it would often bring us a fresh subject to converse over on those Mondays glued to the TV room's sofa.

❀

Inside the clubs, though, we were on a mission. We dispersed and tried our best to distract the curious locals, who never tired of asking, "*Hvor du kom fra?*" If it was a woman, well, I'd drop a line or two to make her feel beautiful and comfortable. But it was not easy at all for a brother with no money, no job, to be competing with the locals for ladies' attention, no matter how smooth a brother was. But if he was lucky, he might find a sugar mommy.

As Cliff had sarcastically put it, "It is the toughest job to find for broddas like us." It doesn't require documents or a work permit, but still, it was a demanding job to keep a busy, divorced Norwegian happy. They say money can't buy love, but believe me, being a miser won't cut it. Even the African women who were awaiting their verdict from the UDI were inclined to find a relationship that ensured a stable future. Few dated fellow asylum seekers. It was enforced prostitution—not of the body, but of the mind in dire need of security. Let's face it; we all mean business.

Thus, a city boy, we looked outside the Mottak to satisfy our needs, be she black or white, so long she provided. A few brothers said they have fallen in love, despite the differences in age, culture, color, and finances—but if it worked out, who was I to judge? Still, some of us just liked showing off with a local white girl, and scoring a couple of points on the stressed and starved asylum boys. Most of them were forced to abstain from sex for as long as they remained in the Mottak, or else handle it by themselves. No wonder why the toilets were so busy at times!

But for others it was more like a job, as Congo had called it: "the night shift." The pay was good for some, depending on the performance. Some of us were dedicated to the cause, and it always showed. If you took care of your sugar mommy, she could really take good care of you. She could find you a job through her connections, if she cared enough. But most preferred to tip well for the night hours. It was a diversion for a couple of hours a day, in addition to the extra favors. And the woman knows it, as well, but I didn't believe they liked to think about it. The older ones knew they were not getting younger, so they made the best of it while it lasted. The fact was, the first minute a brother found a better opportunity, he would be gone. No need to pack, no need to hand in a resignation letter or seek compensation; you just moved on. One could be terminated just as abruptly if she found a better suitor; thus, it was just business, nothing personal. And the more clearly the two parties realized that, there were fewer complications afterwards.

After one stressful affair with a sugar mommy, one friend said, "Dey say wine and woman get better in age. Man, dey meant bitter and rougher!" Understanding the pressure of having a rough night, we would reassure him that it was the nature of the job. Women in Norway were highly empowered and independent; besides, they had the full backing of the law. They, from our experience, loved to be in control. The ones who had been through divorces and failed relationships knew exactly what they wanted and when they wanted it. Worse, some considered men to be disposable sex objects. Once they had their kids, men fell even further down the list of their priorities, unless it was for a quick fix. Yet even when these women meant well, they had to have it their way. Being a broke, black asylum seeker did not help our case, either, so a city boy had to swallow this one real hard. You ended up getting an idea of what it felt to be a traditional wife back at home. Talk about a dose of one's own medicine.

On the very few occasions that we discussed our grievances— or rather, our night shift inconveniences—you would feel like gossiping prostitutes in the end, so we never got that far. Suck it up and man up!

In one of these sessions, a bewildered Cliff cracked us up over an argument he'd had with his sugar mommy. "Dis crazy woman gave me a bicycle as a gift de oder day," he said. "I thought it was for my own good. Was praising de woman all day, mon! Telling everybody: a week of night shift and I get a bicycle for reward.

Was dreaming dat maybe after a couple of months she would give me her car."

We all laughed knowing where he was going.

Still shaking his head, he went on with his story. "But, my broddas, she had oder plans. She call me de oder day to come in the middle of de night, freezing cold. I tell her, it is cold, why not you pick me up? You know what she say? 'Why do you think I gave you de bike?'"

We laughed and laughed for minutes. And because we had noticed that the bike, which he had been bragging and parading around for a week, had disappeared, we gathered his contract had been terminated.

Another friend, who had been seeing a forty-something woman for a couple of weeks, unburdened himself, too. "My friends, I have been with so many women in my life: and believe me, I never met a woman who cannot keep her hands off my zipper. The woman cannot sleep at all. I feel like a cow in a dairy farm. One of these days, my dick is going to fall off, my friends."

After a loud, collective laugh, one added in agreement, "Dey all like dat, my brodda. Mine is even older dan you. But I tell you, I try not to make a sound when I sleep. If I toss or move an arm and wake her, it is followed by another round. No matter how uncomfortable I get, I remain in dat position until dawn."

Once one started to spill the beans, it all came out, but it would never be mentioned again. Someone tied up this touchy issue, saying, "Anyway, we should get our sperm count checked. Depending on the diagnosis, we should renegotiate our contracts."

Deep inside, we all yearned for a stable relationship to which we could give our undivided attention. Even in these troubled times, it would have been nice to have someone special, someone who made all the insignificant problems disappear by just looking at me with her caring eyes. I wanted to unload my soul of all its burdens, and share everything I felt for her. Let the guard down for once and feel the pain and happiness of having a partner for life. Be lost in her love and life, day and night.

Most of us fantasize that our tribulations will end in triumph, given a loved one with whom we bear children and grow old.

Actions speak otherwise. Dreams can fuck up your reality. At times, reality drains the love and life out of you. Most of us had already paid the price of abandoning our loves in search of riches! Some still waited, but most of us knew that our women at home were lost to us; you winced whenever you saw a lonely, bitter, old man, drunk, stumbling from brothel to brothel, seeking for another round of anonymous release.

Some of us might never be lucky enough to find true love. Here is what I learned: You lose a lot when you are constantly on the road. Every time you are forced to move or decide to move, you leave a part of yourself behind—a piece of your heart, especially if you found that other half of you in the opposite sex. The "what if I had stayed longer" scenes haunt you in those lonely nights, even possessing your daydreams. The wear, tear, and travel finally harden you. Not yet incapable of love, you still keep your deep emotions in check. It creates a fear of getting deeply involved, not knowing how long you will be staying in a particular place. It is a self-preservation strategy.

We boasted about our conquests in all corners of the world, but deep inside, we were dying to end the running. We wanted to come back to a one and only, each and every night.

✳

My demons gave me a break for the weekend, and we had a blast. Having reconciled with my sugar mommy late Saturday night, I felt refreshed to face off with another five-episode Monday series. In the Mottak, the weekly auction was underway: a whole variety of products laid out under the watchful eye of the Merchant.

Cliff, who had just woken up from another crazy Saturday night, entered the frenzy of the Sunday market hoping to watch some TV. As usual, the Merchant was wooing his customers with his sleek, relentless way. "*Amico*, you are my good friend. Zis mobile I want to send to my sister. Look, look... ze battery is very good. No charger, but you come to me tomorrow, I get you charger. You take for 400 kroner." He would sell one Samsung to a newcomer desperately in need of a phone. He often targeted the new arrivals, knowing their innocence and desperation. "No, no, *habibi*. *Malek welahi*, zis laptop work very good. I fix for you today. You try give me money tomorrow." And there went another laptop that had been out in the cold for probably days before the Merchant discovered it.

We were watching the drama unfold until Cliff suddenly jumped into action and grabbed one Somali by the neck. Alarmed, a couple others and I rushed to pull the huge, raging Nigerian away from the skinny Somali.

"Where you get dis sweater, huh?" screamed Cliff.

The stunned Somali just happened to just be trying on some of the clothes on sale.

"My friend, you crazy," he protested to Cliff. "I come here now, look at clothes, you fight me. What is the problem? You crazy. You want to fight, huh? I kill you, *welahi.* You don't know me!" The skinny boy had some stamina, to the surprise of all, who was actually gesturing Cliff to go and have a mano-a-mano outside the gate.

"Look at look at dis boy!" Cliff pointed at his fired up opponent. "You want to die, eh eh! I finish you today. Come on, go out!"

By then, there were a lot of bodies in between them, trying to cool off the situation. Cliff tried to push everyone aside and tried to grab the feisty boy by his collar. The boy threw a punch to break the huge grip of Cliff's hand.

"You don't know who I am. I show you. Am a powerful civilian."

Cliff was turning into a bull about to go on a rampage. We finally managed to pull him outside. It took three of us to subdue him.

Finally, standing outside, we asked him what had provoked him.

"Dis boy stole my sweater!" he snapped in irritation. "Did you see him? De boy wanted to fight. Dis Somalis, I tell you, dey are crazy!" Cliff was still astounded by the kid's audacity to fight back, despite the height and weight disadvantage.

"Hey, Cliff, come on, man!" I said, in a pleading tone. "Ze kid was just buying ze sweater from ze Merchant. Talk to ze Merchant where he got ze sweater, man!"

In the meantime, the Merchant was gravely complaining for having his auction interrupted. "Please, please, you will break my things! Hey, my friend, you not pay for zat! Put it down please! You break it, you buy, *kompis. Ingen gratis!*"

He was shouting over the chaos, and finally subdued the crowd and all went calm.

He came rushing outside and shook his head in disappointment. "I don't know why you always make problem for me, Cliff!" he said. "You never buy! You always make problem. Not good, my friend, but I give you zis phone free. Because you are my friend!" He extended a busted-up, worn-out Erikson mobile phone to Cliff, cautiously.

The already-forgiving Cliff snatched the phone and peered at it for a closer inspection. He looked back at the Merchant, whose beady eyes were blinking wildly. "Where you got dat sweater is what I want to know!" Cliff said, and slipped the phone into his pocket.

Relieved the matter had been resolved, the Merchant looked at us, smiling, and said, "Cliff, my friend! You think ze factory only made zat kind of sweater for you only! You see your name zere, Cliff, *welahi*? But I give you free! Don't make no more problem!" He winked, hoping Cliff would drop the case. We all smiled at the cunning Merchant and went inside. The auction was back in business.

Demons in Progress

The Mondays fly by like a plane in the distant sky, as if they had nothing to do with you. Just a bystander to time, you wait anxiously, festering under the eye of ever-vigilant personal demons. It was soon another year gone, on the verge of 2010. The mood in the Mottak was subdued. It was just another reminder of another year wasted, nothing more. To make matters worse, the weather had deteriorated dramatically. The arctic depression had set in: seven minutes of daylight a day. The locals had mostly fled to the tropics, leaving us as guardians. The TV room was packed. Snow was falling hard outside, and the meteorologists predicted more heavy snow in the following days.

Shooting Dogs was on TV. The gripping, grotesque depiction of actual events of the 1994 Rwandese genocide kept the mostly African audience in quiet, uncomfortable suspense, yet none dared to change the channel. The substance of the suspense was a morbid fascination with what we humans were capable of doing to one another. It happened everywhere, in a continent ridden with hundreds of years of injustice stemming from colonialism, tribal differences, difficult histories, and religious disputes. Hatred and contempt for one another were rife. It only took an excuse to stir up all the misfortunes of the past, letting them boil over from where they'd simmered in the collective conscience. I looked at the black faces around me to see the same mixture of pity, guilt, and shame there. It was annoying at times to see that any news coverage regarding Africa was accompanied by a drought-starved child, a child soldier with a Kalashnikov, or an angry mob with bloody machetes. There was a lot more to us. We were so diverse and different, yet the same.

The horror on screen took me back to how politics manipulated the savage mob in all of us. I remembered how dramatically people had turned their backs on us when the border crisis erupted between Eritrea and Ethiopia. Having lived side by side for generations, praying in the same churches, dining off the same trays, suddenly these people vehemently demanded our deportations. The contemptuous stares in the neighborhood, the constant harassment by the police who wanted to hasten us on our way, we were humiliated and stripped of every piece of belonging in a land we had always felt was home. My entire identity was stolen the day I was hauled off to the bus terminal, where thousands of my so-called countrymen awaited deportation to our "motherland."

And I remembered as well, a couple of years after we had uneasily settled in the ever-turbulent "home" country, the border war intensified and the entire population rose up in support of the troops. Following a rapid advance of the Ethiopian troops along the eastern flank to occupy the major town of Barentu, the capital city made a reprisal attack on the remaining Ethiopian citizens, vigilante-style. Targeting the Ethiopians who had lived there for generations, I was one of the many intoxicated by the mass euphoria and coerced to unleash all fury on a selected few. This temporary, mass psychosis was capable of annihilating anything along the way, and my dear continent seemed to relapse into it time after time.

Never will we move forward until we learn to forgive and forget. We just had to get even, and the West never understood that. But it was always easy to judge, sitting safe and sound behind the TV. Payback was always in the back of the mind. The frustrated, disillusioned, warring mob was manipulated by ill-intentioned leaders who riled up support by magnifying centuries-old differences into unleashing an unstoppable killing machine. The worst part was that it was contagious. Where I came from, I saw people who ate the same staple foods, who shared the same beliefs and values stretching back for more than two thousand years, who wrote and read scriptures in the same unique alphabet, who shuffled and danced to the same beat of a drum unique in all the world, who married into each other's families, turn to each other like arch-enemies. They shed each other's blood, but when the corpses were buried and the dust settled, wished no one but each other as a neighbor. Thousands of miles away from home, both out of their comfort zone, it took one look around at the white faces to realize that even though you had loathed him bitterly, only he or she could ever understand you.

The film's antagonist and his strong-armed followers hacked and chopped their victims with a horrifying enthusiasm, yet we could barely look away. With a scene of a young Hutu boy cornering a mother with a terrified newborn son in her embrace, the camera zoomed on her face as the machete struck her forehead. Blood splattered all over. Her protective grip was still firm though, even as she tumbled to the muddy ground. The young boy was undeterred by the blood squirting from the mother's head, and the baby crying at the top of his lungs failed to faze him. The boy spread his legs for better leverage, and lunged again at the woman's head, again and again and again, with a blank expression on his face, as if he was hacking the heads of fresh caught river fish. The woman was long dead, yet the lifeless body was still curled around the tiny body of the baby, fully protecting it from the endless blows. Despite the violence, it was an epic moment that captured the unfailing love of a mother.

And then the boy wiped his face and turned next to the baby.

"Ah, ah, dis people are cruel, my brodda!" exclaimed a stunned, horrified Tallest. "How dis little boy kill a little boy like dat? I don't understand!"

"Sometimes you wonder where God really iz. It iz disgusting: one million people killed in a matter of one hundred days. Can you imagine?" added Preacher.

Cliff, who was hoping anybody would change the channel, said, "It's dis white people who allowed it to happen, I tell you. Dey don't care! Let's watch something else, na."

A pensive Congo, who was squirming and fidgeting in his seat at every strike of the machete, finally said, "You know I am a Tutsi myself," he began. "I seen it happen right in front of my eyes. Dis people, Hutu, believe dey are de natural heirs of de land. We come from de northern highlands and took deir territory for centuries." He paused for a second to regain his composure. "You know how it is, back in de days, we always fought over land and de Tutsis were on top for long time. It is never de first time. Den dis Europeans came with de divide and rule."

"Mtsee, dey did dat to everybody, I tell you," reiterated someone in support. "Na, we will neva have peace. I come from Biafra state. Look what dis British and dose French did to us!"

"Very true, my friend," said a newcomer Somali. "Look at Somalia here, same people. One ethnic group. Same language, same religion! Zis British, French, Italians, and Ethiopians divide us. We still fighting." The remark raised a couple of Ethiopian eyebrows.

Congo continued with his tale about how the hatred had deepened among the Hutu due to the European powers favoring the Tutsi literally over everything, even though they were the minority. The tables turned during independence, when the ever-shifting European policy of handing over power to the majority came into picture. The Tutsis began to systematically eliminate the Hutu educated elites by the thousands. The same was going on in Burundi and Congo.

"Tit for tat, for decades afterwards! When either one of the two tribes was in power in one of the countries, der will always be ripple effect on the neighbors, I tell you. Swinging the power scale to one side or other all the time, mtsee! Things may look better on de outside but, I tell you, de people are always brooding for a payback! Dat is Africa, my friends."

The way Congo related the reality of our continent added to the montage of thoughts that my mind conjured. What was I, as a human, capable of doing? I was disgusted. In retrospect, I realized that I often dwelled on the past and the failures, looking for excuses, even though times tested the character. I somehow had to make peace with myself. Had to stop hating and condemning myself and my fate.

That had to be my priority, because the negativity was such a consuming force. You have to respect pure hatred—it never forms overnight. A true hatred is built up gradually. First, one had to know the person or the issue firsthand. Then get a chance to get acquainted; and then afterwards, weigh the pros and cons of the relationship. If the pros outweighed the cons, yet you felt unsure, it was only insecurity. Insecurity did not constitute true hatred; it only proved one's incapability to compete. Only when the cons outweighed the pros should one think of keeping a distance; thereby, a dislike formed. Still, one could avoid conflict by minding one's own business. A real man was the one who never picked a fight, yet was capable of defending himself at all costs. Only after a prolonged conflict and a threat to one's life or identity could hate form. That is profound, fact-bound hatred. The rest was a mediocre waste of time and energy.

The New Year's blues had gotten to most of the residents. Most withdrew earlier than ever to their bunks. I was well aware of the trauma Congo had been through as a Tutsi minority. During the Rwandan genocide, he had been living in a border town running a small retail shop. From the few comments he made about his past life, I gathered he had always lived his life on the edge. Always ready to be on the move, whenever and wherever disaster fell around him. He had witnessed the hatred that had been simmering over decades turn into killing spree in a matter of days. The genocide spilled across the border, as neighbors and family members turned against one another. Though he avoided the subject, his eyes at times told a different story. The master of disguise maintained the smile on his face, but the longer we knew each other, the more I felt the burden of sorrow he carried every day. He was often jumpy whenever anyone had a big kitchen knife in hand. I imagined the machete scenes came flooding into his mind—that was hard to live with.

But I could only fight my own devils; I had my own issues even if they were not as grave as his. It was a personal battle you rarely shared; we Africans were not that into sharing our traumas with strangers. We'd bottle it forever if we could.

Besides the obvious distinction of residence status, race, or religious affiliation, by far the most oppressing and damaging differences the tribal ones. It was a ghost that haunted us Africans wherever we went. Based on twisted myths, distorted history, recent division, and hearsay, tribal differences created a poisonous cloud in a relatively peaceful atmosphere. We wished to distance ourselves from it in the twenty-first century, yet in failing, it was easy to understand why there would never be peace in Africa in the near future.

Coming from a part of the world boasting thousands of years of civilization, what do I have to show for it? I come from a tribe who prides itself on tracing a direct bloodline to the wise King Solomon of the Old Testament. We had been part of the great Aksumite Empire that reigned over the Nile and the Red Sea, and accepted Christianity before it even crossed the Mediterranean. We had come from the same kingdom that ruled over a vast land across the East Africa and extended to the Middle East. We had invaded and inhabited fertile lands under a dynasty claiming roots in Solomon's time. We boasted about our own unique civilization, with its peculiar alphabets and rich traditions, which were surpassed by only the Egyptians'. A couple of hundred years ago, many missionaries and awed foreign dignitaries had predicted a bright future for the great empire that had withstood all other foreign forces. Who would have thought the first picture that came to people's minds would end up being starving villagers begging for foreign aid?

Times changed, but our proud mentality hindered us from going forward with the rest of the world. While other nations dismantled borders, we were fighting one another over a piece of dry land. Hatred and mistrust destroyed our family. Like two lovers, our country was split in half and we, the children, were caught in the custody battle. In the motherland, we never felt welcome anymore; only like second-class citizens in a broken home.

❧

Labeled upon arrival, feeling stateless ever since, culture-shocked, and still young, I was struggling through a severe identity crisis. I hated my people; I hated both sides and felt ashamed of my history. As always, I found comfort with the Amche, the newcomers, as we were labeled. I lived—rather, I served my term—and lived most of it trying to escape the country I called home. I had no intention of going back anytime soon nor even liked thinking of the lost pages of my life. Once I was out, I just represented myself. I was stateless! The thousand years of history were no longer applicable to my cause. And the friends I made later in life were those who did not remind me of the past; rather, they allowed me to discover and transform myself into someone new.

The mistrust, the negative vibe, the spreading of rumors fueled by one's religion or another's tribe, had followed us all the way from Africa. They had robbed me of my identity and now, often, I felt I had to choose sides. I wanted none of it!

However, there was always that somebody around who allowed you to forget the past and live for the moment, know you as a person, and not as a member of certain tribe. In our case, we had been blessed by Cliff's presence. Even though he was from the proud Igbo tribe in Nigeria, he never cared where anyone was born. Coming from the Biafra region of Nigeria, his entire clan had almost been wiped out during the civil war between the North and the South. Carefree as he was, it was only whenever his Igbo friends were in town that he exhibited a feeling of being unfairly done by the British colonialists and the corrupt Nigerian governments that followed. His demeanor would be transformed, proudly stating to whoever was listening, "I come from the richest country, the Republic of Biafra." Not Nigeria. Even though he embraced Nigerians from other tribes, I sensed a reserved distance in him. Mostly, though, he was the kind of guy who made you forget the negative. He cracked jokes at everything and everyone, and it neutralized the negative vibe all around us.

❧

Congo paced in the entrance gate with barely a sweat suit on, alone and distraught. I made my way out to have a little talk with him; he had always been attentive to others. He was oblivious to the scalding cold outside. Lost in the abyss, the ever-smiling Congo had finally succumbed to the blues.

Disturbingly, I took comfort from the fact that I was not alone. I brushed off the thought, looking at his gloomy face. It had aged a decade within hours. I was lost for words—I never knew he had a dark side to him.

Blowing a mouthful of the cheap LM cigarette smoke into the wind, Congo said in a low voice, "Cold country, cold people, cold fate, man. Frozen in time, frozen in space, I don't know, man. I don't see myself going anywhere." Huffing out more smoke, he added, "I don't know if it is a fucking curse or what. I just got de worst luck in de world. Shit never works out for me. Even if it did, it makes sure dat I never get to enjoy it, man, you know. Always been like dat, as if dere is some devil haunting my every move."

I nodded in agreement. "I feel you, man."

But Congo was in a trance. "I believe in God, man." He choked back a sob. "But sometimes I wonder. If dere is one, I hope he is enjoying it. Watching one of his poor creatures cracking under all unworthy pressure." He looked up in contempt.

I'd never seen him so hurt and so remorseful, but then I couldn't say I blamed him. I patted him on the back, and an attempt to cheer him up, said, "Congo, I never knew you get so poetic when you are cold."

He looked at me and gave me his signature smile. It was short-lived though, and he went on. "Serious, man. It is just not fucking worth it; all de sleepless nights I have to endure, de dreams and fantasies I have to make up for all de fuck-ups. I can't say I did not try, man. Let not dis smile fool you. Believe me,

I tried, brodda. But den I get nowhere, so what do I have to look up for anymore? You know what? Am getting fucking tired of it all. If der is a real God out der, if I had pissed him off for my shitty existence, den all I got to say is you can have de life you given me back anytime. I know I don't deserve all dis, my brodda, but am not begging him anymore!" With that, he flipped the butt of the cigarette into the snow and walked right back to his bunk.

After our little talk, he had me talking and thinking to myself all night. Some nights were worse, though: deep serious thoughts, man, about what the fuck the purpose of my existence was. I thought, I can't be running forever in search of safety and security all my life. Got to be more than that! I was mad at myself for hesitating to at least come up with one decent explanation. I strained my mind for words to define the reason for my being, wanting to understand where I really stood. I felt sure I would disappoint everyone, and myself. My life had been a play without a script, running unnoticed, with no plot, no theme, just a bunch of irrelevant characters. I was the star, redundant and boring at times, yet always in a state of suspense that never seemed to dissipate.

But before the next scene, I'd be fast asleep.

These dark thoughts were getting to be a ritual. They say when life gets rough and beats you up like the neighborhood bully, you had to pick yourself up, even if it meant starting from scratch. Yet what about all these scars?

When I woke up the next day, I put my game face on. I still felt deader than the day before, I would try to busy myself with all the bullshit I could find, just to stop thinking. Just to shut the demons up.

Time flies indeed! The ice began to melt away, along with our dreams. Seasons slid by as we weathered our own prisons. My rage would take over at around this time of the year, bringing in a season of madness.

March was my personal hurricane season. I was always braced for disaster. My moods swung wildly, and the turmoil would last a couple of months until I met with some humbling experience that finally calmed the rage. The ripples and aftershocks would last until around late July. Then all that mental and emotional strength that I had accumulated in the previous months would be razed to the ground again, and I would find myself on a countdown to self-demolition. Year after year, the disastrous cycle I had not been able to avert had made me superstitious and a little paranoid whenever the season arrived.

Times were tough; money was even tighter. I was used to the personal welfare but relations had been strained with my sugar mommy. The contract was nearing its closure. She had been offered a job with a considerable raise in a bigger city with bigger opportunities. I was a surplus good in a small town. Her interest in me decreased dramatically. But then, I had not held many expectations. I knew that the little gifts, the free cigarette packs, drinks, and pocket money would soon disappear, and that I had better look for another suitor before the boredom of the Mottak killed me. You only miss your water when the well runs dry, indeed; the gateway home was getting away. I was stuck in my own bunk indefinitely.

My situation deteriorated at a time when the Mottak was undergoing a massive transformation. The authorities had begun issuing decisions at a breathtaking pace, stemming the incoming tide with verdicts that sometimes came within two weeks. Some decisions came with a residence acceptance letter. These lucky souls mixed easily with the crowd, knowing it would just be a matter of months before they relocated to their own house in another city or town. Their enthusiasm was a slap in the face for the likes of us, whose wait dragged on. I despised the newcomers to a point that I avoided them by any means necessary.

My roommate, Korea, had been granted his residence papers at the turn of the year. He left the Mottak the way he entered; cool as ice. The old man, frustrated by the lack of response from the Immigration Police, had abandoned the system and moved to the capital to fend for himself. Afterwards, my room felt like a brothel, with plenty of guys coming and going, some after only a night or two. With my multicultural, loud friends a constant presence in the room, the suspicious fellow countrymen requested reassignment to a safer environment.

My quarters were pretty disturbing, actually. The basement room window had been hung with two, double-thick, dark curtains, to curb what little light reached our building. Better to embrace the darkness from the inside out, I figured. Plus the two over-mirror lights had been heavily taped with purple polythene shopping bags that had dimmed the lighting into a groovy gloom. The constant, dubbed, reggae music reverberated from an old laptop, purchased from the Merchant, across the two busted-up speakers, and trapped smoke rippled in a thick haze, especially whenever I had company. This was not a place you would really come back to have a nap, anyway, not until Sleepy settled in. We ended up getting along very well in the few hours he was awake.

Sadly, we had also lost a couple of our beloved brothers to deportation. Among the forgotten crew of the dungeon, the loss of Big Man from Burundi was felt the most. Unlike others who were devastated when the escorting police officers knocked on the door, and cried like infants, Burundi was ready as ever.

A loud rap on the door snapped me from a deep sleep. My eyelids felt heavy. In a trance between dream and reality, I could hear that the rapping had grown impatient. Sleepy did not even budge. It would take a bomb to wake up the guy. He had even slept through an entire fire drill, with the fire alarm ululating the whole time. I finally forced myself up and demanded who it was.

"It's me, open up, na. Have not time!" replied Burundi. Still in my underwear, I staggered past the pile of bottle rubble and chairs strewn all over the room from the mini-party the night before. He stood outside, flanked by two giant policemen on each side.

Though I had nothing to fear, I cut my stretching in midstride and straightened myself up, ready to answer questions. Thousands swirled around my sleepy head; *Had I done something wrong? Of course you have done something wrong, with a dozen of demons up in your head. You don't even know who is in charge of you!* The reasoning voice inside argued back, *Just relax and don't panic!*

I requested in a calm voice what the visit was all about.

Burundi smiled, noting my alarm. "Dis people are deporting me today, man!"

Taken aback, I took a good look at his calm eyes and his big smile. He did not look one bit bothered by the surprise visit. Many had broken into tears or tried to jump off the window ledge when they were ambushed by an early police visit.

"So, my brodda, wish you good luck and give me cigarette na. I can't find de Merchant!"

Still astounded at how easily he had taken the news, I ran back to my bunk, knocking down a couple of empty bottles along the way. Luckily, there were five sticks of soggy LMs left in my pack. I grabbed the pack and a lighter; disturbed by the fact that this was the last time I'd ever see the fine man from Burundi, and all I could send him off with were five, soggy, expired cigarettes. The police were explaining that they had a tight schedule to maintain, sounding just like an African taxi driver about the delay. Sleepy moaned and grunted in a sort of a protest.

Burundi slipped the cigarette into his pocket, strapped a backpack over his shoulder, and gestured with a snap of his neck to the police that he was ready to go. He winked at me for one last time with his signature smile and said something that had stuck in my memory, like hair to the skin, ever since, "Mama Africa, here I come. See you when I see you under the sun!" and he had walked off with just a backpack full of belongings. Almost a decade in Babylon and that was all he had to show for it.

Kalakuta Republic

Just a week after Burundi had departed for the motherland, the northern wind carried in the most charismatic African the Mottak had ever hosted. Dudu, dressed up to his shiny best, had just been dropped off at the main gate in a car driven by one of his many contacts in town. I sat, gazing lazily upon the grey sky. Having noticed the gloom on the long face staring at him, he extended a pack of Marlboros towards me. Licking and smacking his pouted lips, he reached out for the duffel bag strapped around his shoulder and produced Jack Daniels bottle, which instantly brought a smile to my face.

The good-timer was back in town after a six-month hiatus. Walking with his signature swagger, he joined me on the stairs. After an exchange of pleasantries, he readjusted his red NY baseball hat. He looked the same, if not better. His clean-shaved, chocolate face still looked like as if he had just walked out of the shower. Scanning me up and down with his commanding, yet warm eyes, he said, "you know what kills you, man?"

"Ze system my brazer," I replied.

"no man, we all in the system. We barely get along with our own system!" retorted Dudu. "it's not people that kill you, my brodda. It's not disease. It's sure not guns that is killing all of us, man. It is expectations that is killin' us." He trailed off, a Marlboro Light dangling from his parted, charcoal lips. He let a hissing trail of smoke through his teeth. Eyes still locked onto the grey abyss, Dudu went on. "We just expect too much from life, man, as if we live forever. In the end, you are just 206 pieces of bone buried underneath. They all going to cry at your funeral as if they care. But uh uh, nobody cares." He wagged his forefinger to side to make his point. "They are just crying out of fear because you remind them of their own imminent departure. Life is nothing but a cigarette. We are all burning under pressure from day one, to turn into ashes. Then tossed away for the maggots to finish the job."

A cold shiver rippled through me, imagining his scene. Dudu tossed the cigarette butt high into the air; my eyes followed its every flip in the air before it hit the wet ground. The tiny ember was extinguished with another soft hiss.

We sure were like a cigarette with a whole lot of expectations. My eyes remained on the cigarette butt, as if expecting it to convulse and fight for the last breath. I felt like I had witnessed its entire life, from the pack to the ground. It was the humbling moment that floored me: the entire, trivial, ego-driven, fantasy-ridden lifestyle would one day be pushed to the side. All things burn down, gradually disintegrating into ashes. Ashes to ashes. I shook my head in a dire realization.

I reached into my new leather jacket for my six finger. There were seven sticks left in the battered pack. Tapping the bottom, the butt end of the next two victims came sliding out. I stuck one in my lips and passed the pack mechanically to Dudu. He pushed it away with disdain. I smiled, knowing Dudu never settled for less. I ignited mine, and the toxic smoke filled my lungs. I was suddenly conscious of the hissing disintegration of the matter stuck in my fingers. As I stared at the burning tip, the ring of reddish flame kindled in the cold wind, and consumed the contents at a breathtaking pace. The elements took their turn to torture you, layer by layer, until you blended in with the very ground. Every passersby, even the ones who smoked your life away, would trample over you again and again.

"ay, let's go in and get wasted now!" Dudu finally said, interrupting the spiraling thought he had instigated. As I followed him inside, I heard Cliff break out in a huge, welcoming roar at the sight of his best friend.

With Dudu around, the Mottak would often turn into a disco hall. The seven Mondays would end up being four Fridays and three Saturdays. So long as one never asked a question and followed him around, drama and fun were guaranteed.

Some called him the pimp, a ruthless individual who took advantage of vulnerable women, talking them into selling their bodies to strangers, yet he preferred to be called nothing but Dudu, his mother's nickname for him. Though some rumors said he has many hos in all the cities he traveled to, according to him, the ladies wanted him around.

"I just handle their finances, my friend. And at times, I set them up with better-paying customers."

In his defense, from what I witnessed myself, he never pushed women around nor made them go out with people against their will. He was smooth and tough to say no to. Above all, he had clear principles about whom he worked with. The money went 60–40 to the ladies, who had to do all the physical work. But he handled the transactions. Dudu set them up with a paying customer, confirmed they were lodged in a safe place, got paid, and made it home safely. With him being short and skinny, he often hung around big brothers in case anything went wrong. But the girls felt safe around him. He had told me once, "they are going to give it up anyway, so why not get paid for it? We are all prostitutes, one way or the other. We all want something in return. And above all, we are animals and we love to fuck, so I don't see what I am doing wrong." He had said this in his fluent British accent, which he had picked up in his brighter, college days.

Since under Norwegian law, prostitution was prohibited and the pimp was likely to face stiffer charges, he was always careful. Dudu wished to keep his head down, but his profession demanded his presence in the crowd and the clubs. Besides, his flashy dress code and his swagger drew attention in a small, northern town. Thus, he moved from town to town often. In frustration, he had said, "man, I don't like doing this, man. I have sisters, you know." Adjusting one of his many trendy hats, he had added, "But these girls can't find jobs, and they still have a family to support. They chose to please strangers sexually and get paid. And I get my cut. But if they get caught and snitch on me, I get locked up. This is fucked up, man. I am not even doing the fucking." The pay was good and after a brief encounter with the law, where he was given a stiff warning, he moved in with his closest girl.

Well, old habits were hard to kick and I got to admit she had the hottest body. Anyone would at least contemplate having a piece of her. Every time I met him, he would be telling me this is the last day he would be pimping his baby: in his words, "am thinking of retiring, bro!"

While the Nomad's intention was to avoid attention by being inconspicuous, there were some who were willing to do anything to get noticed. And some came in pairs, as well; interesting business partners. One solicited and promoted an ancient trade that never seem to run out of favor, while the other provided a luscious commodity for a limited period. They were never apart, always dressed to impress. He was always on the phone taking calls and making appointments, bartering over the price, promoting the commodity, receiving and assuring unsatisfied customers. She stayed at his side, seemingly oblivious to his conversations, biting her nails until he finished up, just waiting for the call to get dressed for a job.

They looked like a happy couple to any observer. They probably loved each other in their unconventional way. They moved around from city to city, usually lodging for a couple of weeks in one of his contact's residences. At the very mention of his name, people would start to smile and tell you a story or two about what happened with one of his ladies or the fights he used to have with men who mistreated them.

I remember my first summer in the north of Norway. It was a sunny warm day. Cliff, Congo, and I went out on our daily long walk around the town. Cliff said, "you never know what you might run into, so better get your ass moving." In the summer, the town really came to life. The smiles start to crack free from the long faces; the cafes would stretch out their awnings and customers filled the outdoor tables. Tourists from all over would swarm the centrum, an yachts and motor boats would bring life to the once-lifeless ocean. It was sure a nice place to be in the summer. So, once in a while, some Norwegian in a good mood would invite us over to his place for a couple of drinks or to one of the bars in the city. So, that particular afternoon, after the walk, we ended in Stiv's Café, just across the parking lot that led to the centrum and police station.

It was a popular hangout for the elderly and the unemployed, and of course foreigners. The owners did not mind much when we even hung out without ordering; I guess we gave it a diverse and busy atmosphere.

"man, I so want to shak and shak today," announced the lively Cliff, meaning his desire to get drunk and go dancing to country music.

I said, "no, no chance today, man. Everybody is broke after ze weekend."

Cliff, however, was optimistic. "man, soon as you finish money and no one to buy you drink, you think it is a bad day. Me grateful for de sun, man. Man, if dis people don't deport me soon, I will deport myself. Don't think I will go through another freezer time in de camp," he declared, in jubilant mood. "It is a good day, got to be grateful. Like the song by Don Carlos, goes all praise to Mr. Sun."

After a while, the pub began to fill up and we felt like idiots sitting there with nothing on our table, smoking one cheap cigarette after the other.

Even Cliff began to get bored of the music. "I don't know why dis people listen to dis kind of music all de time," he bickered. "dat is why dey all unhappy and depressed all de time, mtsee!"

But as we were about to leave the place, a familiar face popped in. Dressed up in dropping brown shorts, white shirt, beach sandals, and topped with classy sunglasses, Dudu sure looked more like a tourist than a local pimp. "my brothers, how is summer treating you, huh?" And he came running towards us with open arms.

Soon the beers were raining down on us. The owner, though he was distant to us, probably had a serious thought about our loitering around and weighed it against the business we brought for his tiny, sad joint. But as soon as we started to order the beers, he began smiling. It is just business, nothing personal!

"man, we don't have job," announced Dudu. "we don't have resident permit. Yet nothing ever stops us from getting fun around here."

After looking at the small crowd of older men and bitter women around our table, Congo started laughing. "what is funny is, they get angry when they see us having fun. As if they never expect us to be here! Mtsee."

That got me started, as I always found it odd, the double standards and stereotypes we faced. Most were aware of our dilemma, but they still turned around and labeled me a lazy-ass, good-for-nothing nigger. "man, I hate zat look. You know when zey see you having fun. I don't know how zey expect us to act. Maybe like one of zos old American movies, man. Yes sir, no sir, and the nigger hides back in the kitchen or the garden." But fact of the matter was, no matter how unwelcome they tried to make us feel, we had been taught in the school of hard knocks that looks won't do you any harm. So we went on with our loud fun.

Some say a pimp is never off duty; maybe that was true. Even when Dudu was totally engaged in a conversation with you, his eyes had the radar on for potential or regular clients at all times, in close range. He was gifted at reading people. When his ladies were not out to show off their goodies, it was all up to the man to fetch customers. Thus, while the rest of us were busy getting drunk, my man Dudu had already made the bread for the days to come. I don't know whether he had already made the proposal telepathically, but before we knew it, a big, tattooed man was standing next to our table extending a hand in greeting.

"*du snakker norsk?*" he asked.

A resounding *nei* was the reply.

"English?"

I could sense his disappointment already.

"Yeah, sure man, we all speak English." Knowing Dudu like we did, we knew it was business time. He invited the man to join us.

The man sat down. He was a huge white slab. Even though Cliff was the biggest of the four of us, the guy literally dwarfed him. I was not really comfortable with him. It was not the size— it was his eyes, dead, still, and grey. He was rigid and said little.

But Dudu had sprinkled his magic dust over the conversation to try to make him comfortable. "you are not from around here, are you? You look too cool, man."

A faint smile. "no, am here for few days. I work on fishing boat!" the man said.

"cool. I hear the fishing industry pays well here, man."

A pause and a look at all four of us, then, "Yeah, it's good."

"so, you work in shifts?"

"Yeah, something like that. One month at sea, one month off."

"that is cool, man. So you must be on a break now, huh?"

"Yeah, I will be off in two days."

"man, if I were you, I would spend the whole month of my break getting crazy somewhere, real crazy, man."

Another pause to consider his answer. Another glance at the four of us, and another gulp from his beer mug. "Yeah, I was someplace crazy weeks ago." He cut to the chase; the guy definitely did not like small talk. "listen, can you guys hook me up with some chick for tonight?"

With a satisfied smile on his face, Dudu said confidently, "you have come to the right place, my brother. I can get you the best chocolate loving you ever had, my man. Just the right one to see you off to sea, my man."

For the first time, Mr. Tattoo cracked a genuine smile. "oh yeah, can you fix it now? I don't care how much it cost."

"where are you staying now?"

"in a hotel just a block from here."

"Yes, sure." with that, Dudu got busy. He dialed a number and slipped past the booth for a private pep talk with one of his girls.

It did not take long. Maybe fifteen minutes later, the beautiful "savannah" walked in. She was, as always, dressed to impress: a tight fishnet brown top that was almost the same color as her cocoa skin, tight, white shorts that accentuated her gorgeous thighs and her round behind. The moment she walked in, all eyes were upon her. Even the women's eyes bulged. Her brown wandering eyes, her bulging pink lips, and her perfect teeth elicited fantasies from all who saw her. Had she been cheaper, or Dudu given a discount, I would have paid all I had for a night with her. But she was one of his most prized assets, so I never pressed it. But Mr. Tattoo was impressed and drooling, and that was all that mattered at that moment.

He got up to buy another round of drinks. The giant had already hit us with one round when Dudu stepped away to make his call. As far as I was concerned, we were heading for another fucking good night for the books.

Savannah sat next to Dudu. I swear, I never met a pimp so gentle, and yet so effective in his approach to women. Mr. Tattoo came back with the drinks and placed them in the middle of the table with his gigantic hands. All of a sudden, the rigid fellow was acting like a true gentleman. "what would you like to drink, Miss Beautiful?" he asked her in the most romantic voice you would ever hear from a man like him. All I was wondering was, *the things we do when we are horny!*

"I will have a Bailey's, thank you," she replied. Dudu must have really coached her, I figured. And the guy was off once again to get her the drink of her choice. For all I cared, I was having another good time, so I had to play my role. And my role was to leave the couple and their manager alone; so Cliff, Congo, and I would get on with our business, which was to keep doing what we were doing and keep drinking, while they got on with theirs. As far as we were concerned, we were set for the night. Not that we were third-wheeling; we served our purpose.

Whenever Dudu was around a few of us, he made the point that if ever any of the guys attempted to play him or his girls, that we were his backup. Even though he took his share beforehand, it provided him more leverage to let them know he would do whatever was needed to protect his girls. The deal was always that he would accompany the client and his girl to the specific room of whatever hotel had been booked for the consummation of the deal, for the safety and security of all parties concerned. Afterwards, he would hand off the other half of the deal to the lady when they entered the room.

The party continued. Another gentleman who was sitting by himself, a Norwegian with an East Asian complexion, offered us a round so we could join his table. It was rude in our culture to refuse a kind offer, so we all got up without hesitation. The man was of Sri Lankan origin and had lived in Norway for more than two decades. Yet we could sense he somehow felt relieved that a few black faces were in the bar. After an exchange of the usual introductions and sharing of origins, Dudu suggested a toast for all the brothers in the struggle: "This is for all the black brothers in Babylon," which turned a couple of local heads, but it made our brother from the Far East feel at home for the night. The guy turned out to be a real fun-loving type, which suited us all.

After we were nearly kicked out of the bar, the brother from a Far East mother insisted we join him for a drink at his place. We strolled down the cobbled street, receiving a few condescending looks from locals taking their midnight-sun stroll. We headed towards the taxi stand adjacent to the bus station. Our friend ordered a minivan taxi. Sitting comfortably inside the van, we were taken down the Storgata and through the Borgata Highway towards our destination in Gansas, at the southeastern end of the island. Just a ten-minute trip. We ended up at his place to enjoy a more relaxed atmosphere, and had the liquor of our choice at our disposal. No one wasted time as we poured glass after glass of every cognac, martini, vodka, and wine bottle he owned.

The next thing I remember, it was the next day, and I was waking up to the sound of Dudu screaming threats over his phone. I must have crashed on the living room carpet. I looked around and Cliff was sprawled over the big sofa. Congo had already woken up; his distinct humming and whistling drifted from the bathroom. I looked around to see some impressive furniture all around. The place was exquisite. The guy did not look that rich from the way he was dressed. He looked rather like a carpet merchant. But most of his belongings were antique and expensive. There were odd-looking musical instruments, stuffed animals, miniature temples, and the Hindu gods, I presumed, set all over the shelf. What impressed me most was that every object was neatly cared for.

He must have traveled across the world, as there were plenty of pictures of him standing next to famous landmarks in traditional attire. Yet while I was admiring the guy's place, Dudu was still screaming his lungs out. "I don't give a fuck! Just bring me back my baby or you would regret you ever met me you stupid fuck... What? I will show you what kind of man I am. You can never hide from me, I tell you... Yes go ahead and laugh. It will be the last one, motherfucker." With that, he snapped his phone shut on his palm with a rage I never associated with the little gentleman I knew.

His outburst startled our host out of his bed, and he shuffled his way to the living room threshold with a long pink robe on. With his thinning hair sticking out like armpit hair, he looked more of a cartoon figure. "*er du gal. Hvorfor skrek du så høyt. Jeg sover...*" He must have forgotten we were deaf to Norwegian.

But we all burst in to laughter as soon as the freshened-up Congo steeped in from the bathroom to join the excitement. "look at dis man. Wearing pink robe, you nearly fooled me from behind with dat hair, man. You are a funny man."

India Man, as we liked to refer to him afterwards, did not find it amusing. He pointed us all towards the door.

On our way home, Dudu explained to us what had transpired the night before. "it was a mutiny, my friends. After all that I have done for her, that bitch repays me like this. I left all the other bitches for her and this is what I get in return."

The hangover still spinning his head, Cliff whispered, "did I miss too much? I don't know what you are so angry about." looking at me and Congo, he realized we had done nothing to set Dudu off.

Dudu was obviously infuriated; he was constantly shaking his head while he strode a couple of steps ahead of us. "you know, she did not even have the nerve to talk to me. She switched off her phone. I knew she would stab me in the back one day, but never had I thought she would do me like this."

We gathered that Savannah had played him.

Dudu mourned her loss like a millionaire would mourn a stock market crash. She had been his livelihood for some time. We found out afterwards that after a night with Mr. Giant, she had been persuaded to move to another small town, presumably to his brother's house, until he got back from sea and settled her for good. It was not an offer anyone in her position would hesitate to accept. I would have done the same.

Days passed and life went on as usual. She became a distant memory, as we all had more pressing matters in our respective lives. However, things had not worked out as well as Savannah had thought. She left the guy after a couple of weeks. I was not sure about the details, but it was obvious everybody wanted a piece of the cake. She showed up and begged her way back into Dudu's favor, though things were never the same. Since his erratic relationship with the Mottak officials had become more strained, they had been trying to get rid of him for some time. Though many could still come back to the Mottak and regain their residence after some questions and paperwork, the constant coming and going infuriated the officials.

But what I really loved about Dudu was his sharp mind and his ability to enlighten others about some deep, real facts about life, camouflaged in humor. You might laugh at one of his jokes, but then it would get you thinking about the issue and his different perspective. I gathered he was well-read, and most probably went to college as well, though he would never admit it; he preferred to give the impression that he had been self-taught, self-sufficient brother all his life.

There was one time, at a party, when someone had said, "the money they give us is not enough. Life is better here, the standard I mean."

Another brother had scoured most camps all over Europe but was never lucky to be accepted by any of them. He added in frustration, "my friend, I have been in Italy; it's fucked up. They give you the papers and tell you off you go. Fend for yourself, they tell you. They don't care if you live or die. Some survive, some struggle but still some make it good. I been to France and Germany; their services are good but the rules are stricter for a refugee. Still, there are some opportunities, be it working labor under the radar or underground biz—you have choices. But here, my broddas, they give you such nice place to live with everything that a tenant needs, more than you could ever get anywhere else in the world. The life standard is high and they at least care about us human beings. But, my friends, no opportunities unless you are granted the papers! That is why we are always complaining!" A resounding grunt of approval came from all sides. "you are right, my brodda, it is not de place, it is opportunity we need!"

"exactly, my friends."

"Yeah, yeah, true said, my brazer!"

Sitting in a corner, fidgeting in disapproval and disappointment, Dudu banged his bottle hard on the wooden table to get our attention, spilling the foaming cheap beer on some of those sitting closer. "Listen to yourselves. You are all so fucking pathetic," he announced, "always complaining about being left out by this system or that! When are you gonna get it into your head that none of them care about you?"

Those of us who did not take Dudu seriously began to protest and tease him. "so what, do you expect us to be pimp like you to beat the system?"

Dudu often got incensed when people failed to take him seriously. But seeing the veins sticking out on his forehead, we all understood he was dead serious, so leaned back to let him talk.

"Don't ever be grateful for who treats you better than the other," he said. "You know what Malcolm X said when they asked him would he be grateful if the civil rights movement was ever recognized?" He looked around. Though some of us recognized the name, none of us had deep knowledge about this brilliant black rights advocate. "he said: 'How can you say thank you to be given back something that had once rightfully belonged to you?' So, know one thing, my friends. They owe us. They owe us big time. If I recall, they came down to our continent without an invitation. No one put them in a concentration camp." A resounding nod of approval stirred up even more agreement. Dudu cleared his throat and added, "They came one by one and took off with everything. Everything, my brothers! Did anyone ever hold them accountable for all their atrocities? Huh? Huh? Nope!" He was on his feet by then, with the rest of us barely breathing, our eyes glued to the refugee philosopher. "It was the needy and the curious ones who ventured all the way down, and for the many who made it safely, it paid off big time. Now their descendants live it all off, mtsee. What do you think is the biggest motivation a white parent gives to his child growing up?"

No one replied.

Noticing the perplexed looks, he said in a softer, mocking tone, "You know, I see it in their eyes, telling their kids: 'We came a long way to have this privilege, and you better make sure it remains as it is. Better get your shit together, as you have it better than the darkies!' The status quo shall prevail. So where does that leave us?" Dudu glared at the quiet bunch in a fury. "Centuries later, the curious and needy black ones make the same journey. Guess what awaited us, huh? The camps! Reality bites back. It is payback, my brothers. The few hundred dollars they hand out every month are not charity, my friend—it is a restitution fee. An unspoken arrangement for having the audacity to strike back. Not the deserved amount, yet enough to survive! If you are looking for more, you collect the tips on your own, my friend!"

All of us were left with dropped jaws, marveling at the flash of history and reality check delivered at a blistering pace. But Dudu was not done. "so, the prize for those of us who made the difficult journey to get here is a place to stay and a handout of loose change, so we won't starve. Remember, it is all a game. It took them months, sometimes years, to make it across the deserts, jungles, and rivers to get to their prize. Many died along the way. So, no coincidence that the same struggle awaited you when you set out to get all the way here! For the ambitious ones who wish to get their hands on the fat repatriation check to make up for the outstanding debt hundreds of years unpaid, you are on your own. On your damn own! You can make it how you choose, and finally go back to wherever village or goddamn hometown you came from, and have it named after you if you wish, too!"

A year and half had passed by; a lot happened some days and nothing happened on others. But you can't deny it was a hell of a test—test of character, test of fate, and test of faith. Though I was mostly confined in the Mottak, I was exposed to diverse cultures, attitudes, customs, religions, and moods. Met a lot of friends and enemies. Within the four walls of the Mottak, seekers of opportunities from all four corners of the world were represented. Many doors of opportunity had been closed to me, yet many more windows had been opened in return. Sometimes, it was just the situation that shaped you and your state of mind. The choices you made in life, too—so it was better to be on a road you have chosen on your own, to face whatever consequences waited for you.

Inside the Mottak, tension had been building up every day, waiting for an outlet. Tribal lines were deepened and consolidated. Wherever there was a lack of progress, trivial matters where often blown out of proportion and the mob in all of us felt more secure in our blood alliances. There were often dominant groups that intimidated the rest of the Mottak with their aggressive "nothing to lose" attitude. Lacking a strong bond with my "people" made me a little vulnerable if I was ever in a confrontation with anyone.

Given a stark difference in culture, appearance, and demeanor, the city boys and a Middle Eastern clan had tense in each other's company. Every second of their waking, the Arabs were never apart. They had built an intimidating force inside the Mottak, trying to impose their rules at will. It was inevitable that we would clash one day.

Early in April, after an extended party from the night before had spilled into the afternoon of the next day, the intoxicated city boys made it to the TV room for some music time. The usual trio of Cliff, Congo, and I, along with Dudu, Sleepy, Preacher, and Tallest took our places in front of the giant plasma TV. Before our arrival, a couple of Africans and the Middle Easterners had a confrontation over what channel to watch. The Arabs, having a numerical advantage and unmatched aggressiveness, had physically launched themselves at the protesting group. The Africans retreated after having being surprised by the united aggression.

Having conquered the reception, and surfing the channels at will, they were not ready to surrender the conquest. Our loud arrival was met by a hostile exchange in Arabic. Congo, unsuspecting and unaware of the foul-mouthed, paler residents, got up to change the channel from Al Jazeera Arabic news to the Voice.

"Ayy, am tired of watching dis news, my broddas!" he said.

We were silenced by the outbursts and insults thrown at Congo, who stood his ground, astounded by the level of animosity towards him.

"you fucking animal, don't change channel," blurted one of them, followed by an Arabic tantrum at which his colleagues laughed.

"what did you call him, you motherfucker?" snapped the infuriated Dudu on behalf of the rest of us, who were just readying ourselves for a fight.

"what you going to do? I called him fucking animal! You have problem?" replied the leader of the clan, shrugging his broad shoulders to flex his muscles. It was like an orchestrated drama, and the TV room suddenly exploded into a mass brawl. The mutual hatred that had simmered, brewing for months, finally boiled over.

Even though I threw myself at the one I loathed the most, I was surprised by a punch from the left that landed on the bridge of my nose. It knocked me off balance. Warm blood tricked down my lip and I tasted it in my mouth. The taste of one's blood awakened an old, pure raging animal in me. I had little recollection what happened afterwards. Blood gushed from my broken nose, but I was numb to the pain even when a second mild punch landed on it. I kept throwing punches and kicks at multiple assailants, who were moving around to avoid our blows. Though we were matched in number, we had the superior physical advantage plus a rush of adrenalin from the alcohol we had been downing for the second day in a row.

The TV room turned into a battleground, with bodies crashing over the TV stand. The flat screen tipped over onto the marble tiles. A heavy, hardwood table was shoved to one end to make room for the melee. The wooden chairs were flying in all directions, crashing onto heads and torsos, followed by a painful grunt whenever they hit their target.

Blood was all over the floor. The folding wooden partition that stood between the reception sofa and the corridor to the main gate got ripped into pieces as a couple of bodies crashed hard on it. A growing number of spectators gathered in one corner, watching the gladiators.

Even though the Arabs had been taken by surprise, they stood up and worked as a unit. Every time one of them was thrown to the ground, another would abandon his man and put his body in the way of the incoming threat, to give the fallen man time to get back on his feet.

The police sirens ululated and the tires screeched to halt. Cops raced in. Yet the gladiators paid no attention to the flashing blue lights that flooded the reception center.

It took a while to subdue the group. The spectators finally assisted the police in breaking up the brawl, and the exhausted gladiators gradually surrendered. The police took down the names and IDs of those involved in the scuffle. Witnesses gave accounts of what had transpired, as both aggrieved parties laid the blame on the other. Separated by the police, we were left to nurse our wounds.

❧

That night, I had the most peaceful night's sleep in a while. I felt like a huge flat rock had been lifted off my chest. The rage had finally been vented; the primal animal was let loose, without interference from the mind and heart. Having drawn blood and shed some of its own, it padded back, panting and satisfied, to its cage. Fighting felt even better than sex. I felt alive, even though it would take quite a while to recollect the entire scenario.

When that animal stirred inside me some nights, it made my thoughts crazy and suicidal. I imagined slashing my throat and watching the squirting blood paint the mirror. Or, at times, I contemplate running out naked in the cold to freeze myself to death, relishing every sharp invisible pain, every misfortune that had befallen me. At times, I would contemplate throwing myself into the dark sea.

In those moments of solitary madness, staring blankly into the abyss, on those unbearable long nights, every movable thing looked like a deadly weapon, every blunt and sharp edge close by was available for the Jackie Chan in my mind. Making a long list, which was extended every day, I retaliated at night bashing and trashing their heads with every available object while they begged for forgiveness.

Those were rare, tipping incidents, though. The scenarios had some sort of therapeutic value, an expression of the inner perverted self. For a boy who had always tried to avoid physical confrontations while growing up, my imagination compensated somehow. As sick as it sounds, it helped me keep my composure,

as no one had ever been jailed for having dark thoughts as long
as he did not act on them. But once in a while, when the urges
manifest, it kind of fortified the will and the mind . The trick was
directing the thoughts to a positive energy. And I would sleep
like a baby afterwards, in peaceful, deep, dreamless rest.

We paid the price afterwards. I was left with a broken nose and
a fractured finger bone. Dudu needed two stitches to seal a cut
above the eyes. Tallest had swollen lips, and knocks and bruises
to the head. Congo had broken two ribs, sprained his ankles, and
received a little cut to his head. Preacher, well, he had taken a
nasty blow to the nose while trying to break up the fight and
retreated early. Sleepy, who had been decisive in the fight by
introducing the chairs as projectiles, had escaped with a black
eye.

Despite his heavy involvement, Cliff had no visible wounds.
"I am too black to have a black eye, my brodda, but am hurting,
believe me," he declared the following day.

In addition, we were issued fines by the Mottak for the damage
to the reception center during those nine minutes of madness.
The local paper ran a story exaggerating the danger by raising
the question of what these untamed savages could bring to the
rest of society, if they did this to one another on a regular basis.
The police had promised to run a thorough investigation into
the case and bring the guilty parties to justice. It would go down
in our personal files and probably seriously hamper our cases
with the authorities.

However, at that moment in time, under the circumstances
and the state of mind we were in, it was totally worth the
trouble. Besides our letting off of some steam, peace returned
to the Mottak. Most residents were grateful we gave the Arabs a
timely lesson. We were considered heroes, not the violent thugs
the local paper and the police had labeled us. Above all, we got
full respect. The Arabs agreed to stay away from our building
and relocated to a faraway camp at the outskirts of the town.

One look at our opponents, though, made all our pain
disappear with a collective sigh of pleasure. They had come
out worse than us. One of them needed an emergency ride to
the hospital to stop his head from bleeding and was still in the

hospital the next day, while another had needed treatment to his ribs after having difficulty breathing the next day. All of them suffered heavy bruises and cuts to their faces, accentuated by their light complexions. And from that day onward, they never looked at us straight in the eye, ever again.

The blowout in the Mottak brought another, unexpected victory for the city boys. Hoping to appease Cliff and keep him away from the Mottak following a number of run-ins with the officials, they decided to relocate him from the central Mottak to one of their many dispersed apartments in the town, run by the Mottak. It was a one-room basement apartment at the center of the town, just in front of our favorite club, Grunder, overlooking the Northern Sea, and behind the open bus station. Thus, they passed responsibility for him to the local police, who actually knew him by his first name.

Cliff's apartment soon became our favorite hangout, along with some young Norwegians. Music blasted constantly. It was an international integration hotspot. It provided a platform for all to express themselves and learn about one another while being entertained. For the first time, we had a place we felt was ours, beyond the dreaded rules of the Mottak. It became the actual Kalakuta Republic that Cliff had always talked about.

Cliff's place took our minds away from everything. It felt more ours than theirs. By then, we had reached the monumental stage of our stay. The sun made a full round trip on us and was halfway through her second. A year and a half had gone by, like the minutes you impatiently watch tick past on the platform while you wait for a delayed train. New faces flocked in and the old faces disappeared, some deported, others deployed to another camp, or worse, the mental asylum. The irony of an asylum seeker stationed at the mental asylum! The rest of us were the welcoming staff at the dock. We were not into making new friends. We were aloof and a little arrogant to the newcomers. They just reminded us too much of our stagnant situation; that's all, no malice intended!

We had expanded our network in the town by then. We knew the shortcuts, figurative and literal. There were a few employment opportunities that trickled to the Mottak for the disadvantaged, undocumented asylum seeker. Some hired cheap labor for a day or two. When a truck drove slowly by the Mottak gate, fifty asylums would rush out to get picked, like those Mexican workers in the movies or like hungry children in a flooded refugee camp in Africa. Either way, we mostly aimed to just put on a good late night shift, twice a week, with a sugar mommy—you'd be set for the weekend. City boy got some reputation to keep!

Thus we lived our lives a day at a time. We could not afford to think of an uncertain tomorrow.

ꗊ

You kind of lose track of the day, or date for that matter; it's insignificant under the circumstances. You feel the long nights, but in the daytime, you fully engage to keep you mind occupied. You scrape up every penny you got and head out to the nearest shop for cheap beer or homemade vodka and then guzzle away the day in Cliff's world. You begin the day watching anything athletic on the TV channels. Cliff, being an excellent cook, would make some delicious Nigerian meal with all the delicacies. We'd all pitch in for the groceries. In fact, there were days when you'd wake to his call.

"hey, mon, what's up? You at home…"

"yeah, man, just woke up," I would reply.

"Ahhh, you know what you can do for me? Bring me two onions, some sardines, and dat spice I tried in your place de oder day, and rice—you know what kind of rice I like, huh?"

"yeah, man. I bring now?" I felt relieved, being saved from cooking.

"eh eh, hurry up. I have guests comin' today and tell de Merchant to bring me something to drink and Congo to bring ehhh cigarettes. Come quick, quick."

"okay, man. So, who is coming later?"

"you just bring what I tell you! Look, look at dis, man, mtsee. We eat first and we see about later!" Cliff's voice would contain a scowl, sensing my curiosity.

"sure, sure, bro. We are coming now…"

"brodda, you der?"

"yeah, man!"

"i forgot. Make sure you bring money. You buy drinks today! You know you have been on two straight night shifts. Understand me?"

"Ha, man. Payday is not yet, my man. But, man, what you think I save some in ze bank! Of course, I come wiz it. You don't trust me do you?"

"my brodda, I don't have much credit to argue with you. Just come here now, we talk."

"yeah, man, coming, coming!" I hung up and headed down to summon the city boys to gather the groceries. We would be running around, door to door, to fill up Cliff's wish list.

"got two onions here, man!" Congo shouted from one end of the Mottak. The Merchant would definitely fix the rest through his excellent diplomatic skills, and we were set for the day and night.

We could already hear the faint tunes of Nigerian music playing from Cliff's basement apartment, even as far as the petrol station across the street. His loud presence and aura reached out to us, and he shouted at top of his lungs, "oh, my broddas, welcome, welcome. Come in, you are at home!"

Every now and then, new faces of all colors would pop by, to add to the already colorful congregation. Cliff had become the magnet to all the lost souls in that small northern Norwegian town, especially on those rainy spring days. The atmosphere was so relaxing. Everyone was at ease and engaged in a lively conversation eating, drinking, and smoking whatever was available.

I come from a long tradition of celebrating each day of the calendar year dedicated to a saint. City dwellers often undertook it as a serious religious duty to offer prayers of gratitude and praise to the saint, preferably in a church bearing his or her name. With times diluting the church's strong hold, it had fallen to housewives and mothers to pay their respects. Yet most people had their own favorite saint or church they revered. On a saint's day, you would light candle, feed beggars, lament and supplicate and beg for the Lord's forgiveness via the saint. Our mothers, mostly being housewives, prioritized paying deities to the Tabbots and commemorate the day by taking part in the conveniently long coffee ceremony, and gossip all day. Some go so far as to brew the local beer and get wasted, all for the saint of the day.

The first day of most months: Ledeta or Raguel. The fifth was either Abo or Abuna (revered saints), seventh Slasie (Holy Trinity), the tenth of a few months was Jacob, Meskel, or Nathanael. The twelfth of every month was Kidus Michael (archangel Michael), the seventeenth of some months Estifanos, some Giorgis. The nineteenth of most months was Gabriel, the twenty-first of every month Mariam (Saint Mary), and the twenty-fourth of many months was Abune Teklehaimanot (another revered saint and servant of the church). It went goes on and on, with the countless saints one could name as an excuse to get wasted.

On the other end of the world, I was lamenting and supplicating every god I had lost faith in, yet couldn't seem to abandon, and found myself celebrating every day like our mothers did. I guess nothing is ever new!

When you are an asylum seeker leaving the Mottak, you don't meet lawyers, dentists, and scientists in your path. Even on the few occasions that you do, the conversations are something neither remember the next day; especially if one was a city boy restricted in opportunities, one was drawn to the underworld. Environment dictates one's company. As some say, crime pays, but never forget that is maybe the only place where a city boy could get some love and much-needed compassion. You don't necessarily have to be involved in it; it just feels good to be part of something active, something evolving. That is the unspoken norm of nature: keep moving as everything on this multiverse is set in a constant motion.

I was one of the millions of lost souls from the isolated Horn state of Eritrea. Having graduated from college in my country, I had figured my future prospects would be brighter in my future life, regardless of where I ended up. On the other hand, suffering equally under a regime that brainwashed every citizen to mechanically obey orders had left me feeling hollow and disillusioned. Military experience, which had been mandated as a way to break down any resilience and inner resolve, had already eroded the perspective I had in life. Living in a police state, running the inner city like the Gestapo, we had been distracted from doing anything that would help us discover our own destinies. It was impossible to express our individuality or respond to the inner fire to explore. The more you are oppressed, watching the dynamic world racing past you, the stronger your wish to rebel individually. Your faith in the system, any system, is put to the sword. Dreams and fantasies begin to take on a new life in your head. The current condition is deemed unacceptable and unsuitable.

In many of the soul-searching sessions, I held monologues in my head, presenting and rebuffing theories to explain the reasons behind my struggles. My demons dictated my mood and thoughts. Whenever pressure and anger fueled rebellious thoughts in my head, I would come up with my own theories that made more sense and justified some of my actions. In one of those sessions, I thoroughly assessed the value education and environment.

I deduced that school taught you theories about the mysteries of life, all the workings of visible and invisible matter, so one could be competent enough to handle challenges in the ever-dynamic digital world as a productive member of society. And that was knowledge, the conventional version of the truth that appealed to our intellect. It was structured and disciplined, and required concentration and guidance if one were to excel. However, it did not imply a person was necessarily equipped to tackle all the challenges in life. Though the set of truths we carried along the way was the basis for most of conceptions we have of our ideal world, all conventional truth is not necessarily wisdom. But all wisdom is intelligence. In a sense, wisdom had no boundaries and no limits. The unconventional even contributes. Academics did not shine light from all angles. The big picture was acquired from exposure to life. It could be the underworld, where principle and loyalty rule above the law, or a state of mind that was open to wisdom from any source. Where the rules were never written, and there was no uniform format to follow. Either way, the individual gained something extra: the cunning to survive, and intelligence. The individual would gain an extraordinary outlook on life. Among many I had run into in life, the ones most flexible and undeterred by pressure were surprisingly those with little education.

No judgments, as "only he who feels it knows it!" as wise men have said. Whichever way we acquired wisdom when we trod out into the world, it was all for the purposes of survival and finding meaning in this life.

The Company on
the Lonely Road

In my quest to spice up my lame existence in a country where I
was not yet sure I belonged, I traveled to other cities—especially
in those times when I felt like a waste of space. Having my dreams
squashed once again, I was more restless than ever. I had hoped
the authorities would grant me asylum, given the turmoil my
home country was undergoing. The social unrest led millions of
the young blood literally fleeing the country in search of better
living. Dreamy as I was, often I was prone to disappointments
that led to mini-depressions. Being born in Ethiopia did not help
my case, either. With thousands of Ethiopians allegedly claiming
asylum as Eritreans, the UDI was suspicious in assessing such
cases like mine. I felt as though I were cursed to be betrayed
over and over again. My countrymen were granted their work
permits, living in a comfortable house, earning a decent income,
while I was languishing at the camp; it was a little hard to take.

First, my family and I had been deported from Ethiopia and
forced to leave behind everything we owned. Then we had
to move into a country where we were never really welcome,
treated as scapegoats and second-class citizens by suspicious
locals. To add insult to injury, my countrymen had spread a
rumor that I was in fact an Ethiopian posing as Eritrean. I had
been overlooked as a victim for far too long. When was the
suffering going to end? I had no idea, but I needed some outlet,
otherwise the anger and frustration in me was going to explode.

Since I had been kicked out of the Norsk language school
after the new year, due to my lack of attendance, I was left
with nothing better to do in the Mottak except contemplate
the disappointing wheel of fortune they call life—or else head
down to reception and rip the system and blame every mishap
in our lives on it. As one of our friends had jokingly stated, when
pressed why he was unwilling to learn the Norwegian language,
"what good would do me to learn your language, if you don't want
me to live here or work until you decide to remove me? I learn

your language and then one day you decide to deport me; what will I do with the language? Go back home and find a job in the Norwegian embassy? If you are concerned about the trouble of communication, don't be. I speak English and you all do, so why bother? If you want me to learn, though, give me permission to work or live! It is the way of the world."

Restless at having my fate stalled on me, I was watching many rise in society. Saving every krone I could spare from the UDI allowances, I was cutting down on my addictions and extra expenses. Trying to maintain contact with the few old friends who had established themselves in Norwegian society, I made a few others, as well, allowing me to travel around to some of the bigger cities and towns. At times, friends would send me invitations with the expensive plane tickets or cover some of my plane fare, which made it easier. Otherwise, it was unthinkable for a person in my situation to make those journeys. Beginning with the bus fares to the Evenes Airport that charge 300 kroner for a one-way pass, I had to cough up every krone I had to make a trip. For the times I was making the flights on my own, I had to ask a favor of people with credit cards to book me a flight in advance, as it was remarkably cheaper than booking from the travel agencies in cash.

On those brief journeys, unless it was on an official season break, I had to report back to the Mottak every two weeks to sign in or else miss out on the allowance and gradually get kicked out of the system. I was lucky enough to experience life from different angles and meet people from all walks of life. Some stood out from the crowd in their unique ability to touch or intrigue others, in even the briefest of meetings. Some had been able to defy expectations to rise up on their feet comfortably. Not only that, but they had been able to extend a helping hand to those in unforgiving, complicated circumstances.

By far the most intriguing character I had met in my life was a West African whom I still have trouble figuring out what or who he really was. I had run into him during my trip to the capital city during the Easter break. To an observer, he was just another laid-back African who was always happy, regardless of what goes on in his life, or his mind, for that matter.

The guy walked into a room and literally brightened up everyone's mood at once. Most asylum seekers are edgy and disappointed. But this guy, a smile never left his face. His wandering eyes sparkled at anything that breathed. The flat, wide nose and the big lips on his round, clean-shaven face and short-cropped hair gave him the appearance of a humble African. His 1.8-meter, imposing figure might intimidate a stranger, yet his movement was more gentle and agile than that of a man half his weight. His loud, melodic voice announced his presence long before he was in sight. His animated way of talking, his jokes, and his detailed stories made him like a magnet to the lost black souls of Babylon.

He was always helping people that he felt needed it and never expected anything in return. He had no work permit, no residence permit; his claim for asylum had long ago been rejected by the authorities. Yet, it never fazed him a bit, nor did he resent others who had been able to secure legal documents to make a living. He sure was making a lot of money. More than many thought he did. Yet he never showed off; he dressed casually, mingled comfortably, and lived in a tiny apartment he shared with two other brothers in a shabby student apartment in Kringsjå. Few knew he was making a ghetto-fabulous living.

He was a medicine man, as some would say, a major drug dealer with deep connections. He was known to supply pushers all over the major cities of Norway with the best quality hashish at a reasonable price. Rumor from the few people with whom he associated say he dealt some other stuff as well, yet no one was quite sure what he was capable of. He was a discreet businessman; few questioned. He never uttered a word about his business dealings or about the money or risk involved. Only after getting to know him well and spending more time, underneath his genuine smile and his gentle stare and animated voice, could one sense a hint of a contained dark side. Some say he was a dangerous man who was capable of doing anything to people who crossed him. Since I was staying at a friend's place in the suburbs, in a neighborhood whose name I never seem to remember except that you take the number 10 train from the central station and get off at the fifth stop, I knew very little about the town. Since my friend spent his day at work, I was left on my own to discover the town. With no knowledge of the Norwegian language, I had to hang out in the areas where foreigners, especially Africans, congregated, in hopes of running into old friends or making new ones.

At first, I tried to get around on my own. I would get off from the central station and set off to different direction every time, so I could track my way back to the station as a landmark. But no matter how straight the paths I took, I seemed to get lost. I had a terrible sense of direction, anyway. Other times, I would get on the city trams regardless of where they were heading and sightsee the beautiful city without stepping out. I was tired of getting lost and searching for a friendly face to ask directions of! So, after a couple of days wandering around and getting acquainted with the city, I was able to locate the places where a broke asylum seeker like me should and should not go.

There were few spots not far from the city center that were favored by my brothers. It was relief to see some businesses owned or operated by Africans. Small businesses like restaurants, bars, barbershops, clothing lines, music stores, and so many others seemed to assure me maybe I had a chance to make it someday.

Seeing the diverse community of Oslo everywhere you turn, Asians, Africans, Latinos, Europeans and so many nationalities getting around, doing whatever they do, and not one paying attention to the other, made me feel more at home the longer I stayed. Having lived in a northern town for some months, this was a load lifted off my chest. Besides, everyone was a guest on this earth; none of us was here to stay. I began to make all sorts of friends, and that was when I met this enigmatic man.

It was on a Saturday night. My friend and I had been going around to bars and cafés, meeting friends all day, as Sunday was his only day free. Guzzling beer and checking out new spots, meeting new people, was my kind of thing, so I was enjoying the evening. Since it was sunny and warmer, we ranged from one spot to the other like postmen. We finally decided to chill in a trendy bar owned by some black man from West Africa. It was a couple of blocks from the Oslo central train station so I had no trouble of finding it the next day, maybe on the second or third trial.

It was a cozy bar, with red, dim light and loud hip-hop banging from the speakers hanging at all corners of the rectangular bar. The mahogany tables were set not far apart, as one could literally make out what the others on the next table were saying. The bartender, a gorgeous black girl, was serving the beers with a smile that urged you to finish your beer in haste and head back for another round. I really liked the place; besides, there were plenty of black faces around from all over, with occasional white ones. It made me forget for once where I really was, at least for that night. When I was heading towards the toilet, I heard many languages spoken at different tables: Nigerian, French, Amharic, and some other language I could not place.

In one of my trips to the toilet, I bumped into my man. He just said with a smile, "sorry, my brodda, my mind was somewhere else."

"no, it is okay. Shit happens!" I replied, trying to be friendly.

"yeah, shit happens. So where you from?"

"I am from Eritrea. Where you from?"

"Am from all over, my brodda." He laughed. "So you been here for long?"

"you mean in Norway or zis bar?" I asked, while we were still peeing.

"no, Norway."

"no, not for long, just a couple of months. I am now, huh, sort of living in the north. You know, asylum thing."

Sensing my shame, he looked at me straight in the eyes and in more of a whisper said, "it's okay. This too shall pass!" He said this with a sigh and a reassuring nod before he headed back to his seat.

Well, the sigh said it all; he looked like he was so sure of himself, and genuinely cared for my feelings. I thought it was weird but the most positive, brief toilet encounter I ever had with a stranger. On my way to my table, I scanned the room to see where he was sitting. On the corner to my left there were two beautiful white women and one stunning black girl, along with a skinny brother sitting around him. Their table was full, with a finished champagne bottle and a bunch of glasses.

Back at our table, my friend was engaged in a deep conversation with a friend of his whom he had not seen for quite some time. The drinks kept coming, the music was to my taste, and I had nothing to complain. Occasionally glancing towards the other tables, I was trying my luck to get some intimate action for the night. Once a city boy, always a city boy.

The bartender had smiled at me twice or so, so I thought I would try to make eye contact with her. My eyes followed her from table to table. She had a great figure. She was wearing a sexy, knee-high, wool skirt and a revealing, grayish top. After fruitless attempts to catch her attention, I realized she was just being nice to me as a host. She was smiling and giggling to every customer. Disappointed, I focused my attention on the rest of the women in the bar.

Unlucky me, though, as all had company already. Finally, one girl showed some interest. She was one of the white girls sitting at the West African's table. I waited long enough for her to look my way and smiled at her. She smiled back. Had it not been for the nice African I had just met in the toilet, I would have hauled my ass right to her table in a minute, but then something held me back, so I decided to play it cool and keep drinking. *Maybe tonight is not your lucky night*, I told myself and pretended to pay attention to whatever my friend and his squeaky-sounding friend were babbling about.

After a while, I stepped outside for a smoke and there outside was my man and his girls having one, as well. I introduced myself to the girls, taking a welcoming cue from him. They sounded nice. The usual talk about the cold winter ensued. As I had mentioned I was new in Norway, they asked me for my impressions of their country.

"I like it. I never felt so safe and secure in my life," I lied, thinking I would earn a point or so. But looking towards Big Man, I kind of sensed a shake of his head.

The girls finished their cigarettes and went right back in. Big Man, as I heard some passerby address him, stayed behind and offered me a seat at his table if I did not have any company. Though I was pleased, I had come with the friend I was staying with, so had to decline. We exchanged phone numbers and split back to our tables.

Back inside, my friend was getting ready to go. He must have noticed my new friend as he jumped at me with curious questions about who he was before I even sat down. I just told him it was just the black thing, that we needed no introduction, and that we hit it off as I always did with any African anywhere we met. He did not like any part of it. He stared at me for long seconds, trying to figure out something, and finally just told me that I had to be careful in making friends around this town. With a worried glance at the table where Big Man was sitting, he told me I had to stay away from those kinds of people if I wanted to live a trouble-free life in Norway. He had always been a suspicious man, but I kind of sensed he knew Big Man very well. As much as I wanted to clear the air, I did not want to drag out the issue. We hastened back to the sunny night.

My friend and I go way back. We had been through a lot in Eritrea. We shared a lot of memories together; all the good and the bad in that little, troublesome country. We had finished high school together in Asmara and later on served in the same regiment during our mandatory national service. Mine was a short stint, though, as I was lucky enough to achieve the minimum grade required to join the university. It was the only way to get an exemption from the military; my friend had been agonizingly close, but missed the cut. Just another D, even in General Knowledge, could have altered his life radically.

After years of toiling and slaving under the brutal military service in the treacherous, hot location of the eastern lowland desert for nearly half a decade, my good friend had made up his mind to desert to neighboring Ethiopia. He left the country in 2003 and after making a lot of detours like the rest of us—crossing the Sudan and then the Sahara across Libya and finally crossing the Mediterranean to Italian shores—his fate had finally brought him to Norway. He had long been accepted and integrated into the Norwegian society but still struggled to make ends meet, working two jobs in one of the most expensive cities in the world. I was not sure, but I felt like he resented his situation or maybe believed he deserved better. For all, I was sure was he was not happy. Still, he was the one close friend I had in Norway. And when I had planned to come to Norway, I relied on him for accommodations and information before I handed myself in to the authorities. But circumstances had changed our friendship; maybe I was expecting a lot from him.

A flashback of our first encounter in Oslo began replaying, as if it had happened the day before. I landed in Oslo on a cold night in the beginning of January 2009. After cautiously avoiding the airport security, who often target nervy foreign passengers for illegal entries, I made my way out and grabbed the airport express that led to the inner city. My friend had agreed to meet me upon my arrival at the central terminal. My nerves were calm. So far, everything was going according to plan. I was not new to border crossing and entering countries illegally, not by choice, but mostly forced by the circumstances. The worst-case scenario was that I could get apprehended by the airport security, who would waste no time deporting an illegal suspect back to his airport of origin. Having avoided that, I was in a festive mood and imagining a bright future.

I stepped out of the train carrying a light backpack, and ventured onto the freezing, busy platform. I headed straight for the gate that led to the exit. Making my way past the crowded station, I spotted my friend seated anxiously in one of the benches overlooking the big screen of the train routes. With a satisfied sigh, I strolled with ease towards him, knowing I was safe and sound.

I was to remember afterwards that it was not that easy to make it, given how cramped my friend's living apartment was. It rather looked like a compartment space in a student's flat. For a while, I never left the apartment, unless once or twice accompanied by friends. I did not want anything to go wrong before I handed myself over. As well, I was mentally preparing the case I was to present to the authorities. I was briefed about what to say and what not to say, as well as what documents to bring. Some had even advised me on what to wear on my way to the "Politi," so as to create the impression that I was a helpless African in need of protection.

There were plenty of stories that actually raised hairs on my neck. Some just overdramatized the situation into an action movie, with lots of interrogations and surveillance. But I gathered, then, that Norway had become the new oasis for asylum seekers from all corners of the world; thus, national security would be their major concern.

The fact of the matter was, they normally handled cases more efficiently than any other European country. In addition to the decent temporary residences they provide, along with the services accessible being of a better and higher standard than those of other European nations, it attracted the needy like fire attracted moths. From my understanding, people from crisis regions, where they faced threats on their lives, were given priority. As I had fled my country fearing for my life, in addition to my country being in political and social turmoil for so long, I was hoping to get acceptance soon. The last night I spent at my friend's house, I was really in a jubilant mood, smelling recompense for all the troubles and misfortunes to which my fate had subjected me.

Judgment day arrived! I never knew why, but I always hated Thursdays; well, no wonder, now that I come to think of it. After a lousy breakfast, and packing the few things I needed inside a small backpack—not anything new and flashy, just to follow advice—the friend and I took the train to Oslo's central station. The friend, who had been distant and very occupied during my stay, was giving the last pieces of advice before I walked into custody. He said, in Tigrigna, the language of my country, "*welahanti tsegem yelen, zekone shiger telo deweleley, zetrefe nebretka kea kesedelka iye kulu meswedaka.*" (There is nothing to worry about! If there is any problem, you have my number, you can call me, and the rest of your stuff I could send it to you as soon as you are settled.) With that, we strolled side by side, lost in our thoughts, towards the Politi.

Though I was accustomed to walking into police stations in many countries, willingly or unwillingly, this time it was different. The expansive building that served as the reception center for asylum seekers looked more like a hotel from the outside. Where I came from and most of the countries I had been to, one could almost smell the police station from a mile away, with the noisy police vehicles and the cocky uniforms swarming all over to make their presence felt. But this one was disturbingly quiet and very neat as I climbed the stairs of the front gate.

Afterwards, my train kind of fell off its track. But what disappointed me most was that my friend was in fact a kind of happy to get rid of me. I understood afterwards that life was difficult in a big city. If one failed to secure a reliable career or attain a higher education during the two-year introduction phase, one was more likely to struggle. Besides, living in the capital did not help him, either. Without any acquired, high-paying skills, some of my friends got stuck in the sanitation business. But due to the mass influx of foreigners, there was stiff competition even in that department. Regardless, he was working way too hard and supporting his family back at home. As a result, he was physically emaciated and mentally strained.

He even felt a bit of resentment, I thought, seeing my relaxed state of mind when I passed through during my vacation.

❧

So, I was doing my best not to push his buttons; otherwise, I would have headed off with Big Man for the time of my life, probably. Once we reached home, my friend kind of implied that some Africans here were making a lot of money, mostly illegally and living a good life, while the likes of him were struggling. I knew where he was going with it, so I just headed to the sofa where I was to sleep, to avoid another lecture.

❧

The next day, I woke up late with a hangover. After revitalizing myself, I left in haste, as if I had a business appointment. I had to leave that place fast, as my friend's roommate had not been that thrilled to see me in their cramped crib. He had been giving me the silent treatment. It seemed everyone was brooding. Since the roommate had no work permit, times had been tough to find black jobs. Still, we all got problems. I didn't know why anybody should blow off steam on me.

After a short walk around the train station, I headed straight for the barbershop, where people from my country hang out. There, I could kill a couple of hours and meet very funny people and joke around for a while. While chilling there over coffee, I had a sudden urge to call Big Man. Though I did not know him well, he seemed like a very interesting person. So I took out my busted-

up Nokia and dialed his number. He picked up on the third ring. He sounded cranky, so I figured he had a long, long night. "hey, man, remember me? I am the Eritrean guy from the bar last night."

"oh, yeah, man. From the toilet in de bar."

"Yeah, it's me." I was surprised he remembered me at once. "am in town, and I thought if you were around, maybe we could hang out or something."

"sure, brodda. You know Grønland?" he said, after second's hesitation.

"am not sure, is it around the Somali shops?"

"Uh huh, der is a small pub under the bridge called Downtown. Me and me broddas come der sometimes. You come in two hours. We talk den."

"sure, man. See you zen." not really sure exactly where the place was, I hung up the phone. Thought it would be stupid to ask him again where exactly to find it. I figured I would ask around and eventually get there.

In Downtown Pub, I paid for one beer and sat close to the door, where I had full visibility of the outside. The bar was cozy and homey, and the customers were mostly old and lonely. The beer was cheap. A trio of Latino customers at a far corner was gazing at the overhead TV where a rerun premier league game was playing. A mixed couple was having an intimate moment at the next table to mine. It was nice to see a black man and a white woman sharing their affection in public. Love knows no boundaries, I reminded myself. A white bum was drunk, mumbling something incomprehensible at the other end of the bar. The Asian bartender seemed to be bored with his job, as he passively poured the beers into the glasses and slid them in slow motion to every order. Before I noticed, Big Man and another bigger friend of his walked into the bar and were standing next to my table.

After two hours and many beers, we were joking around as if we had known each other for a long time. The guy had been everywhere; he had been to Ethiopia some time ago. I gathered from his stories that he was older than his looks suggested; maybe late thirties or early forties. In the middle of our conversation, he asked how I knew the person I was sitting with. "we go way back," I replied. He did not seem to care. He told me that he was always happy to meet any African anywhere he went. He said it beautifully, as well. "you know, my brodda, all we have is each other at the end of the day. We are all unwelcome guests in Babylon. But some broddas think dey are better dan others. Big mistake, my brodda." He wagged his pointed forefinger in the air. "We all trying to survive here. And survive by any means, especially if you are denied of all opportunities. But some people never seem to understand dat, mtsee!"

I understood him. Whatever he did for a living was not my business. If he could handle it, why should I care? Besides, he had shown me more courtesy than anyone ever had since my arrival in Norway.

It seemed everyone who stepped into the pub seemed to know him or recognize him. Some would come by and shake his hand with respect. Others would either nod or grunt their greeting from afar. But it was enough to give me an impression of how well connected the man was. Besides, he was never able to finish a sentence with the dozens of calls that rang from one of the three phones he carried.

I was humbled by his hospitality. Every person he talked to, he looked them in the eyes with genuine concern and attention. He seemed to be knowledgeable as well. I was not sure if he had been to college, but his deduction skills and his open-mindedness made you want to listen closely to whatever he was saying.

Afterwards, we went to a house party at his friend's home somewhere uptown. Once again, I had no recollection of the location. All I know was we got on the 168 tram to Majorstuen. All I remember was that we ended up in the fifth floor of a high-rise apartment. The place was filled with a variety of people from all over, and they knew Big Man very well. The host was a guy of mixed race: black, white, and some traces of Asian. He was already drunk when we got there. The music was playing at full blast. A teenage-looking white boy was playing the music from a laptop, crouched on a corner of the overfilled sofa. The table was full of half-empty beer bottles, and half-full glasses of cocktails. There were few black faces—most looked from West Africa—a bunch of Arabs, and of course many Norwegian men and women. There were only three African girls, who were isolated form the rest in the kitchen, talking animatedly to one another. The magnificent place, though still organized, seemed to have borne the brunt of endless parties, with the stench of stale beer, spilled spirits, and cigarettes butts still lingering in the air.

Since Big Man had already disappeared in one of the bedrooms, I stood hesitantly by the living room shelf, talking to one Norwegian who kept bombarding me about where I came from, what was I doing in his country... I interrupted his interrogation and asked him where I could get a drink. He pointed me to the kitchen to help myself.

In the kitchen, one of the Nigerian girls seemed to have understood my dilemma, as she poured me a stiff Jagermeister with some coke. "hey," she said, "just pick and pour any bottle, when you finish. None of us live here, okay?" She handed me the paper cup with my drink and glided her beautiful figure back to her friends. I took a sip and slowly made my way past the guests and stepped outside to the balcony to smoke a cigarette.

Dragging on my Marlboro cigarette, I looked out to the city, its nighttime skyline in a haze. *It is a beautiful city*, I told myself. For the first time in the many months I had been in Norway, I was not a bit ashamed of my asylum situation. I even forgot that I stayed in the Mottak. I was really grateful I had met Big Man. I guess your situation dictated what the eyes could see. Had I been living in a camp, even in the capital, I would not have had the pleasure of admiring the view of the best of nature and man's modern city. Aesthetics went hand in hand with a feeling of stability and security.

Afterwards, at the party, some guy came up with hashish, which almost everyone smoked. By midnight, everyone was laughing and joking harmoniously. I had even begun to understand some of the Norwegian conversation, miraculously; maybe it was just the hash. Big Man was the center of attention, though; all the girls were competing for his attention and the guys looked up to him. I was enjoying my time; met an interesting woman and once again I had altered my alias to accommodate her interests. Even Big Man was surprised when they asked him where he'd met the journalist from South Africa.

Though I barely remember everything that happened that night in detail, it was one of the best nights of my life. We had been going from one club to another, drinking and dancing our hearts out. My dear friend even had called me at some point late at night, worried about my wellbeing. Hearing all the commotion of the club, in addition to my mumbling about where I was, he did not at all sound pleased as he hung up.

The club was soon followed by an after-party. Those of us lucky enough to hold onto our dates ended the morning with a blissful lovemaking.

I spent three days in Big Man's apartment with his friends. He was one of the nicest men I have ever met in my life. He could read one's mind and understand, even if he didn't know you that well. Above all, he was very diplomatic. Sensing my desperation for some direction, he assured me that he could squeeze me into a corner if I was willing to make some decent money. "I know I can trust a person like you, am good with telling personalities, my brodda. Just call whenever you are ready. I even know some people in de town you live. Just let me know," he had said, as we exchanged information on how I could contact him if I was ever to be part of the business. After three wonderful days and nights in all sorts of places, I said my goodbyes and headed back to my friend's place, to a cold reception.

Had I not had two more days left before my flight back, I would have preferred to have slept in the train station. I admit that I had been reckless and a bit rude, yet I was no child. At heart, he did not like the fact that I had been able to make other friends from other cultures and have fun while he was working his butt off. Well, if I had a work permit, I would have spent my time wisely and productively, but I was in limbo. A prisoner would have more rights and recognition than I had. Besides, I was covering for my expenses, and it seemed the friend did not appreciate that.

As he once again saw me off to north, I realized it would never be the same between us from then on. But it would be a big lesson in the future: it is not necessarily your blood brother who comes to your rescue when you are in need; it could be a stranger. Thus, anybody could be my brother in life, so long as I kept an open mind. Times change, people grow up and apart, even best friends become strangers. But life will always go on!

Big Man, whom I would later meet on many other occasions, was a real survivor. Though he made his living selling destructive, addictive, mind-altering substances, he meant well for others. But as Big Man put it, "you know, if my asylum case had been accepted in one of de countries that I had applied, I would have taken a different path in life. I have not always been like dis, you know. I was a truck driver one time in my life, with an international driving license; I could have worked as one anywhere. I have been in college; I could have advanced myself, you know. I always had an eye for business; I mean legitimate business. But dey denied me dat opportunity to be productive for myself and deir society. Den they go ahead and call me a drain to deir economy. You see de double standard here. Den, after brooding and recklessly wasting some time regretting my fate, I realized only me can deliver for myself, me brodda. At first, I thought it was only about de money, but after making so many mistakes, I learned it's about maintaining friendship, love, and family and be dere for each otha. I know one day all dis is going to end, but I know dere will be plenty who would be dere to help me when I really need dem. And I don't regret anything I have done so far! When your rights as decent human being in life are never respected for you, I don't believe I should bother respecting deir laws. God damn it, am a man and a man gots to eat." to which he left us speechless for a couple of minutes.

❦

One time in the Mottak, during one of our endless chats with Cliff, we were surprised that most of us knew Big Man. He seemed to have touched each of us with his compassion and his generosity. He had bought Cliff the plane ticket for his way back, after he had run into some problems in Oslo.

Many others recounted the favors he had done. Cliff had said, "I know dat man. He been doin' dis business for so long but dey neva caught him. It is the good deed dis man do dat keeping him safe. Believe me."

Congo, who had met Big Man in Bergen while visiting his girlfriend, added, shaking his head, "I tell you, he make a lot of money. I know he is rich. Probably stashed somewhere! But de way he treats everybody de same amazes me!"

We all nodded in agreement.

Another Nigerian friend, puffing the smoke of his cigarette, declared sarcastically, "If I was him, I would be driving a nice car, live in a big house, fuck beautiful women every day, and never talk to asylum niggas like you. You will always want favors from me!"

An outburst of curses rained on him. "look at, look at dis man! Greedy, always thinking of himself. Dat is why you will never be with money."

"you would have been caught long time ago, my friend..."

But we all know it was his strategy of staying humble and under the radar that helped keep him safe. Maybe he had some spirit looking after him too, or whatever; voodoo, juju, degimt. In whatever culture, it was working. But the truth was, if you were too flashy and showy, you would never last long in the streets. Besides, helping out friends and making as many of them as possible could neutralize potential enemies as well as spread his influence even further.

But the longer we speculated about him, the more we were astounded. Though many accounts of his nationality are unreliable, some close friends said he was from Ghana, though I had heard Nigeria, Mali, and Senegal, among many others. But the amazing fact was that he supported nineteen immediate and extended families in his homeland, or so I had heard. He had financed his families to set up a small business that generated a healthy income. Big Man had taken care of his old friends along the way, helping them get to their feet in Europe. Though he had also helped hundreds of strangers, I was not sure his family knew what kind of business their beloved son did for a living.

Some said he recruited his street pushers selectively in different cities through his connections, which supplied his customers at fixed prices. His brand was often noted for its quality at a reasonable price. We gathered that he had been able to evade the authorities by not keeping stock in any of the places he stayed, and he rotated those places often. And when he felt he was being watched, he changed cities or even countries until the heat simmered down. Thus, with the help of loyal subordinates whom he took good care of, he made sure no trace of the dealing could be tracked back to him. Some of his boys had been caught, but none had confessed their supplier. Appearing and disappearing in the open, he had been able to survive the scrutiny of the authorities longer than most.

Every time his name was mentioned on any occasion, every city boy in the Mottak showered words of praise on that enigmatic black man who had defied the odds and made it to the top without being detected. Of course, what goes up must come down, and he would one day be caught, unless he decided to retire and head back to his homeland to a hero's welcome—but he had left a mark on many. He sure had made a lot of money out of it, yet he never forgot where he came from nor got carried away by his riches. Once one made it here in Babylon, few ever look back; and he earned our respect for being different.

The Landlords

I once dreamed of the sons of the sun trekking years and years, braving the treacherous desert and the raging seas, in search of the Northern Lights. Destiny was calling. Yes I, a son of the sun—may the epidermal evidence reaffirm my claim—followed the trails left hundreds of years ago to get my share of the riches. Sons of Kush, Cousins of Sem, Igbo princes, and Bantu chiefs were along in the caravan. We'd been in the sun for far too long, in search of shade. The load on our shoulders was getting heavier by the day. The sun was unforgiving; the nights brought cold and storms.

We finally ran into sprawled awnings with their frowning occupants relaxing in its shade. They looked like they'd been in the shade for far too long. Contempt was their welcome.

Sweat dripping from all earthly shades of our brown skin, we approached humbly, hoping. A favor had been owed to us for more than half a millennium, yet they scowled at our "audacity" to even contemplate the thought! Sure, sure, we were as guilty as they were in a blind participation of the soul trade. We sold the bad eggs but they mistook our kindness for a weakness and they wanted it all. They stretched from Fort Augustus to Zanzibar and usurped every glittering thing, from the diamond to the smile. But only the middlemen from the east made profits. Is it rude to ask for an outstanding debt? Okay, forget the interest! Let bygones be bygones, if you say so; but cut us some slack.

I woke up, still in the Mottak. The debt was still outstanding.

City boys had us a motto: "You can only be a guest for a night." The next day, you had to feel at home, even if it was way away from home. Regardless of one's status in any society, you would eventually run into the friendly ones, if you kept looking. Some might be tired of the same faces and same jokes; others shunned you of their own will, and still some others ended up making you a friend just out of curiosity. As it was the case of misfits trying to fit, it was not a surprise that we ran into other misfits. Maybe two misfits might fit in just right.

On one of our endless weekend excursions, one never knew who we might see. Some just bored you to death with their persistent questions, "where do you come from?" "how long you been here?" "where in Africa is you country found?" Ufff! It felt as if we were on CNN's *The Africa Hour*, bombarded from all directions. "woman, why don't you buy me beer? My mouth is dry from answering your questions," Tallest once snapped. We did not mind the questions when they came accompanied by the beer; in fact, we gave an elaborate explanation with some dramatic, spicy stories you'd never forget. But on a balcony of the Grand Hotel, where we had been stranded purposefully outside, we complained how slow the night was. Then in walked this stocky white man, in his mid-forties, smiling his way past the balcony door towards us. He stood half a meter between our group and kept smiling before saying warmly, "my African friends, how are you enjoying the night?" and he walked straight into our group with an extended hand.

Within seconds, the ever-welcoming Cliff and Dudu were conversing as if they had known him for years. The man was in a surprising good mood as he rushed in and came back with four beer glasses foaming down his wet hands. Our interest instantly grew. However, we were genuinely interested when he stated that he knew how we felt about how the Norwegians treated us, as he had been subjected to the same end of the racist stick. We were bemused by his statement, thinking this guy probably forgot to look in the mirror or must had been smoking some strong stuff for far too long. Then he went on to state, in a hushed manner, that he was from the Indigenous Sámi tribe that was colonized by the Norwegians. We were left stunned for a couple of minutes, trying to process what he was telling us.

"so are you telling me we living in your land and not ders?" questioned the stunned Cliff. "ayy! Dese people are wicked. Mtsee, did you hear dat, Mr. Man?"

"Yeah, man!" I replied, with my curiosity suddenly taming my tipsiness. I cocked my ears to hear more about the indigenous people.

"so you people, what are you people called again?" Congo looked at the tall blond man straight in the eye, hoping to decipher if the man's story was genuine.

"Sami. We are called the Sámi people," the smiling man replied, noting the curious faces that were scrutinizing him from head to toe. "we have been living in this part of the world for more than five thousand years. All the northern part of Norway, Sweden, Finland, and some parts of Russia used to be known as the Sámiland."

"cool. So you people have your own language?" said another one of us. The fascinating white man looked no different from any other Norwegian.

"Yeah, we do, actually," he said. "It is very different from Norwegian language. It sounds more like the Finnish language. You know, from Finland." He sipped his beer and looked around. We were still puzzled by a new revelation. There stood an ordinary white man with a blond hair, grayish blue eyes, and all the common features we associated with the locals. He dressed and acted like them, but claimed otherwise. It was food for our thoughts, as we each ran a couple of scenarios to make sense out of the conversation. From my point of view, an indigenous tribe was distinctly different from other settlers; from physical features to cultural traits.

"so, let me get this straight," began Dudu, straightening his dark grey fedora. "you people were occupied by the Norwegians, like the Aborigines in Australia and the Red Indians in America, or what?"

"Actually we were treated exactly like them," replied the man. "They took our land; we were considered primitive savages," he recalled, a hint of resentment lingering in his conversation. "they forced us to learn their language and naturalized us into their society. We suffered for years and years, in fact, from racism and their attempts to Christianize and civilize us. But unlike other indigenous tribes in the world, the government here is doing its best to make up for its past mistakes. And hey, you move on, right?" He threw his hands in the air nonchalantly, to indicate that he harbored not so much hatred towards other Norwegians.

Norwegian country music blared from inside the bar every time somebody pushed open the door to the balcony. Indeed, something about him was a little different. He was dressed in blue jeans, a light, striped shirt, and a black blazer, yet he was far more relaxed than others we had met. His eyes had this fire in them that we didn't see in the local people, who were quite opaque and difficult to decipher. An older man then came from behind and playfully groped the indigenous man's shoulders from behind. Surprised, he turned around to face the other man and they embraced as though they had not met for a long time. He broke into a heated, hilarious Norwegian conversation.

"tomato, tomah-to! He is white at de end of de day," snapped Cliff and led the way towards the bar, leaving the indigenous man to converse with his countryman. Once inside the bar, it was business as usual.

At the end of the party, though, we all gathered outside the hotel entrance, checking out the surroundings and figuring out a continuation of the night's celebration. Dudu was cajoling two women in their mid-forties. The longer they were exposed to his charm, the more likely they were to be smitten; he knew how to work his way around women. Cliff was engaged in his drunken banter with the security guards, arguing over why he had to take the bar's glass along with him. Congo and I waited for opportunities, contemplating moving towards the taxi stand where all the drunkards of the night congregated for a ride home. Then our dear indigenous white man showed up, along with two friends of his. He invited us over to his place for a couple of drinks. We did not hesitate, as we left behind the lover boy and trudged along to the taxi stand's long queue.

❁

The indigenous man lived around the Trondenes church that was about a seven-minute taxi ride. According to his explanation, he was married, divorced twice, with children all grown or living with their mothers. His two-story expansive house sprawled near the beach, and the cold sea breath gusted all around. We soon settled in his modern living room with our beers and cognac. After he stepped inside the adjacent kitchen to fix himself a sandwich, we looked around at the ornaments and pictures that adorned the vast living room. Strange-looking garments adorned the wooden pieces with distinct blue, rose, and purple braids in most of the pieces. Skin garments were suspended on the wall of what we presumed were the winter clothes of the arctic people. Black and white, expensive-looking, wooden-framed portraits were displayed, hung evenly all over the wall. Some looked like they were taken a hundred years ago, with the heavily bearded, short, high-cheekboned subjects standing defiantly, clad from head to toe in fur garments, as if facing the firing squad.

Later on, the indigenous man told how his people were deeply married to the spiritual and natural worlds, paying their tributes to various gods that blessed and cursed them accordingly. And that no matter how civilized and Christianized his people had been for the past hundred years, they had maintained their spiritual essence all along. He went on to tell us, even though he had been a converted Lutheran at one time and an atheist of late, he was devoted to the Sámi ways of connecting with supernatural forces and the ancestors for guidance.

With Cliff constantly interrupting the narration with a funny remark that drew smiles from the host, we had the most enjoyable night for quite some time. Our host was nonjudgmental, an insider–outsider who really understood how we felt. It was informative, as well: There lived a spiritual, indigenous white population living so close to the land of their forefathers so far up in the north.

We exchanged farewells and numbers with the man. He promised to pay us a visit in the coming months, after a much-needed visit to the ancestral land where some of his relatives still lived. He mentioned that he frequently visited a sacred site deep in the arctic, where some of his people maintained the old ways that refreshed his soul.

"Ah, dat is not white, I tell you," remarked Cliff, in admiration. "I met so many white people in my life but neva seen man like him. Mtsee, dis man feels de spirit like real Africans do."

Trotting off toward a splitting hangover from the free booze I had been gulping all night, I recalled a saying from an elderly man a long time ago about land, passion, and people. The more territorial they got, the less likely they were to be indigenous. The invader often treasures the land, but the original cherishes the land like its dear life. The original knows you can never own the land; you are just a guest for a little while until you become part of the very land others step all over. You probably could get a decent burial, but sooner or later, somebody was going to need that piece of maggot-fertilized land.

The encounter with the aborigine conjured memories of an astounding people who had shaped my perception: the aborigines of the land of my forefathers. The beautiful wooden houses with green, well-trimmed lawns on both sides was the exact opposite of the images my memories had transported back to me as I shuffled along the endless pavement back to the Mottak.

How could one know the life one claims is really theirs? Maybe it was just an illusion; one is just a nominal physical figure in a master plan that one is not quite aware of. Maybe when one had some bearing over one's destiny and the so-called will power, maybe then it feels like one's own grand plan. For some, the path had been paved by their forefathers for generations. Their livelihood had been ensured. Their survival had been secured. Yet, disaster still could strike anytime, and the fear of it was what brought the suffering. Regardless of how well prepared and organized one was, one thing was for sure; it would all end. Can't live it all on one's terms! Unless one wished to end it by himself. Either way, we all lost in the end, to rot underneath.

But then, when the suffering was too much, when all forces were working against you, testing and pushing you to the brink at every turn, when nothing but curses and debts had been passed on to you, where every day was a burden, even when one had long given up, one was not left alone. When it felt like it was too much for a day, still you made it for another. Well, one gets numb in the face of intense moments when catatonic movements could only count as a mere functioning. One feels no fear, no pain, as if one is in a trance watching his own self moving about, performing tasks he is quite unaware of, like a robot. Medically, the pulse in the veins might prove one's existence, yet it felt like lights all lit up in an empty house. Still not a home though, until the day someone moves into it. Funny thing was, one kept moving. No matter how alone one felt, we were somehow connected to one another.

The suffering, though, was part of the lesson, the message, or maybe the vague answer to the never-ending doubts. Though every man felt his burden was the heaviest, we all knew deep inside who had it worse. Yet, one forgot; a grave error. Every step counted; there was no such thing as a coincidence in life. All is a learning process. The nightmares and all the ugly scenes in the suffering were a process, a test, a challenge, to find out if one was worthy of the next challenge. We all wished for the days to be normal, to sleep peacefully through the night, and wake up to live another day. Yet, reality was nothing but ordinary. It was a stark and ugly string of scenes that one could never out run or hide from. Some escaped it by creating tight, narrow, and, at times, shallow comfort zones to keep the evils in the dark.

For others, seeking asylum in fantasies temporarily shielded them. It happened everywhere, whenever one felt insecure, one would taunt and intimidate others who were different, either to persuade or force the victim into accepting inferiority.

Yet, those labels felt truer the longer they were beaten into you.

❧

All life was a passage. And the sorrow and the grief shall all pass like the joy and happiness that came before. If it did not, well, one thing was for sure: We will all pass away one day, or the other. As some pass away, others pass on and life goes on...

During my passage, I was blessed enough to be exposed from many directions. A decade ago, living under difficult circumstances in a country where uniformity and conformity were the order of the day, I enrolled at a higher institution without a crisp motive or purpose (yet I would find out later in life that it was lost due to my inability to find a meaning into my existence). At that point in life all life was meaningless. All concepts were deception. Images manipulations. Sounds, distractions. All I had known before was dissolved into a massive ocean of confusion. None of the academic theories captured my imagination or even rewarded my curiosity. I just could not relate. It was just another sort of debt I was paying back, this time to my parents. Where I came from, it is the second-best thing, after making them grandparents. Otherwise, I felt like I was wasting my time.

I was desperate for something meaningful, something fresh. It was bad enough that I would rather pay attention to a drunkard's philosophy than a prominent professor's lecture. All they offered were speculations on matters which mostly were irrelevant to me at that point.

However, in retrospect, I believe the mind is like a giant sponge that sucks in every bit of information from any experience, regardless of how attentive or interested one really is, to finally squeeze out meaning, one drop at a time. Thus, nothing is wasted, so long as one is constantly moving and engaged in a direction. It all depends upon one's recognition of one's velocity.

As all life was suffering, and all suffering was an ongoing process, the process made me a kind tourist in the safari of life. Thus, I, the tourist on my first outing from my comfort zone of home, found myself in a strange land with strange people. Though a place was only strange to a stranger, I was taken aback by what awaited me barely 100 kilometers away from my second hometown of Asmara: Shambukko.

Though there were two routes the bus companies use to get to this exotic part of the country, I took the direct one that was supposed to take eight hours. The first route, the smoother one, took longer but only a quarter of its path was a dirt road. The route circled around the northern towns of Keren and Akordet before it headed back to the southwest. Then one had to spend a night at Barentu, the seat of administration for the entire western region of the country (Zoba Gash Barka); the trip took approximately six to eight hours. It all depended upon the bus, the driver, and the weather. If one was lucky enough to hitch a ride to Shambukko, clinging to truckloads of cattle and firewood, one still had to spend a night for an early departure along the treacherous dirt road farther to the southwest to reach Shambukko in four or five hours. The second and rougher route, though, took a direct approach, but with only a tenth of the way being tarmac road. The route cut through the southern towns of Mendefera, Debarwa, and Maidema, and headed farther west, passing Molki and other small towns along the river—making for an unpaved, flood-washed, bumpy, rocky, and dusty journey along the way.

Shambukko, being located in the southwestern part of the tiny horn country of Eritrea, was an administrative town for the districts (sub-zones) surrounding it. Twice receiving the blunt devastation of the border conflict that had taken place between Ethiopia and Eritrea between 1998 and 2000, the recognizable modern structures of the town—its hospital and administrative buildings—had been left in ruins. Only the newly built junior high school stood out, with its modern designs.

The town was founded along the perennial river of Mereb that stretched along the edge of the town to meander its way down south of the border before it eventually made it to a wandering rift of a valley. The river was the livelihood of the people who relied on its waters for their cattle and small family-owned farms and plantations. Due to its location in the lowlands and the rising highlands on all sides, it was at times unbearably hot and humid for most of the year. Since the war that had stagnated its development, the town lacked all sorts of facilities. There was no water, except for the recently constructed water wells that served the town, from which people transported it by mule. Yet most fetched their water from the river. Electricity was a luxury, with only the town's privileged members owning the loud generators that illuminated their places like sore thumbs among the small, scattered habitations.

Even the rich had to limit their generators to scheduled periods; two hours during midday and a couple more during the evening. A telephone was unthinkable; electronic contact was handled through radio by higher administrative officials, the military, and the police. Public transport linked Shambukko to the rest of the country daily. The public often traveled to the capital or the nearest big town of Barentu by the abundant buses, minibuses, and pickups that crisscrossed the dusty roads. With a heavy military presence in and around the border, the local traders transported their renowned honey and aromatic spicy butter to the big cities.

You could actually feel all your organs shuffling and switching positions along the way from the constantly bumpy road. The treacherous route was such a nightmare and so unpredictable that you would be as exhausted in the end as if you had been traveling for days. The buses or minibuses assigned to that route were the old and busted-up ones designated to bear the poor souls across the unfriendly terrain. Though there were dozens of checkpoints along the way to inspect valid passes and IDs, the soldiers barely cared about the safety and number of the passengers. Buses heading to remote areas would cram as many customers and as much property as they could along the way. In fact, there wouldn't be a space even to move one's feet by the end of the trip, with kids and the local folks sitting all over the floor with their belongings, some asleep standing, even a few others leaning on the door; you would fear if the door ever burst open, two or three passengers would fall out like beans from an over-packed can. Had it not been for the goods lashed to the top of the bus, I was sure the driver and the conductor would have been thrilled to tie some of us up there, instead.

Dust and dirt that sneaked through all the invisible cracks, windows, and doors left you with a sore throat and bloodshot eyes. The stench of all the perishable goods, carelessly stashed underneath the seats, mingled with the sweat, body odor, spices, homemade snacks, vomit, and baby excrement. You would get accustomed to it after one or two hours. Besides, the heat and humidity was so intense and depressing that you wished to open the window and let some fresh air in, but then the dust would blow right into your face. The sounds were an onslaught, too: the constant rattle of the windows, the gurgling and grinding of the vehicle's metal parts, the crying babies, the music from the radio of unbearable, high-pitched songs in languages you never heard of, multilingual conversations, loud debates, women arguing with their young ones, hens and cocks tied together and stashed underneath their owners, crowing at the top of their lungs. It would drive you insane. It was a trip I dreaded to make with a hangover or even after eating breakfast, but hey, I had to make it for a living.

The most frustrating part did not end there. What would normally take eight hours might somehow end up being twelve or even an overnight trip. Some sections of the road had to be constantly ground level by bulldozers to make them traversable. The riverbeds would be flooded, nearby paths would be washed up, the hard gravel road would turn into a sticky muddy plain when the rainy season arrived. When that happened, one had to help the driver and dig the path for the bus to cut through, or line up rocks through a shallow pit left behind by floods. Of course, there was also the unfortunate possibility of flat tires, meaning one had to wait in an outdoor tearoom until they changed it. Then there were constant arguments between the checkpoint guards and passengers, and the bartering over unfixed fares that tempted some to persist in haggling over forever. The best one could do was wish to arrive in one piece, no matter how long it took.

The Kunama natives, the original sons of that piece of land, were what called me there. As I said before, a place was nothing but a setting suspended in time; pay too much attention to the background and you will lose focus of what was most important—life and love. The Kunamas were the most exciting and down-to-earth people I had ever met in my entire life. They revolved in their own orbit, oblivious to the rush around them.

It was like walking back in time, yet thinking about it now, it might be more like taking a stroll into the future. Given the proximity, it was unbelievable to run into a culture with a totally different rhythm of life. It had a slow pace but was well organized. They harmonized, as if they had been spared the pollution of civilization that had disrupted so many other souls. Though there was a slight infiltration of the inevitable, they still could take comfort in their way of life among themselves. Yet, they seemed quite settled and barely interested in what went on outside their sphere. They had their own perspective on the world, but above all, they believed in Mother Nature. They celebrated and cherished her. They lived, fed, and slept so close to nature. They talked and walked so naturally. Meanwhile, I had always felt like the Congo, full of factions and rebels fighting for control deep inside of me.

Come to think of it now, it was just a case of the digits. My life was a compilation of numbers. The race against every lost minute and those boring, long hours was just a case of numbers—fucking numbers! The need for company, even for a one-night stand, the friends I kept making and losing, they were just numbers at the end of the day. The money I chased in dreams or for real—just numbers. Even after I was long gone, I would just remain a number underground, if I was even lucky to get a decent burial. Otherwise, each of us was just an insignificant digit; think of all the billions who went before you.

But out there, they had no value for numbers. Their heads were clear. You ask one his age, and it would take him a couple of moments to check his memory before replying. For me, my mind was and still is full of numbers and passwords I was expected to automatically regurgitate. The numbers were my identification and direction. Without the numbers, I was invisible. I could recall the exact time and day of the significant events in my life immaculately. I was programmed to keep track of the time, hour by hour, and account if I could, every painful second ticking in my mind. My age was a constant reminder of my failures and expectations. The older I got, the more digits I piled on to be counted and given value

These people, though, they were aware of their existence and the rest of the world's fascinations and obsessions, yet they had stayed out of the race. They managed to account for events in a natural sequence; they were content adhering to the rules and rhythm of nature, adjusting accordingly.

First impressions did them no favors, but that only underscored what a flawed thing our perception is. At first sight, they looked so odd to me. They looked unattractive—they smelled odd, and they dressed weirdly and talked animatedly. As I stood and scrutinized them, trying to find some faults to make myself feel better, they barely acknowledged my presence. They were never bothered by others' stares or perceptions. They just went about their lives, at ease.

But then come the five senses; no matter how much we relied on them, they misled us. We saw what we wanted to see, we barely knew how our own selves smelled, and textures and sounds and tastes were not uniform, either. Each culture had its unique scents and colors. Costumes are meant to cover and protect the body from harm, with each culture having its own style . Those are culture-specific, with a priceless meaning for the bearer, with each costume being expressive and self-explanatory, yet maybe a little ridiculous to a stranger's eyes.

Like most, my fears got the best of my consciousness, and I gave in to stereotypes. The "they are like this and like that" thoughts—of course they were! They had their own rhythms. Theirs were totally surrounded by other, mighty rhythms, forces of nature in that could spread harmony and ease to all, if we let them. Yet in the eyes of the civilized and semi-civilized world, they were just primitive pagans, with no purpose or any trace of intelligence. As expected, I fell into that trap and felt superior in their presence. But never had I sensed any judgment towards me. They just kept their distance. I observed a welcoming indifference in their faces. They were accustomed to having strangers around them, but they had not much adapted the ways of the invaders, even though they had been outnumbered.

Even though the Catholic Church had relentlessly attempted to convert them, they retained most of their beliefs. They paid tribute to their gods in lavish ceremonies and rituals that were exotic and intriguing. As strange as it sounded, compared to the strides and struggles the feminist movement elsewhere, Kunama women had always been ahead; they called the shots in this matriarchal society. The woman was head of the family, basically the provider. The man was a peripheral figure in the household; no wonder why they had fewer altercations. When a girl turned sixteen, the elders would communally build her a hut near the family lot to announce her independence. Thereafter, she had the responsibility to decide upon the right man for her to marry. Moreover, she would handle most of the home tasks, even the physical ones, without his help. Coming from a traditional Orthodox Christian society, I was baffled by the independence and freedom a Kunama woman enjoyed in a society I had once presumed to be backward and uncivilized.

In my society, unless it was a modern household, the women's domain was the kitchen and childbearing, while the man put food on the table. As for how decisions went, it would be shameful for a woman to question her husband's authority and judgment, especially in front of company. Times had changed and women played bigger roles in every department in our cities, yet they were never the dominant figure. That experience shook up my perception of where I stood as a Habesh city boy. It was too strange; I just could not find a term to define their lifestyle, seen through my shallow scope of perception. They were just natural, enjoying their lives on this earth. Thus, I could not find any use in labeling their existence when I had no idea what mine was is. In the end it was all –ions, -isms and schisms, anyway.

Their unique, colorful, traditional outfits were perfect for the hot and humid weather. Over time, they had adapted modern-day clothing to fit their tastes. The woman wore knee-high decorated miniskirts made of fabrics that clung tightly to their behinds, revealing lanky, long, dark chocolate legs. With their torso barely covered by the colorful, tight-fitting t-shirts, they were a joy to watch at all times. The carefree men spent most of their days relaxing in their small hut unless summoned for errands. They wore shorts or modern outfits that often were very colorful. However, it was the shiny ornaments and beads they wore around their necks, ankles, and wrists that caught the eye; and the combs and bands on their heads colorfully reflected their unique identity to outsiders like me.

Growing and breeding whatever they needed, they were dependent on nature and not on the stores run by the settlers. They barely consumed any processed products, though I am not still sure whether it was because they perceived them as artificial, unnatural, or a luxury.

❀

The Kunama celebrated life in almost every occasion. To my surprise, they even celebrated the departure of one of their own joyfully, just as they welcomed the arrivals. There was one time I'll never forget, where we heard loud chants and music, constant stomping and screaming that went on for more than one night around the camp where we lived. Not used to this kind of commotion, we asked the reason, and found out that the villagers were celebrating the passage of the oldest elder woman of their tribe, thus the elaborate the ceremony. I guess there was no time for sorrow, in stark contrast to their Habesh neighbors, where funerals were as loud but full of sorrowful tears and agony and mourning lasting weeks, if not months. But make no mistake, they grieved in their own way. They were indeed peaceful, yet if one of their own was unfairly treated or their pride threatened, they would respond violently—however seldom. Mostly they went about happily, sometimes tipsy from their home-brewed beer, daga.

The ironic thing was that they were fully aware of the misconceptions of others and they took full advantage of them, as I was to learn the longer I stayed and lived with them. Their indifference and non-alignment principles, with no conventional religion to follow, no centralized administration to obey, gave them the freedom to move across borders without any sort of papers. With their community stretching along both sides, the Mereb River had split them into two countries. Even though there was a small militant section that had taken arms to secure and protect the interests of its people and the land, they were not political, from my point of view. They just wished to be left alone and they did not need papers to prove that. Besides, if you think of it, "paper" was no proof of existence; it was a just a conventional illusion, just like the imaginary lines that serve as borders. On the ground, no matter which country claimed them as part of theirs, with constant interference and utter lack of influence, it never won their natural hearts. They were too in sync with nature; their rhythm and bonds were too strong to be disrupted. They only sent their children to school to appease the authorities. If children refused to go to school and were of better use at home, they were never pushed. As a teacher, doing my national service, I had met a few who came to school fully dedicated and sharp, but they stayed home if they felt bored or had something better to do.

Their indifference was a remarkable defense against outsiders' ill intentions; they belonged to none but their own culture. One can call them savages, uncivilized, pagans, wild, untamed, or whatever labels came to mind. I could not ignore the fact that their way of life just suited them. I guess it was all a state of mind and conviction. If one held firm to what one felt was the right and only way to live, that would make one's life meaningful.

On the other hand, one is more relaxed and at ease with nature when one truly belongs to the earth. They breathed and cherished the earth. They lived so close to her. They were and still are content despite constant intrusions. The Kunama were the indigenous inhabitants of that part of mother earth. Habesh, my people, were the invaders and it was we, the Habesh, who were fighting over the land with other invaders for a piece of land that never belonged to us, anyway. They had seen regimes come and go without ever taking a side. The constant battles left their scars on the other side of the land, the settlers'. They were barely touched.

⠀⁂⠀

The longer I stayed, the more respect I had for the Kunama people. Still, I always wondered what went on in their relaxed heads. I would try hard to decipher the secrets to their ease in that unbearable piece of land they called home. Coming from the substandard comfort and spoils of convenience, I could not fully appreciate the all-natural treat that had been presented to me, by the most humble natural people I had ever met. As much as I found it to be educational and refreshing, the longing for the comfort was too strong at times. But the simplicity of their lives never failed to fascinate me and gave me temporary peace of mind. No sophistication, no complications.

It would take me a whole lot of suffering to finally understand them. All life was simplicity. All life was a cycle. But back then, I was confused. The new experience opened a new door, added another dimension to my shallow perception. Fear and inexperience had clouded my vision all along. I was only focusing on the ideas that I was shaped to believe, yet I realized that real life was in the periphery. Images could be deceiving; we see what we want to watch. But real perceptions are by far deeper and wider in dimension. Maybe I was trying too hard in searching for the needle in a haystack, but on closer inspection, all the haystack could have been a pile of needles. When one tried too hard, one loses faith in one's mind, and emotions take over, clouding one's vision and causing the misinterpreting of simple wisdom. But then, if all could keep the experiences in the back of our heads, our tribulations might have been trivial.

❀

Headed back to the very land I shuffled about, one fact was undeniable: maybe envy was what had been driving me blind over the things I had taken for granted. Reserved as the Norwegians were, maybe it was the weather; it was not easy trying to make the locals close to you. Some were not at all used to seeing chocolate faces. They would just stare at you as if you had been dropped from the sky. There were also those who were offended when they saw us in numbers, thinking probably that we moved way up north, braving the cold, thinking we were safe from any intrusion, but were somehow ruining it for the others who were born here. Funny though, after all the five hundred years of contact and all the Internet networking turning the world in to a small village, we still turned heads. Congo once joked, "man, I feel like a superstar, man. Looking at me everywhere I go, like the paparazzi. Maybe I should start signing autographs."

But one thing we all agreed upon was the governance. We did not blame the people lacking faith in the gods; the rest of the world was still killing each other. Napoleon was rumored to have said, "Religion is what stops the poor from killing the rich!" Instead, the rich had built nice churches in which the poor were to pray the problem away, or so it seemed at times. Walk past the town, one saw poverty. It was astonishing: row after row of almost identical wooden houses. The owners had cars, boats, and bikes. And that was just an ordinary middle class neighborhood. They had every material thing any family in the rest of the world would wish for, even an American one. Despite the weather, they were beyond safe and sound; they were very comfortable!

Had we had leaders or parties in Eritrea that really took care of citizens even half as well as the Norwegian government did, no citizen would have ever thought of leaving. Even the farthest town had every facility a modern city would have. I had lived in some border towns where the people were not even sure which country they lived in. Despite the weather, comfort was guaranteed at the other end of the world! Something must be really wrong on our side of the world. At times, I contemplated whether I should blame the high brows; it was pride and a natural state of being territorial.

The Boiling Point

The Mottak had never been the same since Cliff relocated; the pressure was piling up on me. After the recent visit of Big Man in June to our town, I felt as if I had let myself down big time. I felt that I had squandered a big chance, probably my only way out. I had never felt so lonely in my entire life. Even my closest friends around the Mottak had a blood brother close by to rely on if something went wrong. There were times that I wished I spoke French, such as when Congo and his French-speaking buddies got into a heated conversation in French, and I sat staring at the dull ceiling until someone bothered to explain in English. Or whenever we got together to watch some Nigerian movie, Cliff and his countrymen would giggle and converse in Igbo and pidgin, while I smiled along like a stupid kid. I was not on the same wavelength as my countrymen, who had long been assimilated into the society as they chased the greens; I was a misfit trying to fit with the unfit. Sure, there were a couple of guys I could converse with in my mother tongue, but none to whom I talked as I sometimes had with Cliff or Congo. None to whom I could pour out my soul. There were times that the West Africans in particular felt aggrieved by the prejudice of some of my countrymen, and would vent their frustration whenever we went out together.

In one induced occasion, listening to some good old reggae, Dudu had blurted out of the blue, "You people are Arabs!"

"What do you mean by Arabs?" exclaimed Preacher, who was still mourning the authorities' rejection of his case. I echoed the question.

"You are mixed with Arabs and think you are better than us."

"We respect your tradition and history more dan you," Cliff added.

"What?" I was not quite sure if that was a joke, and I waited for clarification.

"Why don't you people show respect to King Haile Selassie, like any other black man do? Tell me."

Preacher came to my rescue. "You have no idea; ze man was revered by some tribes, while he was a hated figure among some tribes whose people were oppressed during his regime. Believe me, was I an Eritrean, I would have hated him as well; he broke international agreements and forcefully annexed Eritrea wiz Ethiopia. But not everybody in Ethiopia is proud of ze Tribe of Juda thing, my brazers!"

"but here in Babylon," Congo commented, "it is dat man who fought for your black skin. You have to look at de big pikcha. Not in tribal lines, me brodda. You see de white man only teach its young about the good deeds of deir great man. But us, in Africa, we never appreciate our idols. We always like to bring down deir name, and most of the negative is passed on to de next generation."

"a hero is never celebrated at home. Never forget zat, my brazer," I added, in agreement.

"So why do you people think you are better than us?" Dudu questioned coldly. "I even hear someone from your country with a darker skin than me calling me 'black man' in the same tone the white man use. Tell me why, I just want to know!" His rage and fury hissed through his nostrils.

"it is history, man," I replied. "We still suffer from zat prejudice in our country, my man. Tribes wiz superiority and inferiority complexes..."

"I am not talking about tribes," interrupted Dudu. "I am talking about the same look. Not all of you, but some, give the rest of us Africans the same look we get from non-Africans. Like looking down or something." Dudu was on his feet, with a furious look on his face.

"hey, man, we were never colonized," Preacher retorted. "we had civilization zat stretched for thousands of years. Ze white man taught us nothing. Zey came with ze bible, we showed zem ours. We accepted Christianity way before zey did. We had and still have our own alphabets and calendar. Don't you forget zat? Maybe zat is why some feel like looking down on ozers, who had everything taught to them by ze white man!" Preacher eyes were nearly jumping out of their sockets.

"no, no, no, my brodda, don't go there," Dudu cautioned, wiggling his pointed fingers towards Preacher. "The white man came and we all had our own civilization. Maybe some way more advanced than others, but we all had our established ways that were working perfectly for us. Maybe you should educate yourself about the rest of your neighbors, instead of taking too much pride in your own history. Okay, you were not colonized and you preserved your culture, but my friend, the white man might have renamed our rivers and mountains, but dey never took our spirit. We still have our colorful culture and most lost their written language with Babylon alphabets. Have you ever heard of the Benin civilization, my friend? That is where I come from."

"Yeah, I know little," replied Preacher calmly. "My brazer, but our culture is very different from ze rest of Africa and even different in religion and tradition from ze Arab world. Since we had lived secluded from ze rest of ze world for far too long, some still are a bit suspicious of others. But make no mistake, we are Africans."

"Ayy, African when you are only rejected by the white man and others. I have seen some of you, my friend. You would rather be with white people or other non-Africans than with Africans."

"no, don't forget, my man," I said. "some Eritreans who live by ze coast have been more in contact with the Arabs zan Africans, zeir tradition is ze same, so don't expect zem to relate to you just because you come from Africa. Ze same wiz some coming from Muslim tribes along ze Sudanese border," I came in defense, as the attacks were becoming personal.

"so you telling me some of you are Arabs and some are not? Which ones are the Arabs? The light skinned ones or what?"

"no, people have been intermarrying for centuries, my brazer," Preacher stated calmly. "Sometimes you have three different shades of skin in ze same family. But I know some claim to be full Arabs, some say 50 percent Arabs, some say pure Africans or Jews."

"Yeah, I hear you people are Semites, like the Jews in Israel." Dudu's inquisitions kept coming.

"No, we are not Jews, my brazer," Preacher retorted, "but zere are black Jews zat had been living in ze region for centuries, called Felashas. But our history claims we may have migrated from ze land of Solomon thousands of years before, maybe, and intermarried with ze local tribes. But ze white man classified as Semites some Kush and some Nilotic, based on ze language. Otherwise, we look ze same, eat ze same food and most have ze same religion."

"so, which one are you? Are you the one who thinks he's an Arab or a black African?" he asked, looking towards both of us, as the rest were quietly observing every word of the conversation.

"I am black on both sides, my brazer," I replied, hoping the subject would cease at once.

"I am a proud Habesh, but make no mistake, I am no Arab. I see myself as a black African!" remarked Preacher, with a gleam in his eyes.

"now I respect you, my black brodda!" Dudu extended his hands for the both of us, as if he just confirmed our blackness.

"don't forget some who forget to look at the mirror and look down on others," Preacher added. "And they come from all cultures, not just Habesh. I have seen many other Africans who married white women, have white friends, and suddenly zey forget zey are black, and look away when you see zem!"

"I know, my brodda. Many have sold out. Dat is why we even sold each other out in the first place. But believe me, when dat man would neva see himself at the mirror. Be proud of who you are and stay strong. Our time will sure come one day. Now, drink. We are talking too much." with that, he raised the half-full glass of homemade vodka.

"amen, amen, my brazer." The relieved Preacher raised his glass, saying, "But know who you are. Besides, no matter how light your skin looks, zey still will call you a nigga anyway! But cheers, my brazer!"

Unlike me, who wished to end the subject about identity, the ever-carefree Knut fidgeted in a corner before dragging himself into the conversation, when we least expected him to be interested. "let me ask you this, ahh, why do you people keep sayin' Babylon that? You understand me, every reggae song blames everything on Babylon..."

"Babylon is de oppressing system dat fuckin' de world, my friend," the exasperated Cliff snapped, hoping the interrogation would end there.

"but Babylon was an old empire somewhere in the Middle East. I think it was in Iraq. What's that got to do with black people?"

"No, man, not the historical Babylon," Dudu responded. "Rastas refer Babylon to Anglo-Saxon domination of the world and they impose their system to continue their oppression. So, it is only a metaphor. You know, a lot of people take the Rasta philosophy either too lightly as free-spirit, ganja-smoking hippies, or just too literally. But the Rasta philosophy is rich with myths, ideologies, and metaphors from their positive point of view. Understand me." Dudu was back to his composed, "enlighten the crowd" mode.

"okay. That is cool. I like the Rasta stuff, you know. The 'one love' philosophy. But I don't dig the Jah Selassie stuff." Knut wanted more.

"like I said. It's complex and diverse. You know, it is not only Jamaican; it is a worldwide movement. There are like different sects and houses of Rasta faith, with similar ideologies but different interpretations and rituals. One thing you should know is not all Rastas consider Ras Tefari, Haile Selassie, as the prophet. He sure was a messenger. You must understand the significance of Jah Selassie in those times." he paused to drag a long puff of the rolled ganja before he continued. "When the black man was striving to be recognized as equal all over the world, the story of an Ethiopian king who had reigned over a vast fruitful land, surrounded yet untouched and respected by white Europeans, was a myth. A glint of a source of pride in those dark times, broddas, they used to tell the young that there lives a mighty black king in a castle guarded by fierce lions and thousands of loyal army, and all white men cower in his presence. And imagine what those people felt when that witnessed majestic emperor descended down the plane in his graceful attire."

"what about the dreadlocks? What has that got to do with the movement?" Knut's curious eyes were even wider this time around.

"the roots of the tradition come from different corners of Africa, my man," Dudu continued calmly. "The Mau Mau Kikuyu rebels had distinct dreadlocks. The rebels that hid in the bushes from the European colonizers in the early days of Jamaica were said to be dreadlocks. They give the British some hard time, my man. The British finally agreed with them; they would leave them alone. In exchange, they would not allow any slaves in their territory."

"cool! You are killing the rotation, man!" smiled Knut, in awe, while extending his right hand to receive the herb from Dudu.

"Yeah, man," I said. "But monks in Ethiopia, we call zem Bahetawi, still have long natural hairs. Ze beard also grows down naturally, like ze disciples of Jesus. Many Bahetawi had traveled to Jamaica to spread the word of God after Selassie's visit. Zey still in ze monasteries up the hills, you know. Maybe zey had also some influence on ze followers as well."

"Yeah, even in de bible, Samson," Cliff contributed. "His natural long hair was de source of his power. He lost his power when dat bitch cut his hair. De natural hair is spiritual, I tell you." Cliff shook his head in recognition, while dragging the tiny roll, merely hanging by the tip of his gigantic fingers.

"ayy, too bad your hair don't grow more dan two inch, Cliffo," chided Congo. "Never seen his hair grow, I tell you, my broddas."

to which we all laughed.

The timely, soft tune of Culture's "Humble African" played on the speakers, to which we all swayed in harmony.

I am a humble African
Passing through Babylon
I am a humble African
I trouble no one
Some say am a Rasta man
I am a humble African.

"Aay, the old Rasta man was all natural, my brothers," said Dudu, moved by the song. "They cherished nature. They just allowed nature be, knowing they were just guests. In respect of appreciation to nature and confirming to the natural ways, they let de hair grow down and form dreadlocks. But it's an all-African thing, I read, in many instances. I tell you, I found out that in almost every African country dreadlocks were related to warriors. It is like paying tribute to all the ancient warriors, you understand me. Like getting closer to your roots through the natural."

"eh hey, I told you, we have dem. Dem born wi dada," Cliff interjected. "Before de went to war, our forefaders used to dreadlock de hair with clay. Gave dem fearsome look, I tell you," he said, while struggling to roll the overstuffed rizzla.

"we have people in our country, man," I said. "Ze Kunamas and some Coastal tribes still dreadlock zeir hair naturally. And zeir women, too. Zey apply some clay to it, some spiritual thing, I tell you," I said, conjuring all the images of the beautiful Kunama tribe experience.

"but in Congo, and some Rasta people I been wid, tell me de Rasta represent de mane of de lion. De natural crown of the king of de African plain. Lions live and reign in Africa, when de are taken away in captivity, de still wear de crown to show no one can take it away. De remain kings. So de blacks in captivity all over de world felt spiritually connected, but dose who realize of der roots grew der hair to show dey were once kings," said Congo, before taking a long drag of the shambolic rolled ganja.

"you guys know about the Buffalo Soldier, right?" Dudu said, looking around at the fuzzy but attentive bunch, who all nodded in recognition of Bob Marley's famous song. "it was actually the red Indians named them Buffalo Soldiers when they marched in the fields, segregated from the white solders. With their dreadlocks and their full-grown beards, they looked exactly like the buffalo. They were promised freedom after the war; they were fearless and marched forward like a buffalo would. Ze Indians, though they hunted it, had huge respect for that wild tenacious beast, my friends. Ze dreadlocks made history in all corners, my friends," Dudu narrated.

"You know, it's funny," Congo said, with a smile. "Dis Rasta man I met in Amsterdam told me one thing, very interesting, my broddas. He asked me why I grow my hair. I said, it's because I like Rasta. He asked me the meaning of the dreadlocks. He said when you see more than three full-grown dreadlocks; it signifies the assembly of kings of kings. You see, der is only one king to a pride of lions. And no full-grown lion would allow another full grown male lion to be around his territory. But in Zion, all de kings shall gather and be together peacefully. So, he told me, be proud when you see de gathering of many Rastas. It is a rare blessing," he said.

We all nodded at the new piece of wisdom.

Dudu ruffled his back pocket for his wallet to unveil a tattered brown piece of paper and raised it up for all to see. "I read this on a book a long time ago and I had to tear this page from the local library."

we all laughed at that as he cleared his throat and read out in a grave tone, "If the white man has the idea of a white God, let him worship his God as he desires. If the yellow man's God is of his race, let him worship his God as he sees fit. We, as Negroes, have found a new ideal. Whilst our God has no color, yet it is human to see everything through one's own spectacles, and since the white people have seen their God through white spectacles, we have only now started out (late though it be) to see our God through our own spectacles. The God of Isaac and the God of Jacob, let Him exist for the race that believes in the God of Isaac and the God of Jacob. We believe in the God of Ethiopia... We shall worship him through the spectacles of Ethiopia."[1]

We all beamed in the wisdom and the vibe that had transformed from the tense beginning and blazed the night away until we headed out to town.

The ganja had become a preferred method of medication, of late. As every time I held the beer bottle with my thumb and my forefinger, it somehow had begun to feel like a loaded gun with the end of the muzzle pointed at my gaping mouth. The drinking was losing the ability to dissipate my latest mini-depression. Every gulp that drained down my throat felt like a rash of liquefied bullets. Hesitantly picking up the bottle with my index finger pointed as far away from the bottle, I slurped the least amount possible. Never had the loaded bottle felt that heavy. The beer tasted so warm and vile, like a stranger's bile inside my mouth. The very thought of swallowing down another's bile nearly forced me to vomit. I choked and held it down. I felt the bullet hitting my gut. To make matters worse, I had not had a decent meal since the night before. I looked away, hoping to brush off the thought, and caught a glimpse of the gaping fridge where Congo's chubby hands were trying to rip a beer from the hard paper rings. The dripping beer bottles, lined up in perfect rows, looked like a firing squad.

The mood inside had simmered down, with heads bobbing rhythmically to Peter Tosh's "No Sympathy" playing from Dudu's iPod, the melancholic deep voice echoing the sad piercing lyrics felt like the soundtrack to my thoughts...

> *I cant find no love, no sympathy,*
> *what kind of love they got for me,*
> *I am on my way,*
> *to happy day*
> *where I can find some peace and rest...*

I kept going, though. My drained soul bled in squirts that never leave a visible mark, only a blaze of sorrow. Yet, I just could not

---

1 Erskine, Noel Leo. "The Roots of Rebellion and Rasta Theology in Jamaica." London: Equinox Publishing Ltd., 2007, p. 118.

get myself to stop from once again reaching for the bottle. Did I have drinking problem, as well?

Later on, wounded from the rain of bullets in an empty stomach, yet alive in stupor, I would kick and spray my hands on the dance floor, like a call for help from a drowning fellow. Yet nobody ever comes to the rescue.

❦

Though I had begun to get tired of our outings, they had become a duty I could not afford to miss. Maybe it was a cry for recognition. To remind people that we were still out there. It had become more of an obligation, so my waking moments were spent in the company of Cliff and Co.

When the awkward moments of my situation alienated me and put me under the most pressure, I would contemplate joining some of my countrymen who had turned to God for salvation. Some had become ardent followers. Some people turned to God in times of trouble, but they often took full credit when things were going their way. Tired of running away from my own demons, I had contemplated visiting the chapel for some spiritual guidance, but my faith had long ago been shaken, and shaken hard. The divisions and the politics involved did not help, either.

As an Orthodox Christian, I'd grown up going to the nearest church, Saint Michael, for Sunday sermons, and dreaded most of them with a growling stomach. For some reason, the Lord did not like full stomachs. During the endless fasting seasons, you had to give up meat and milk, if you were from a strict family— that was nearly half the year.

The Great Lent (Abye Tsome or Hudade, Day of Duty) was the longest fasting period. It began eight weeks before Easter. This Lent was observed as a remembrance of the forty days and nights fasting of our Lord Christ after His baptism. Later, the Ethiopian church added fifteen more days to it. Therefore, the Great Lent consisted of fifty-five days total instead of forty days, like the Catholic Church.

Then came the Fast of the Prophets (Tsome Nebiyat), observed from 25 November to 6 January. It is called the Fast of the Prophets because the prophecy about the coming of Christ was fulfilled and Christ was born.

156

The Nineveh Fast was a three-day fast, Monday, Tuesday, and Wednesday. It fell at one time in January and another in February. It commemorated the mission of Jonah and it was a fast of the repentance of the people of Nineveh.

The Fast of the Apostles (Tsome Hawariat) started the Monday after Pentecost and ended by 12 July, which is the Feast of Saint Paul and St. Peter. The reason was because the two apostles were murdered on that day. The length of this observance varied depending upon the date of Easter and could be a minimum of fourteen days and a maximum of forty days. The apostles observed this fast after the manner of Moses and Christ. Moses fasted for forty days after he received the Ten Commandments, but before he preached the Law to the people, and Christ fasted for forty days right after He was baptized and before he preached the Gospel.

The Assumption of the Virgin Mary (Tsome Filseta) fast was kept strictly by the church from 7 to 21 August.

On January 21 of the Ethiopian Calendar (29 January on the European Calendar), the Virgin Mary died.

Wednesday and Fridays were observed because on Wednesday, a counsel took place together to put Christ to death and on Friday he was crucified for our salvation. Besides that, the apostles found it necessary to observe fasting for two days in the week for the remission of whatever sins may have been committed during that week.

The vast majority of the older generation still actively practiced most of these demanding rituals. The global influx of modernism and the effective Protestant movement had caused its influence to wane among the young. The church, with deep roots to the monarchy, still had influence and a vast property in both Eritrea and Ethiopia. Though years of independence struggle, the systematic suppression of religion by the dictatorial state of Eritrea, and the considerable impact of well-funded Protestantism, the faithful Orthodox Church followers were weakened, but the churches were never empty. Deeply engrained in the mentality of these Christians was a fear of the wrath of God that hovered thickly in everyday life. At times of trouble, especially the mothers turned to their favorite saint.

Though I had not been to church for quite some time, in desperate times, I had bowed down and asked for guidance. But the teachings, I had found them to be misleading and very contradicting. With the church's blighted past of often meddling with politics and at times openly alienating certain sectors of society, my trust had been eroded. Besides, I was too conscious of my sins to nonchalantly step into a church and shrink through the stinging words of the head priest overplaying the fear factor. The good book had said it was what came out the mouth, but not what went in, that was an abomination to the word of God, so I did not see the whole purpose of malnourishing myself with a heart full of tainted intentions. The books I had been reading poked at the inconsistencies of the holy book and the church, and further provoked the questions and reservations I'd had before.

The obsession with other religions and factions would, at times, be part of the sermon. Hatred and division often stemmed from the priest who twisted the holy books to reinforce their misconceptions about others. Congregating just for the sake of being labeled a faithful churchgoer, to be playing hide and seek from neighbors, to conceal one's lifestyle—these all contradicted the strict Orthodox way of life, but were common and hypocritical. Living a double life was an order of the day for many, just for the sake of being a part of the community.

It was too easy to forget that the whole purpose of religion was to give comfort and deliverance, not fear and anxiety. Instead of the message inscribed in the holy book, it was its messengers who were feared and revered. The message was clear in all religions, delivered in different times by different messengers. Who cares which postman delivered the letters, so long you got yours on time? Instead of striking fear in the believers by telling us that we should avoid the devil, why not teach us that we were all capable of conceiving evil deeds and the devil actually lives with us? Instead of expecting miracles, why not teach us to find peace by containing the devil inside? Only a man at peace with himself can find peace with others. Prostrating in public won't cleanse all the demons inside.

Facing my own devils in the quest to find out what my fate held for me, I did not need more stress or to starve myself for the next life. I wanted it all here and now. I'd lived through hell so I wanted my piece of heaven right then. Yet, I was conscious and at times superstitious of His omnipresence.

But there, in the Mottak, rather than the desolation camp, I was definitely aware of the waste of time, ticking away in slow motion. It dawned on me that all my daydreams were baseless. The dream setting had become the reality; yet, it had turned into a bit of a nightmare. That tiny glimmer of hope was extinguished. Besides, everything around us was in order, running on schedule; everybody else was on the payroll, paid handsomely by the hour, just to watch us self-destruct in time.

Everything about the Mottak reminded us of time and our failures. The ticking could be heard louder than one's own heart, and you could try to hide but couldn't get away. The order was everywhere, so better to sleep through most of it if you could, as the jury had long been out, almost two years, still waiting for the verdict. Could they have found something I did not know about? Maybe I had been switched in the hospital and that my real parents were from a faraway, safer land? I had no idea, but I seen one after the other move on, while I remained glued to my bunk. I had been in the same room ever since my arrival, with my bunkmates changing, one after the other, every couple of months. I got to a point where I did not even bother to welcome or greet a newcomer. Got fucking tired of it; meeting and getting to know the roommates. Some I liked, but then we all got sick of each other. Before you knew it, you didn't even talk to each other, unless it was to remind each other of the mandatory chores we did in turns.

Two summers went by, and I was still hassling, processing, grinding thought after thought. It was bothersome to have all the time in the world to think. I was not sleeping much, unless I was high or drunk. As a human, maybe I was a victim of my own inability to relate my worst experiences into reasoning and to cheer myself on to keep my hopes high. But you know what? I was just tired of hoping all my life. When do I get to live it, man? Maybe I was a dreamer who never stopped for a minute to appreciate my blessings. Sometimes I did, though, appreciate life and the journey I had traveled, but mostly when I was high. I didn't smoke much, and had no addictions except for cigarettes.

I was not raised up to end up a ganja smoker. It was just that circumstances had pushed me leftwards in life. However, when high, besides the occasional paranoia and confusion, it had a serene, reflective, self-tuning effect, without the ego.

In that atmosphere, with soft reggae music on, simmering in my mellow state, I felt alive. Time lapsed. Space and all barriers collapsed into shapeless colors and patterns. All that breathed became breath itself, dancing along casually with the colors. The fusion was harmony, all rippling like trapped smoke trails. Damn, I wished it was always as peaceful as that.

Then you wake up feeling blue, wishing to lay back and relax, but got the greens to chase. It was not easy being brown, with them pinkies labeling me black, doing things in black in their white-run rag, constantly on the red light to be reminded of what was white and what was black while I struggled, colorless like water. Such a shame, though, even when you got to choose what kind of black you wished to be.

They say life is all about choices. I had made my fair share and it led me to a dead end. Except for random fantasies and unsynchronized dreams, I had begun to lose my zest for life. I no longer had any ambitions. If I had the balls, I would have diverted my path every time I had the chance, as some of my acquaintances had done; they took their destiny in their own hands and walked on tightropes. At least they were going somewhere. I was just in a limbo state, just waiting...

❈

You know, when you really give up on something after strenuously waiting, you finally exhaust the glimmer of hope you had and gradually start to look for other options. When that happened, even the imagination refuses to choose a different future. The mind enters the non-ambition mode. You eat and shit as usual. You start to feel more like a harmless zombie, waking and walking for no purpose at all.

Though sleep was the most favored pastime in the Mottak, I had not slept a decent sleep for long time. Once I lay down in bed, the routine had been the same: tossing and turning; listening to the melodic snoring from my roommate, the faint Somali conversations from the sleepless neighbors living next door, the loud banging of the doors, the loud Arabic and

Tigrigna curses, the few cars that passed by the Mottak. All this eventually simmered down to a still night. It was peaceful when it finally fell quiet. The silence would put me in a trance, and I would gradually surrender to the cousin of death.

But on that Tuesday morning of August 2010, the caged feelings of stashed anger, frustration, disappointment, and the desolation were unleashed. Even I could feel the lava inside through my nostrils every time I breathed. I could not pinpoint what tipped me over the edge, yet I knew I was in for a long fucking day.

Going back to bed had crossed my mind, yet I was starving. I had skipped dinner the night before, so I forced myself up. I did not even bother to wash my face. Lazily shuffling in my underwear, I headed towards the fridge. My worst fear was realized; there was nothing to drink, no bread, no leftovers; just a roll of ripe salad rolls, onions, an opened can of tomato sauce, expired peanut butter, an almost empty strawberry jam bottle, and a pile of spices, but nothing I could munch on. I slammed the fridge door so hard that I startled my roommate, Sleepy. The other two had been granted their approvals and settled in other communes to get on with their lives. He mumbled something and went back to sleep; I figured it was a cuss word. We had not been the best of friends lately.

I paced around the room for a second or two, trying hard to remember what to do next, and realized I had not had my morning smoke to clear my mind. I reached out for the chair near my bed, in search of my cigarette pack, which I had placed on top of the load of dirty clothes. *Have not really been taking care of myself, of late,* I noted, in disappointment. I picked up the pack so delicately, like an egg, just praying there would be one stick left. It was empty. I figured I'd had a long night, dragging on one cigarette after the other, lost, sinking deep into myself. I fumbled through my jeans pockets in search of loose coins. Once again, a mere 14 kroner, most of them in ones. I cussed in my mother tongue, barely muffing the words. Sleepy gave another disgruntled sigh.

The Merchant would not give me credit, since I had failed to pay him back for my last few packs on payday. And I was not in the mood to smooth talk my way for a pack; I was not in the mood to talk to anyone at all. I fumed and contemplated how many days of this fucked up pedigree I had left in my life. I hoped I had lived through most of them. I figured I'd had my share; somebody had to take over. I had been standing in the middle of the room, facing the wall and shaking my head. I sensed some movement from behind and realized my sorrow mate had woken up, probably startled to find me standing in the middle of the room, as if I was crammed in a long queue. He had his reservations that maybe I was losing it; there were times I caught him staring at me with genuine worry and suspicion, but no malice. I had been keeping to myself, and spending more time in my room. I did not blame him. Besides, we were on the same boat, waiting and waiting for the rescue team. It was hopeless, so I decided to take a shower and see the day out.

As expected, both the shower booths were occupied. I waited my turn, sitting on one of the crappers with my towel hanging over my shoulder. My turn came and I went in. I turned on the showerhead to the max but only cold water flowed from the pipes. I readjusted the heat and waited and waited. What were the odds? The fuckers must have finished all the hot water in the heating tank. So I had to wait longer. It was August; it was not that cold outside, even though it's never hot in the arctic. So, what the hell, and I jumped in. It was breathtaking, yet soothing. The water raining down on me like splinters, and cooled off the lava that was still boiling up inside.

After ten minutes in the shower, some Arab started hollering for me to hurry up. Trying to put my clothes on, I slipped and fell awkwardly on my back. I banged my head against the door and it burst open. The Arab, who was a nice new guy, peeked in and almost laughed out loud; it was a hilarious scene, wet and flat on my back, holding my head with both hands, nothing but my underwear on. But he restrained himself, noting the fire in my eyes.

I have to get back to bed before something really bad happens, I thought.

I hustled two cigarettes from an old Iranian veteran of the Mottak and shuffled my way back to the room. I was hoping I would run into somebody returning with a sizzling pan of anything edible. No one in sight, just long faces buried in their PC's, probably on Facebook, lying to somebody in Africa about how great their life was in Europe.

My stomach was churning and growling like an old angry street dog. I lit one cigarette and once again drifted back to nothing. My mind was overwhelmed, yet I felt empty. I could not focus on any singular thought. My mind was randomly jumping scenes like an over scratched DVD. My demons were on a rampage. I kept shaking my head at the way things had been shaping up in my life. When I was in deep, waist deep, in the endless drama of life somewhere in Africa, hanging by a thread, with death staring me right in my face, somewhere from the deep recesses of my hardened heart, a glimmer of hope would sprout to keep my mind sane. Sometimes, I would think of it as divine, yet again it would soon turn out to be vile! Yet again, I would fantasize my life being so fine and glamorous somewhere in the Western world, free from the tyranny of the self-deprecating, mentally exhausting, physically emaciating test of faith by my own fate, somehow, someway. We used to say, "mot wey America," (America or die!) the ultimate goal for any African dissatisfied with the endless miseries and mishaps in our lives to the land of opportunities. If not there, at least I would make it to Europe or South Africa.

That dream kept me alive through even ridiculous circumstances. It lifted my spirit to overcome any sort of difficulty. Then you begin to think, *After all this trouble I have been through, maybe God would ease the pain and it is time to count my gain.* You plan and re-plan and still plan. No matter how hard it would be to reach that goal, nothing would faze you. You have been hardened like a cornerstone. All the trials and tribulations will end one day. Then, you reach that goal after more hardships and endless lessons you have encountered along the way.

Reality was harsh. The trials never ended; in fact, they got harder! At times, despite technology, the only change I wanted in life was the switch of analogue problems for digitalized modern trends. If one was stranded in a limbo state where one led an invisible life, the dream began to fade. Some used this energy to divert their focus to alternatives. However, for those who wished to stick to their plan, they were in for the ride of their life. Stuffed and fed periodically, monitored and secluded systematically, one began to disintegrate. When the dream finally died, and you gave up, what waited a state of confused, loud, disturbing silence. Some confused it for depression, but I had long realized it was more a realization. It meant, *think of the days and nights you have wasted daydreaming to get here...*

Lying like a prosthetic leg leaning against the wall, waiting to be picked up by a handicapped person and put to some use, I hated my life and being so helpless. It could have been worse; I could have been dead somewhere in the desert like some of my friends. The death of a dream, though, was a death one lives through every day. *Carrying a cadaver around is not considered living,* I concluded. I dragged the cheap LM so deep, hoping the smoke would at least curb my growling appetite. As starved as I was, all I wanted was some ganja to simmer me down. *I just can't live like this, anymore!* That was all I knew at that moment. I had to do something about it or else it was going to kill me.

The longer you sat and stagnated, the richer of a breeding ground you became for negative thoughts. My demons would rap anxiously inside me, urging me, *a sitting duck, you are my friend. It is a personal battle not a social solution. You know what to do; pray for manna or prey after money! By any means necessary, remember!* Trapped and hanging by a thin grey thread of morals, I was on the brink of desperate measures. Anything would do, just a way out. On the other side was a not-so-reassuring voice, *this, too, shall pass, bro! The worst is behind you. Just remember: Good things come for those who wait. Just got to keep your head up!*

The raving thoughts had camped permanently in the park of my head, keeping me awake. Insomnia plus paranoia drove me to crave intoxication of any sort. I was constantly out, with or without invitation, with company of any sort. Misery loved company and I was never alone. In a losing battle inside my head, I was obsessed with negative thoughts radiating towards all who reminded me of any authority. Lashing out in every direction, in hope of relieving myself of the stress, I had been entangled awfully, like a fly trapped in a cobweb. Scene after scene of savagely violent reactions played and replayed in my head, like a Chinese karate movie. I would meticulously construct a scenario whereby I literally bashed some guy's head over and over again against a metal door for presumably talking behind my back. The rage would somehow dissipate, even though I would not dream of really enacting the scene. Times were that bad. I trusted no one and made quite few enemies. Still, I could not bear to be by myself unless I was in a chemical haze.

Some of the friends I had, whom the state had denied the legal means to make a living, had already swerved to underground means. No judgment—the end justifies the means, and besides, it had been said, "you can only get rich in the dark."

My stomach growled again. I knew my life would be different from that day on. It would be the day I would start evolving. I literally felt that last, thin, grey, moral thread snap inside my conscience. It soon became a mesh of dark. There were no more lines to cross.

❧

I finally made the call, the call I had been contemplating for the past couple of months. Big Man was in town; for some reason, his visits had become more frequent. Was it temptation, a coincidence, or more of a confluence? He already had a couple of brothers connected in town. After witnessing how we went around, he had said sarcastically, "hey, my broddas, wid de connection you have in dis town, eeey, you make big money. Mtsee, you people know everybody! You don't even have to stay in a corner, customers come to you!"

His words had been ringing in my head for quite some time. Intoxicated as I was, I had asked, "for how much you give us? How much can we make?"

"my brodda, Cliff's big brodda is like family to me. I could give you 100 gram for five K. You know it cost a lot. Eh, hey, we pay for the mule to bring it all de way; it is expensive, me brodda. But I don't want to see you suffer like dis, mtsee."

Congo had somehow stopped me from inquiring further, but Big Man had told me to contact Cliff whenever I was ready.

I had spoken to Congo the next day, knowing it would remain between us. He was never warm to the idea. "My brodda, it is small town, you know," he argued. "We live in de camp; de place is full of nosy, jealous refugees. De hear of us making money, ayy, dey snitch on us, I tell you. I don't like it at all. At all, my brodda."

I was disappointed by what I heard. Though he was realistic, I did not need him to confirm my fears; I needed him to back me up. "you are just a bitch, man," I had snapped. "Just because you are afraid does not mean you have to scare me."

But being the ever-diplomatic Congo, he had made up some funny jokes about the gang signs and running after the police; hypothetical scenes that had brought a smile back to my weary face.

But then, I was made up, no going back. I made the call to Cliff and told him I would come by to his place about a serious matter. He picked up my gist and told me to rush down the hill to his hideout.

❧

It was a more constructive and professional meeting than I had attended in a long time. Big Man was perched on the bed of that tiny apartment, with a sight of the window overlooking the town and the TV on the far corner. Cliff was making his signature rice with spicy chicken. The aroma had flooded the entire apartment.

"my brodda, I see you are ready to talk business, now!" Big Man got straight to the point while he stared into my eyes, reading my intentions.

"yes, man, it's about time," I replied, shaking my head in dismay.

Cliff was awfully quiet for a change, paying full attention to the conversation, yet kept his mind on the thick sauce brewing in the pot on his stove.

After an awkward silence, Big Man said, "you know we are broddas." He folded his hands closer to his chest, looking grave. "and dey all speak highly of you. Dat means I trust you. But, brodda, business is business! Never forget dat!"

I nodded in total agreement and show of commitment, but I sensed he was a guy not to cross.

"You know dis town very well, so you have no problem, ah?"

Running the scenes from my endless daydream as a kingpin, I was convinced I would manage very well. "I have no problem, my brazer. I can handle it."

Big Man nodded and muttered something incomprehensible under his breath. "You know de product and de price?" he asked, hoping for a positive response.

"Yeah, I know very well," I said too quickly. Maybe I was showing too much enthusiasm, I worried.

"Okay, my brodda. We talk about oder arrangements some oder time, but you discuss de rest wid Cliff and someone will give you de stuff next week!" With that, he offered me his hand as if welcoming me warmly to the family.

I got up and shook the hand firmly.

I declined the dinner offer, as tempting as it was. I just needed to get some fresh air and take a long walk to process what had just transpired. I crossed the street towards the bus station. A cool breath brushed past me from the open sea, sending shivers up and down my spine, yet all I felt was relieved. Two young blondes giggled past me, clad in their miniskirts. I had no idea how they coped with the weather so well. I changed my mind about the need for a long walk; the ocean was more inviting. I skirted my way around the dock, towards the library.

The seagulls were circling the abandoned benches facing the ocean, picking up leftover junk food from the bin. I startled a few of them as they squawked and wailed away, to hover right back. For such an amazing open spot, the benches were often lonely, except for a few students from the nearby campus who loitered around. I felt like a bird at that very moment—not a seagull, but at least somehow free. I sat on the cold bench, buttoning up my sweater to the top.

What a day it was!

I breathed out a gust of relief and looked around the surroundings and remembered what Dudu had once said. "Fucked up situations stifle your sense of natural appreciation, man!" he told me, when he recalled how tourists would get so excited over little mysteries of nature that we often walked past, oblivious, burdened with life. But the scene in front of me was breathtaking. With the late arctic sun on the horizon, the submerged hills were transformed into a magnified Japanese moss garden pruned immaculately by the ever-busy hand of nature. It sure was a delight to be out in the sun, surrounded by the bright green, which had once been covered by ice, even though it was a little cold.

It was freezing all year round up at the rim of the globe, in fact. In the winter the earth comes into a halt, a salute to Mother Earth and the mighty darkness. Everything underneath the blanketing pitch blackness is sheathed in ice, a total contrast, a black on white like the print letters abstractly suspended on a rugged white sheet of paper. It was just waiting for one to decipher the mystery; those who fail were punished by the endless, cruel, excruciating, deep depression that crept in and lingered seasonally. The darkness was just a beauty concealed, never abandoned. Even the whisper of the skies left a trail of fusing colors some nights. Sometimes I heard the voices; so charming, soothing and so melodic, like the blues of the skies above, with the music of the night illuminating the endless night sky like a new celebrity hot spot in town, but this time it was just the lights that dance to the beat of the night sky. It was a sky disco—or the Nordlys, as the locals call the Northern Lights phenomenon.

And in the summer, it was breathtaking. It was a mystery how nature shape-shifts like a slow-motion kaleidoscope to mesmerize over and over again. You look down, lost in the endless season of human drama, and in a moment the whole sky would have changed. The trees were the most tenacious of all, though. Wished I was one of them. They sprang to life always on time, biding their time out in the open down to their bare bones, withstanding the wrath of the darkness for showing off too much on those bright days. They never protested, though, standing still until their time was due.

There was something magical about the midnight sun. Ecstasy, a climax of a momentary occurrence, was a foreign affair in this part of the world. Something about this place was too consistent to be ecstatic. A mild, clear, serene moment suspended endlessly like the simmering yet never scalding sun hovering mildly in the bright blue sky was almost like the memory of a majestic, crystal chandelier of a dome you have only stood under once, replayed over and over.

Redemption

Every door I banged on and kicked in desperation was bolted shut. It was dark and the hounds were hot on my heels. I could feel their panting on my neck. I screamed out for help. No one except my own screeching cry echoed in reply from the tiny, dark, narrow, slippery, dead-end, muddy alley I was running through. I could feel peeping heads and heaving curtains in some windows, yet no one came to my rescue. I realized my doom was near and I had been abandoned by all.

Then they went quiet, as if saying their prayers before a meal. I waited, hoping and praying to the forty-four tabots and saints in my head. Then, with one howl, I felt them all rip into me at once, thousands of sharp teeth digging at once...

I woke up gasping for breath. I was drenched in sweat, cold sweat.

I looked over at the silhouette of a still-curled figure of Sleepy, barely moving, from across the room. I was sure I had made some noise, but it took a grenade to shake Sleepy of his vegetative restive state at night. Fuck! The nightmares had never gone so far before. I often had bad dreams when I was anxious and in crisis, yet never had I been torn apart by beasts. This was a sign I could not really figure out; then, with a flash, I recalled the blood test I had taken months ago. The reply had taken too long! Had they found out something worrisome, something like HIV? I breathed heavily, blurting in my mother tongue, "this is just too much!"

Sure, I was lethargic as ever, but it was normal under the setting and the circumstances. *Besides, I'm just stressed out; there's nothing wrong with me,* I assured myself, with a hesitant glance up to the shielded sky.

Or could it be something else? Something to do with my recent activities! No it was just nerves, it was just a dream, only a bad dream. But some dreams had come true in the past. Even nightmares had been replicated in my reality. As a firm believer in instincts, I often felt bad news coming. Whatever step I was planning had felt bad, as well—very bad.

Congo had taken the place of my moral conscience, repeatedly discouraging me from pursuing the other way out, after I had confronted him after my glorious visit with Big Man. "my brodda, don't forget: blood is always thicker dan water. On good days, he might be your brodda. But when disaster strikes, we all race back to our countrymen. Dey have each oder; besides, you know de can get back to deir country at der will. But can you? Think about de consequences and de escape plan, my brodda. If you are ready, den, my friend, good luck. But I play no part. I don't have de stomach for dis shit, my brodda, to tell you honest!" His watery white eyes were glued to mine for some time, as if he was trying to sync some sense in to me. But I had decided otherwise. I was just waiting for the next shipment and I was in business. I had never been that excited in my entire life. The adrenalin kick had bolstered my confidence. It was a fresh start. I wiped off the sweat and went back to sleep this time, directing the scenes of my dream.

Congo and Cliff had already been connected to the network, so I had no trouble getting into it. Cliff had been the first to make the link, after our first year. Congo had been a late entrant. Even though I was not in the business, I knew most of the connections, the deals, their nature, and the price of the commodity very well. There was not much discretion when it came to business among the brothers. In fact, you just learn to respect what they do, and keep your nose out of their business. So there was no need for orientations; it was in its making.

There was no introduction to the game. You buy a good quality hash from the supplier and cut it into grams and deliver it to your customers at a reasonable price. The locals already thought I was a pusher; maybe they saw me with other pushers, or just as the usual stereotype—they label blacks who hang around the town. Regardless, I was in the game with no trouble at all. I had dealt once or twice on behalf of some friends before, so the nerves were all right. Operating in a small town was a risk, especially as obvious outsiders. You know one day you are going down, so you make the best of it when you are around.

Another problem was there were so many pushers. They were from all cultures, all with their own tight circles. Most kept a low profile, keeping loyal customers on the regular. Ours was different; we were doing it in the open. With most of the clients based in the few bars and clubs in the town, we had to often hang around the scene to maintain availability. It was hell of a risk, yet it was more profitable and more fun. With us being out on most nights, we were constantly having fun, keeping our minds off our other problems, and often spreading our network, while keeping a wary eye on the police.

The thrill was exhilarating; I could never deny that! The attention very tempting, the money was reassuring, and the adrenalin was an all-time high. Sure it could fool you, but then you never know when you were going to die, so why stress?

It did not take too long for me to get the hang of the business. Before I knew it, I felt as if I had been doing it forever. Though there were plenty of brands in the market, our brand was the most expensive and its quality was unmatched. They called it the Alonso, after the F1 driver.

Running the Alonso in the narrow streets of a small Norwegian town, I felt like a new man. I was more at peace with my demons; ever since I handed over all responsibility, they had not stirred my anxiety for quite a while. There was just a dangerous silence inside. Sure, once in a while, my will and conscience, buried deep under the rubble of demons upstairs, would instigate uncomfortable thoughts regarding the consequences of my recent actions. But then my demons would squash the thoughts: *You want to get back to the vegetative state you had been for the past two years?*

At least my demons were keeping me on my toes. Any outlet was fine at that very moment.

You know beginners luck? I was making easy money with fishermen and locals from smaller towns nearby, who called me regularly for a bulk supply. That eased of the risk having to peddle in bits and pieces in the open. With the newfound money and boosted confidence, I felt like the man. Since I was able to acquire my goods without many middlemen involved, my profits were handsome.

For the first time since my arrival in Babylon, I was in the position to be thinking about others' welfare—my closest friends, whom I had shut out for a long time, and my extended family whom I seldom contacted. I was calling and offering any sort of assistance now. I would be able to send a couple of hundred kroner to the stranded brothers and close ones. The gratitude coming from desperate friends would fuel my ambition to get more; more money, less problems, I figured.

Our headquarters were at Cliff's. Every businessman and the rest of the entourage were literally benched there throughout the day. Every once in a while, somebody's telephone would ring: "hey, who is this?... Yeah, I remember you now. How much... You know the price for one, huh... in fifteen minutes? Okay, see you!" That was the regular service center conversation that would set off a run to meet the customer.

There was always competition and backbiting involved, especially if one was a newcomer stealing an established customer. The old guard, paranoid and cautious, was suspicious of everyone. After a couple of run-ins with the authorities, some were on their last strike. They had established customers to whom they were just a call away at whatever time. They enjoyed making fun of our enthusiasm. "I was like you when I began, running around like I own the streets! Den, when the police catch you with your money and the stash, eh, you start to get a hang of de real deal. It is no easy, my broddas! Keep your eyes open at all times!"

For the fresh princes, creating your own sphere of influence meant meeting new folks. Risky as it was, the adrenalin made us feel a little invincible. It felt like I was a part of something for the first time in a long time. I even began to sleep like a hooker after a long weekend in the streets. I was no longer worried about my asylum case. I was a self-employed citizen making a good living. I no longer felt like a refugee in need of handouts.

Our shift, the fresh princes, was during the nighttime. After a drop by Cliff's place for a couple of refreshments and catch on the gossip, relevant to our area of expertise, we would then head out to town separately. If we were on duty, we often avoided bunching together; that would be a jackpot seizure for the police. Loaded with ammunition of every size and price, in separate secret pockets, I headed out to the local bars.

Here's how you do it: Keeping an eye on the frequent police patrols, you take a seat and order a drink, preferably outdoors with views from every angle. Acting naturally, like an ordinary fellow on a regular night out, you maintain eye contact with potential customers. Trying to pick out any suspicious characters in the meantime, you initiate conversations with those you presume are party guys. With the drinks loosening up the reserved tongues, conversations at times run for hours. Manipulating the conversation halfway, you tell them how crazy you used to get in the parties back at home and how easy it was to get any substance suitable for the moment. Taking the cue, most would either decline at once or hesitantly ask if you have something along. The bold ones cut to the chase and ask for it right away. Once they fall into your grasp, you play cautious and state, "I don't sell, but a friend of mine got some good stuff you should try out!" and head out, take a stroll, and come back to the same spot as if you had done them a favor. *what a nice guy,* some would think, and you go your way, having exchanged numbers and made a little something along the way, plus the free beer for your selfless services.

Cliff, Congo, and I ran into each other's way for quite a while, tipping and warning each other off. At times, we borrowed products or lent off a customer, just to keep the flow. Eventually, after making new acquaintances and meeting old ones, we headed back to either reload or ease off the cash pile, make quick calculations and head right back to work. As taught to us by the veterans and through our observations during our night out, we are well acquainted with the places and type of fellows to avoid. But the first rule was, never stay put with your stash in hand. You had to constantly move around, mingle, and act natural. In the meantime, you should enjoy yourself; it was a great job. At some point in the night, we got together in a bar and relaxed ourselves, shooting pool and guzzling beer. I could tell from their eyes what kind of night they were having, so no need to ask questions.

The night would end at home, locked in the toilet, doing accounting.

By the time I felt like my shift was up, I was a bit tipsy. Every pub I went to, every club I entered, I had to buy myself a drink like a regular customer. The week would fly by like that. Every day was like a Saturday. Customers flocked to me. Once I built a core list of them, it was all about maintaining the demand and availability. They always came running back.

The gang would get together on some weekdays whenever the Big Man was in town. Big Man, who had extended his services through an associate of his, would come around to collect royalties. The guy was sure expanding. We had heard the cops had hit him hard the past couple of weeks, with the seizure of major stashes in a couple of cities. Rumor had it, though, those were acceptable collateral losses for a guy who reportedly had connections as far as South America. Once we were under his wing, though, his attitude had become more assertive.

All the underground paperless hustlers would congregate for a huge party to somehow recognize and appreciate each other's progress despite the circumstances.

If the cops had ever ambushed us, they would have had the bust of the year, literally. Dudu would show up with a couple of new recruits. Young and feisty, something to feast the eyes on at times, knowing how much they cost. The Merchant would often drop by with some new merchandise to auction off; new watches, phones, iPods, and all sorts of accessories that we could afford by then. We felt truly invincible...

A loud bang woke me up from the best dream I'd ever had in my entire life. It was that sneaky cleaning guy reminding me of my chores. I waited for some movement from the other bed, but none came. Realizing Sleepy had cleaned the previous day, I marched out of bed with hope and energy for the first time in a long time. Some dreams had come true before—why not this one? It was not just attainable, it was right under my nose and I was full of conviction as I snatched the half-full bucket and the mop from the Arab and headed for the kitchen.

I heard the Arab hollering from behind, "you clean the oven good. *Det er skitten! Jeg kommer og kjekke den senere...!*"

I did not even reply. I was sure I was doing it for the last time.

In retrospect, I had been one of the luckiest motherfuckers, given the circumstances. I was still alive, for starters. I had lost some friends along the way. I came through my military stint unscathed; some had been mauled for life, while some had paid with their lives. I was young and healthy; they said the best was always yet to come. I was just too impatient: That had always been my undoing in life. I was restless at all times and reckless sometimes.

In the process of searching for another fresh start, I had stumbled into unchartered territories, some unwise and dangerous. I had faced my devils, had me a lot of sit-downs to reach a compromise with them. They had been relentless, but still they were my own demons, just trying to push me forward. *The end justifies the means,* they had screamed all along.

The next Monday, I had slept well into the morning when Sleepy, who had woken up abnormally early, marched in to the room with a gleam I had not seen in such a long time. On his heels was one of the ladies who worked at the office.

I hissed out a sigh of disgust and looked away, readying myself for another fine for violating one of the endless Mottak rules.

"come on, I have good news for you," she said, giggling. "Your asylum has been accepted by the UDI."

I kept looking at her. In fact, I never really paid close attention to her. She was in her mid-forties, still fit, liked wearing bright colors, and was aware of and loving the horny gaze of sexually frustrated residents. She sure was despised; the strict rules were enforced mostly by her, safely confined behind her office doors, with a personal exit door two meters away to her car. She had a bright smile yet a deep gloom in her eyes. I looked at her, up and down, for a couple of seconds, rubbing my beard, dumbfounded by what really happened.

"*ante congra,* man!" Sleepy jumped at me for a bear hug. "You are free, man!"

I remained on my bed for fifteen minutes, numb and processing the turn of events. Life sure was a bitch; it works out when you finally give up. I was outraged, relieved, and confused at the same time. The lady was even disappointed by my reaction, as I barely could utter a simple, "thank you." and I kept rubbing my beard, lost in my own thoughts. She slipped out unnoticed.

My time had finally come. The authorities had finally accepted my asylum. I was eligible to mingle in and contribute to society at will. The doors that I had felt been bolted had just shattered open. It was a new beginning. A fresh start. *How I will fare, only time can tell.* But excuses were no longer excusable. I had to take a stand, and stand firm. *How would Cliff and Big Man take the news?* Questions flooded my brain.

Almost three decades I had been soul searching. In the process, I had reinvented myself and incorporated ideals that I had presumed to suit my momentary goal. Never had I pursued one ideal or principle with total devotion. Each momentary zest soon ran out of favor. I switched from one state of mind to the other, like the cyclones in the Caribbean. Soon, I would run off with another, at times totally abandoning my prior convictions. With new ideals came new friends, new styles of impression and expressions, a shift in attitude and perception, at times polarizing yet engaging in the moment. Circumstances were not helping, either; they just happened too fast.

The very fact was, I was rebelling against myself and running from my own demons. Like a virus that had been left unattended, they had festered and multiplied, vying for their own airtime in my thought train. Worse than if I suffered ADD, my attention span even shorter than my short fuse. The dark, dramatic, extreme thoughts caught my undivided attention. I had always been a magnet for the outrageous and the anarchists, who lived their lives on their own terms. Fantasy-wise, I had the image of myself I was dying to project, shape shifting from year to year as my ideals took new forms. Taking on a character at a time, I was confusing myself and all around me. It was endless drama.

Now, I was supposed to even celebrate my break, a huge break, the very reason I had embarked when I had trekked fifteen hours, crossed a flooded river, nearly lost my life a couple of times to cross the border from Eritrea to Sudan. *When will I ever be grateful? Or has the news not sunk in yet?* I was just too confused!

❧

As my status in the camp was transformed, things changed dramatically among my friends. I understood how they felt, as I had experienced this situation exactly as they did then. I had become a reminder of the system. Every time I ran into a former camp resident who had moved on and up the social ladder, I had felt a flash of resentment and contempt flood my system all at once. In trying not to reveal my emotions, I had either minimized or severed contact with some. Though some infuriate you intentionally, knowing that you resent their situation, some others feel sorry for you and try too hard to be nice. Their effort, though, enrages you even more; their pity makes you feel like a cripple.

So, at best, I maintained civil contact but never sat down for a lengthy conversation. Any instance where the status of my residence was to be raised was avoided, even if that individual was a close member of family. I was an expert in evading questions and problems, so I had no problem in that manner.

I was no longer the victim of the "flawed" system; I was a beneficiary. My future was brighter, with the freedom to move and the opportunity to earn a comfortable independent life just around the horizon. The resentment and rage that had consumed my thoughts and emotions had begun to lift off like a fog. I was thinking and reasoning more calmly than before. Like a thick cataract had been removed surgically; I was seeing everything around me in new light. It was a huge burden off my chest. All of a sudden, I was cautiously thinking and planning about tomorrow with confidence.

In the beginning, I was so wrapped up in my own surprise that I had not been able to notice the impact around me. Being congratulated by well-wishers and even from those I never had comfortable relations with was a humbling process. It kind of knocked down the walls I had built around myself. But it all comes with a cost.

The small comfort zone I had built with fellow sufferers was corroded. Unintentionally, I had gotten a little too carried away in my emancipation. My overzealous sense of adventure suddenly dissipated. I had become too cautious, maybe, for a person who was often the instigator. Under testing times, when my crew was under severe pressure from the authorities, I was in heaven, celebrating my fortunes.

"ayy, Babylon, now dat dey have accepted you, you are becoming too careful Mr. Norwegian," joked Cliff, with a hint of dissent on one occasion where I had hesitated to receive the roll of hash.

Just a week after my good fortune, the police raided Cliff's apartment on suspicion of narcotics possession. It was just a start of a series raids and harassment by the police, who had been patient in their handling of the refugees, despite the public outcry. Harmless transactions that were openly carried out as an ordinary occurrence and even tolerated by the Mottak administration had suddenly become serious legal violations. Even the sixth finger of the Mottak, the LM cigarettes and the likes of expired Russian imports that had sustained the paperless lungs and a few disadvantaged locals who frequented them, were being scrutinized by the police.

The police had intercepted some locals in possession of the expired contraband brands, to be let off with a serious warning, suspending the heavy fine unless they were ever charged in the future. Having discovered the source, the police were in full pursuit of a "contraband ring" that was making huge profits by subjecting unsuspecting victims to expired toxic products. Though the profits were made somewhere else, the Mottak distributors barely made a living out of it; the least they did was cover their own consumption. The real profit makers were always invisible, but it was always the little fish that made it to the dinner plate.

Suspects living in the Mottak had the rooms ransacked. With every smoker in the building blowing the same brand, the police pressed the weaklings for leads. "where did you get it, this cigarette? Who sold it to you?" As if many had rehearsed the answer, it was always, "some guy I met in the city!" Still, there were rumors of some snitching on others in return for favors.

The Merchant was taken into custody and fined heavily for multiple charges of selling illegal goods, stolen property, and contraband cigarettes. With that disappeared the credit system and a further 5 kroner were added in hope of coping with the recession. "my friends, *welahi*, zis people finishin' me. Zey took everything, *welahi*!" he moaned in despair.

Fear gripped the Mottak. At the same time, the residence permit rejections were raining down like a plague. Three residents were forcefully deported within two weeks. A further two who had evaded police were under constant surveillance. Mistrust of the officials working in the Mottak and each other was at an all-time high. Police had suddenly become constant visitors.

Despite the fracas in the camp, I was at relative ease. The police had ransacked my dorm as they had done to others. Having none to worry about, I had passively stood by as they ran their hands through my things. Sleepy and the other roommate were nervous, as if I had planted something incriminating in their possessions. Strange how someone's impression of you is revealed in times of crisis. Though I had nothing to worry about, it hurt to realize that I was seen as a liability.

But the atmosphere at Cliff's place had become tense, too. The police, Narcotics Division, had randomly held raids and confiscated even his phones; he was taken in for questioning on several occasions. Cliff being Cliff, he was unfazed by the sudden surge in attention.

Big Man was elusive as ever. He had vanished into thin air, hours before the police had struck Cliff's place. None of his stash was in jeopardy; the guy had sniffed trouble and moved on.

⚭

Still, the situation on the ground never abated for Cliff. Though relatively subdued, we were just having our get together. The puns and jokes were thrown at me once in a while, but it was to be expected. Cliff had dubbed me a new name Mr. Norwegian. Even though I had been a little hesitant, I kept showing up with the old crew. They had been my best friends at a time when I really needed them. I was a little conscious of trying not to confirm their suspicion that I had indeed changed by distancing myself from the circle, so I showed up as I used to. The crowd had thinned, though. Things were just not the same; besides, in truth, I was uneasy about putting my newfound freedom at risk.

⚭

The next three months passed by like three days. A lot more new faces arrived at the Mottak. A lot more disappeared. Preacher had gone south for the summer break and never came back. Dudu, after being repeatedly harassed by the police for his past involvement with prostitution charges, took off without notice. He had called me afterwards, unwilling to divulge his current location, and had sarcastically said to me, "You will be my contact wherever you end up. I will show up without notice, my nigga!" The Nomad had bid farewell and headed to Finland. After a memorable simmer-down, meditative night at Cliff's pub, revealing his soft side for the first time, the Nomad was gone.

"I not see my mother in ten years, man," the Nomad had said, in a pensive whisper. "I move all ze time. *Welahi*, it's not easy. I never had a home. I want to have wife and children. But I trust no one. I am a good man, *welahi*." After shaking his head in dismay, the Nomad continued, "Like a Bedouin, I crisscross Europe, always looking for something better. But even a nomad has a home and a woman to come back to. But me, I don't even have friends. Zis is not life. Running all the time."

We were left stunned by a sudden emotional outburst from a man who was impenetrably ice cold. So they say we all have a soul, and time indeed wounds all heels. His usually impassive, handsome face was contorted as if he had aged a decade within a matter of minutes. His blushing cheeks trembled, and sensing pitiful eyes locked upon his, he looked down, hoping to disguise his tears. Apart from a faint suppressed sob and the occasionally blubbering sound of the shisha pipes passed around, a tranquil gloom engulfed the tiny apartment. Grounded, we reflected upon the harsh reality without the macho ego in the way; it was like a passed-out, degenerate, hopeless drunk waking up on a pavement with his own children looking down with disgust and apathy.

The Nomad mechanically grabbed the shisha hose from the extended hand of Tallest. Adjusting the charcoal on the aluminum foil with the deftness of a Bedouin, he placed the wooden mouthpiece between his teeth and dragged the strawberry-flavored tobacco with the force of a tropical storm. Flavored smoke billowed out of his open mouth moments later, like a sandstorm in a desert town, clouding the circle for a couple of seconds. By the time the smoke cleared, the Nomad had regained his composure with that indifferent look we had been accustomed to seeing.

"You say you travel like Bedouin, ahh, Mr. Man," Cliff said, "but I thought you people travel wid your camels. Aay! Where you park your camel? You sell it for the boat ticket to Babylon or what! Tell us na!"

"you are crazy, my friend." a smile returned to the Nomad's face. "you think I lived in Sahara. I go there sometimes; it's beautiful, I tell you. *Welahi*, people live simple life. Move when zey want. But zey are never lost. Zey know ze desert very well. Go from oasis to oasis."

"and you, my friend, are going from camp to camp in Europe," interrupted the snickering Congo.

"*Welahi*, I am tired of being refugee here. Is no good I tell you!" bemoaned the Nomad, in an honest, revealing manner. "I live here for ten years. Everywhere in Europe, but no document. But I come here for de money, not for papers, anyway."

"now zis is ze Nomad I know," I added. "Always business, never personal."

It was nice to see the human side to each one of us. When the pressure of life was too much, it was better to heave some of the stress out, where it could be collectively relieved. With the therapeutic humor often lingering in the air, much-needed laughter was often around the corner. Those thoughts might come back to haunt you, like they often do on those cold long sleepless nights for sure, but better smile at their expense when you have the chance, we figured.

"Dis guy has to be searched like dey do in de airport," said Cliff, pointing at the irritated Nomad. "Hey, na. I saw you, de way you look at my pocket. It is like he counting de money inside my pocket like X-ray in de airport! Hey, dis man. You are very dangerous!"

Cliff remained natural as the very cliff, hanging the mood of everyone around him. He sure was a blessing during the darkest hours of my arctic episode, lost way deep in myself. He was genuinely happy for the change in my residency status. He was a true friend. Well, with Congo, he was giggling as usual, in love with a Zambian girl who was very spiritual.

"I found me my African Queen," he had announced one day, when we inquired where he had disappeared for some time. "I don't think about any problem when I am in love," stated Congo in a romantic trance. "I tell you, my brodda, I don't care about money. I don't care about document at all. Just thinking about her makes me appreciate life!"

"you don't care about money, you say!" inquired Cliff. "why don't you give me every money dey give you, huh!" He waited for a second or two to provoke a response from Congo and added, "aay, look at dis boy. You stingy—when do you stop care about fokin money? Tellin' me you no care about money. Dis stupid boy, you na vex me. You cannot afford to fall in love when you don't even know how long you will live here. Mtsee, dey deport your black ass one day and we see if she comes following you! Ay he!"

"come on, Cliff!" retorted Tallest, in defense of Congo. "Just because you have no one to love don't mean oders can't. Dat is very selfish. God knows only we don't know when we die. You might die in your sleep tonight, you know. And I think it betta to die loving dan alone."

"look at Tallest!" Cliff laughed out loud at the ever-optimistic Nigerian and continued, "better die loving, you said. Mtsee, all I care is I want to die after I eat all my money! I want to enjoy life. I don't like leaving off money. You only share it when I live!"

"Yeah man, zat is ze spirit. Live every moment when you can," I added, in a jubilant tone, with the emphatic upbeat assessment of Cliff's principles.

"come on, what's that life if you never had someone you really love more than life itself to share it with?" appealed the smitten Congo, in hope of getting to the soft side out of the hardened, loveless company around him.

"what you talking about?" snapped the agitated Cliff, rising to his feet like an old-school dictator. "Look at dis boy, spoiled by Hollywood movies. Talking about sharing you life to one woman foreva. If one goes, the oder one come. Dat is life. You move to anoder place, you meet anoder woman! Why suffer? Dat is life for you, Mr. Lover."

"No, man. Fuck the money. What's life without love?" Squinting in the corner of the room slumped in a depressed state, Knut barely whispered. "I mean unconditional love. No responsibility. You think alike. Do what you like whenever you... ah, ah, wish, you know..." and he trailed off.

"oh, Chucky, you still here?" Cliff chided, with a friendly wink at his white friend. "who is going to love you na? Have you looked at de mirror lately? You look like a ghost on one of dose children books de Indians used to sell in Africa, I tell you."

Knut had already lost interest, withdrawn back to his induced trance long before Cliff began cracking up over his own joke.

⚌⚌

When it rains, it pours, they had said. The good news kept coming in the mail, as my blood tests came back all normal. Despite high blood pressure, totally understandable, it looked like I was given a clean start. My hands were trembling, though, as I opened the letter from the doctor in the reception toilet. I took a moment to regain my composure, promised myself that, regardless of the result, I had nothing to worry about, as I now was a beneficiary of the country's universal healthcare. But the ordeal was something to remember in the long run, if it ever crossed my mind to engage in unprotected sex.

The long walk to the local hospital for the tests was a nerve-wracking experience. Questioning why every day had to be a D-day, I had shuffled my way towards the town's health center on a rainy mid-March day. All the careless unprotected encounters flashed in my head, one after the other. I was trying to remain positive, yet some suspicious moments always stick out when paranoid. My heart raced faster when I stepped inside the clinic; while I was cursing myself inside, *Why don't I ever learn?* I had a lot more shit to think about, about my long prosperous future that could be cut short. You could never be sure of anything in life. I guess it was the heavenly deities showing off their powers, saying that we are nothing but humans, in hopes of keeping us grounded. Life was a wallet; even when it was empty, you proudly carry it along, bulging from your back pocket. You could get mugged, though, any day.

Some say they see a wave of white light just before they depart from earth. Well, seeing the all-white tiles and the bright white lights and the doctor's white nurses was in some way a reminder of how close death lurks inside the premises. In fact, it was not the medicines and the disinfectant that nauseated me every time I entered a hospital; it occurred to me that is was actually the stench of death.

Tromsø

I moved to the new town Tromsø, the northern Paris; an elegant multicultural town. Cliff and Congo had bid me farewell on a cold November Thursday at the early morning ferry to Tromsø. Wanting a clean, fresh start, I had left behind most of my belongings and packed my essentials into a backpack and one old duffel bag I had bought from the flea market. Though a three-hour boat ride away, I felt like I was heading to another planet.

"so you go now, huh!" Cliff said sarcastically. "Don't disappear on us like everybody else, Mr. Man!" He firmly shook my hand.

Feeling like it might be the last time we would ever meet, I replied, "you know my number now; just call me when you feel like coming by. My place is your place, you both know!"

They both smiled in acknowledgment.

Snickering as usual, Congo poked, "ayy, you hear dis man? We have to call for appointment to come to your place. Is it a hotel? We come for vacation, I tell you. Reserve de sofa for me, you hear me na?"

With the final call for boarding sounding behind me, Cliff reminded me, "your people waiting for you now. Go, my friend!"

I bumped a clenched fist with my two good friends and trod off with my belongings towards the flock making its way to the belly of the ocean beast.

❁

On the boat, I was suddenly engulfed with a déjà-vu of feelings that often took over me whenever I was on the move.

Unlike the past, my destination and situation were safe and secure. In the past, my mind would race off to a fantasy, goody-goody land to get my mind off the uncertainties that awaited me along the way. Crossing borders for a better life, be it on foot or by bus, train, or plane, my destiny was never in my hands. Gazing up the skies for a blessing once in a while, I would start to construct a smooth transition with the comforts of riches and bitches. My heart would sink once in a while with a sighting of a threat. On foot, crossing the Eritrean–Sudanese border, the armed bandits might rob you, the flash flood might sweep you away, the military police might shoot you on sight, the Sudanese border police might deport you, but that inexplicable glint of light keeps you going. It was not courage; it was just something written on the wall. Regardless of the obstacle, you were just meant to get across it, maybe like Moses and his people felt when they crossed the Red Sea.

❦

Leaning back by a window seat, next to a middle aged man, I gazed out into the cold night, into the sea. It sure was alive and feisty as the boat glided across it. I'd had a brush with death, caught up in a flash flood a couple of years back, so I had the utmost respect for the indefinite mass surrounding me. As some friend had said, the ocean stands for the depth of wisdom, unsurpassable, yet unknown and infinite. My thoughts calmly floating along with the boat, I was heading to a future and town I had never been to. I looked around to see if anyone shared my excitement.

As usual, all were buried in their own worlds. The ferry looked more like a hotel lobby. It was spacious and very illuminated. Four rows of three seats each lined the spacious, high-ceilinged, cream body of the passenger cabin, with windows on every side providing the natural treat of all treats. The magnificent, carved mountain ranges, in spots and stripes of the prominent ice, lined the journey until the boat disappeared into deep seas. It had an arresting presence, magnified by the mighty ocean that skirted it. Even in the misty morning, no one would be disappointed: Nature at its best, away from human folly, protruding into to the endless nights of the winter. Still as ever!

Being a weekday morning trip, it was no surprise to see many seats empty. As it was customary to maintain privacy whenever possible in this part of the world, it was rare to find two strangers sitting in the same row. As the boat had crept its way up north, even my seatmate had switched seats.

It was retroflection time; three hours of undisturbed soul-searching and inspection. It occurred to me that every time I had moved to a new place, I always had good intentions and a focused frame of mind. But somehow, along the way, it had not helped that with the ever-complicated circumstances and roadblocks that littered my path in life, I would lose my composure and get carried away in the moment. Maybe I was making too many damn excuses to rebel against myself; I had been seriously critical of myself of late. Sure, no one came with the scripts in hand, sure some had it easy; to tell the truth, most had it worse than I, but we eventually harvest what we sow.

My eyes once again drifted back to the open sea as I leaned over the high balcony near the bow. All of a sudden, I had an urge to feel and smell the water around me, the overwhelming scent. An old fisherman lazily fishing on the Red Sea coast near Beilul had once said to me, "do you know why the sea is so salty, my son?" while snapping the cord of the mosquito-fabric, improvised fishing net tied to his right forefinger.

The frying sun of mid-July sizzling my head, I'd looked around at the peaceful sea that once in a while rocked the tiny kayak. I shrugged and said nonchalantly in Amharic, "I heard a joke that after every invasion, natives of the land would dump tons of salt bars into the sea before they abandoned the town, so that the enemies can never drink the water."

finding my untimely joke not so hilarious, the fisherman rearranged his keshuf with some deft swift movement, tightly around his waist in one hand, and replied, "they say it's through the tears of thousands of years. The slaves that had made their way to the Arabs, the pirates, the storm-stricken fishermen, all the terrible men and men of God, the courageous, the cowards, the children and women that died on sea, all shed tears before they breathed water as their last breath. Respect it and it shall respect you," he had said, and snapped his finger back and forth, hoping to lure a fish or two for lunch.

Once again, lost in the vastness of the mass full of tears, I contemplated my fate and state of affairs epitomized by that emaciated old fisherman on that kayak on the Red Sea over a decade ago. Life and wisdom was the sea. And all humans, natural-born fishermen! The fish were our fate. All catch the sardines, yet all wish to catch a shark who had fished more fishermen instead. Indeed, dreams and fantasies eat us from inside out. A day and a fish at a time, it's a hand-to-mouth affair. You've got no one to blame, though, as every one of the fishermen knows the fish are always there. It's all about the patience, the timing, and the setting.

❦

The past had no bearing on my future. I had to move along. It wouldn't define who I will be, and what I had done in the past was done. I would not hide it in regret nor run away from it forever. Instead I would wear it like an amulet, a crucifix to a real believer, to constantly remind me of where I had been and how far I had come. I would not show it off nor use it like a badge to identify myself, rather I would wear it like a protective vest, concealed by whatever I wore on top. Every layer, every misstep, and every stumble along the way was part of the process of my being. It was part of the formulas, the twists to my making and my unmaking. It was just who I was, but didn't necessarily have to be repeated. That was the lesson.

Threading through a complex path of labyrinth, I definitely had to master the trick of not hitting the same dead end more than twice. Like a good friend of mine had once said in Amharic, "if you hit the wall once, you are a human. Everybody makes mistakes. If you hit the same wall twice, you are a little stupid, but still it is expected once in a while. But if you hit the same wall three times, then you, my friend, are definitely a mistake of a being. A waste of space." I definitely had to learn to stop hitting the same walls over and over again, I reminded myself, as I tossed the butt of the LM cigarette in to the open sea. *Full of tears and butts*, I figured, counting mentally the millions of butts that had been thrown into the sea throughout the millennia. And I headed back to my seat, a gust of sharp wind nearly knocked me off balance.

Back in my seat, still shivering from the cold, I ran the last thought as if I were about to reach a revelation. I knew I needed to resolve some issues. Had to mark where I had stood and be aware of where I should be heading. I was a man of many dreams. A Liberian friend of mine had told me once he had been having recurrent dream of him breathing his last breath on his deathbed. "I tell you, my friend, it feels so real. Am lying in bed with all the flesh disappeared, the skin clinging to my bones in a dark room, all alone. Very scary, my friend." That image had been lingering in my mind for far too long. For sure, when my moment came, I would gracefully accept my departure, but the question of what had I done with my life bothered me. It was a frightening thought. Looking forward, the way I had been toiling in search of a meaningful existence, I had lost the meaning of it all. Who knew what the second half held for me, if there was even a second half.

In the later stage of my adult life, even though I was yet to resolve it, I had realized the two fronts of my state of mind. The boy and the man. The boy wanted to be free and loose, while the man wanted to contemplate, reason, and plan ahead. Meandering from one front to the other like a stray cat had cost me many sleepless nights. Though I was capable of staying in one frame of mind for quite some time naturally, there were always awkward moments that made me feel like a stranger to myself. When I was merely giving in to the natural urges, there was just no suppression; the filter was enabled only for emergency cases where the self was in danger. Otherwise, it was all about liberation. The boy in me was the green light. Though by far less stressed and more sociable, he was harmlessly just getting by.

On the other hand, when the man stepped up and marked the borders and the principles, it felt like a total regime change. The shift was never smooth. Random rhythms that had served me under the lively boy frame of mind would be dismissed as invalid, to be replaced by a routine and self-imposed structure. Censorship of the self was given prominence. Urges were suppressed by the rational animal that was in control. I would tell myself, *What is a man if he cannot control his urges? Give in to all the urges, and you are left with nothing.* It was not a syndrome. I had no psychological issue; it was a battle I had to settle by myself. There were no losers; there was just a balance of power.

If I could let the boy and the man to coexist inside me, I would have a good night's sleep. I had thought of killing the boy inside me and following through with the structure I had set as the incomplete man. Yet I felt so out of place and so artificial, plus depressed. I felt like a robot. If I could merge the regular irregularity of the boy in me to coincide with pattern and schedule of the man, I would be invincible, I assured myself. Like nature, life was all about the balance. And that balance was the essence of life. If I were to lie on my deathbed, I didn't want my last breath to be a sigh of disappointment, but a gust of relief.

Consistency was a major element missing from my character. I was always looking for a new adventure, a new challenge, as if I had finished the last one. Every time I was met with a roadblock, I would instantly turn back as if I had met a dead end. Looking for endless excuses was not helping, either. The thing with an excuse was that you always could find somebody to agree with you. The wicked always sought comfort in other people's weakness. My mother had once said to me that if a friend agreed with your excuses twice in a row, you are looking at your own reflection in the mirror, not a friend. Searching for friends who think alike had always left me prejudiced and blinded. A real friend was someone who offered you a different perspective from your own, not a reflection of your own twisted thoughts.

Having lived my life without a concrete plan, just dreams and half-realities, I realized that now was the time to sit down and take a note. Shit always popped out on its own in my past, or other people made plans for you. I was, at times, a mere spectator of my own undoing. It was not a matter of ambition, though, but attitude.

Structure was another element sorely missed from my character and vocabulary. The "shit happens" attitude had served me well at times of survival. However, one has to restructure his state of mind to the current state of affairs as soon as survival has been ensured. And in my case, I was way past the survival stage. I had now entered the construction phase—not dreams, but reality. "Live for the moment" was not a conducive strategy; I had to step up my game to the next level. I was just tired of excuses!

As observant as I was, I had been reflecting on the environment and its effect on my outlook. Back home, where I grew up, adjustment was the basic skill required in an unpredictable setting. The buses never came on time; the rent was never paid on time. Appointments were never taken seriously; expectations were limited to moments; ambitions were restricted to ordained networks; limitations were never challenged, nor at times even spoken of—no witness, no crime; work was not for the worker but for the boss... Everything to do with time and space was negotiable. Everything and everybody had a price! And if you were not a player of the game, you were just a bystander living for the day, and that was it. You just created a safe comfort zone and took comfort in each other's misery. Chanting the mantra "sharing is happiness," the longer you live through it; the bitter reality goes down like beer.

Only the resolute stubbornly cling to their principles against all odds to tough it out, while the rest adjust. Was it because we didn't care or that people are addicted to inconsistency? Well, we are habitual animals.

❧

Tromsø was a beautiful town. The magnificent, arching bridge, Bruvegen, linking the mainland to the main island, stood out from afar like an extended forearm in an inviting manner. Nature was undeniably at her moody, yet creative, best in that part of the world. Having arrived at a time when her painting wand had stroked dark gloom and mist abstractly on the northern tip of her canvas, I still discovered attributes that captivated the newcomer like a veiled beauty in black hijab from head to toe.

They had named it the Paris of the north for no reason, the sailors a century ago. You had to respect the early settlers: braving the unforgiving winter frost to even contemplate a settlement, let alone a town, showed some tenacity. The ferry from the south docked at the southwest end of the main island, Tromsøya, sandwiched between Tromsdalen and Kvaløya. Situated a stone's throw away from the sentrum, at the intersection of Kaigata and Strandtorget, the ferries delivered you right into the heart of the town.

❧

I settled in a cozy second floor apartment, on a wooden block right at the intersection of Arbeidersgata and Storgata. Thanks to the efficiency of the locals, which you take for granted the longer you live in this Nordic country, the kommune had arranged my settlement more smoothly than I could have hoped. With a coordinator assigned by the Refugee Settlement Center of the kommune, I was given a guided tour of the town upon my arrival. After handing me over the key to my apartment and getting me acquainted with the landlord, a graceful older couple living in the first floor also shared a thick handbook of

190

the residence regulations I was expected to maintain. Then we went for a ride around the town.

"*Kunne visste deg til fot, men det blåser mye i dag.*" seeing me a little dumbfounded by his Norwegian remark, he repeated in English, "it's a windy, cold day." pointing towards the looming dark cloud, my coordinator added, with a smile, "If you were around in the summer, we could have taken a walk down the main street. Anyway, I will drive around slowly and show you the places you need to know!"

"no, it's okay. Will take a walk by myself and get to know ze town," I replied in English, still a little embarrassed that I could not even respond to a simple Norwegian weather conversation, after having lived there for two years.

After two weeks in the new town, the demons were back with a vengeance. I tried to remain calm, reminding myself how far I had come. I was afraid of jinxing it, but had to be grateful for so much change. I know the dark days were lurking right at the corner; still, the better days outnumbered them for the first time. I hoped they'd keep up.

I promised myself not to fuck up, but I was still unsettled. I missed the craziness in a crazy way. I missed Cliff and his jokes. I missed the waking up at whatever time and heading to Cliff's place to dine on the famous spicy chicken and guzzle all the beer, joking all day. But then I would remind myself, *I have got to come to grips with reality; remember the sleepless nights, as well, the suicidal moments too, bro!*

Things simmered down, right now—almost dangerously. Was it because I was not used to the tranquility, or worse, was I accustomed to the thrill of unexpected adventures? I was not quite sure. Dangerous drama that had embroiled my existence must have been embedded in me somewhere. For all I knew, its disconcerting, uneasy feeling was just to keep me on my toes. I never laid back; besides, I had sky-high ambitions to keep me awake. I felt something big was on the way. Often, this time of year was when my season kicked in. I was heading for a milestone, as well, about to turn thirty in a couple of weeks.

The fact of the matter was, there was no clear-cut solution for a balanced state of mind. Life was like the arctic seasons, so extreme yet often on time. Coping with the extremes and handling transitions in turn was the key to the struggle. It was all about being at ease in most circumstances. That was real inner stability; rocking along the tide and not fighting it. The ease under pressure only came when one flaunted the papered cracks of one's inefficiency to handle the pressure as part of one's character. Maybe some were made to be as consistent as the tropical sun, but not I. But then, happiness was just a momentary state of ecstasy never meant to last long; just a transition from one state of despair to uncertainty, restlessness, and numbness.

Pursuing endless, uninterrupted moments of pleasure in one's life was a delusional fantasy that stole even the little happy sparks, taken for granted by the weight of expectation. The truth was in nature—ever turbulent. In one day, I could live through all four arctic seasons. I might wake up morbidly exhausted from the coffin of a bed in a dark gloomy winter state, lighten by a little after springing into a cold shower, feel like the arctic summer sun, mild and bright the whole day, having tuned myself into the carefree mode, and then grow moody as the autumn wind with trivial things flickering along my state of mind like a street lamp in a rundown neighborhood. Finally, the cold winter might settle down on me as I headed to bed, like a dust settles down after a storm. But remaining functional under the changing circumstances was the ultimate goal. I guess I had to tune myself to adjust every day, as sulking under imminent pressure was taking its toll.

Each day now, I would tune in with the real self every morning, reminding myself of the real important things like a mantra, like having my own Buddha moment to gather the self. As if a mudslide had struck the night before, I would dig my way up and clean up afterward, every day for a better day. Every day was a new day, but once in a while, I had to reflect and be grateful for how far I had traveled in the mind, and how much time it took to get to where I was. In retrospect, it was most definitely worth it. Maybe life was not about the prize; it could have been about the ride—the ups and downs, the bumps, the dead ends, the shortcuts, and the lessons in search of the meaning. And what a ride it is...

THE END